THE FIFTH DOLL

THE FIFTH DOLL

CHARLIE N. HOLMBERG

Text copyright © 2017 by Charlie N. Holmberg
All rights reserved.

No part of this book may be reproduced, or stored in a retrieval system, or transmitted in any form or by any means, electronic, mechanical, photocopying, recording, or otherwise, without express written permission of the publisher.

Published by 47North, Seattle

www.apub.com

Amazon, the Amazon logo, and 47North are trademarks of Amazon.com, Inc., or its affiliates.

ISBN-13: 9781477806104
ISBN-10: 1477806105

Cover design by Kimberly Glyder

Printed in the United States of America

*To Marsh—may you always seek truth
and never doubt that God loves you
(and so does your mom).*

Chapter 1

The chest was one of the finer things Matrona's mother owned. Its sides were sanded and smooth, edges rounded, lid inlaid with an embroidered satin pillow trimmed with yellowing lace. Though the chest had sat, unmoved, at the foot of her parents' bed all her life, Matrona could almost pretend it was a rescued treasure from a foreign land, owned by a lady who wore pearls, left behind when some great storybook monster kidnapped her from her balcony.

Matrona blinked the fancy away and ran her hand along the lace before opening the lid, selecting the chest's cherished contents one by one, determining which of them she would make her own.

It was not her mother who knelt beside her on the rag-quilted rug, but her dear friend Roksana, who taught the nursery school near the center of the village. Matrona's mother had not wanted to be in the room for the opening of the chest. *"Too many memories,"* she had said, shaking her head and retiring to the front room to sit in the splintering wicker chair.

"What's that?" Roksana asked, pushing up onto her knees for a better view of the chest's contents. Her round belly pressed into the corner of the chest, full with a child that would arrive any day now.

Matrona lifted the stretch of white satin from atop the treasures. "Just extra fabric." She folded it and laid it beside her. Beneath the satin rested the *kokoshnik* from her mother's wedding: a crown of stiff fabric with a bronze sheen, dozens of small silver beads stitched into the tall, looping coils. Folds of red satin fell from behind it, trimmed with tiny brown tassels.

Matrona held the *kokoshnik* in both hands. It was heavier than it looked. She tried to picture her mother young, her hair as dark as Matrona's and elaborately braided, her cheeks pinched red, and this headdress pressed over her hairline. The image quickly warped to Matrona herself.

I'm getting married, she thought, tucking the ends of her hair behind each ear—the short bits that did not fit into her braid. Marriage was the one thing that would finally mark her as an adult to her parents, as age never had. The ceremony couldn't come soon enough. Her own father would perform it. There was no priest in the village, but her father was well versed in the Good Book, and under the eyes of God, that was authority enough.

"Oh, try it on!" Roksana urged, and when Matrona hesitated, her friend snatched the *kokoshnik* from her hands and pushed the headpiece over Matrona's forehead, arranging it to her liking before sitting back and examining her work.

"Well?" Matrona asked. It fit well, at least.

"The colors are perfect for you." Roksana's smile turned sly as she added, "Feodor will think so, too."

Matrona chuckled and pulled off the *kokoshnik*, setting it carefully beside her. "I'm sure Feodor doesn't care what color my headdress is." Her engagement to the butcher had been settled last week, and her parents couldn't be more thrilled. Matrona wasn't sure if the thrill came from Feodor's family esteem or from the fact that, at twenty-six, Matrona was well past marrying age, as her mother often reminded her. Needless to say, it would be a short engagement.

Roksana's slender fingers danced along the edge of the chest. "What else?"

Matrona pulled free a twine-wrapped package and carefully loosed its knots, opening the thick paper to reveal her mother's wedding dress. It was a long, traditional gown of off-white, with bronze stitching trailing from collar to hem to match the headdress. The dress, too, was heavier than expected. Matrona stood and held the gown up to her shoulders, relieved to see it would fit, though she had always pictured herself marrying in a gown trimmed with black and red.

Roksana stood as well. "Oh, it's so pretty. I wish my mama had kept hers."

"She didn't?"

Roksana shrugged. "Even she doesn't know what became of it. Try on the gown!"

"Not right now. I've chores yet to do." Matrona smoothed out the fabric of the skirt.

Roksana rolled her eyes and took the dress from her, folding it.

Kneeling at the chest, Matrona picked through more items—a pair of shoes that would certainly be too small for her, a christening dress, a silver crucifix on a chain, a small wooden rattle. Near the bottom of the chest, she found a carefully sewn rag doll the length of her forearm, one that matched the style of the doll she had so often played with as a child, though this one had lighter hair and oval eyes instead of round, with a simple brown dress instead of blue.

Matrona lifted the doll and ran her thumb over the embroidered face, identifying it at once as the reason her mother had chosen to stay in the front room.

"Esfir's." She combed her nails through the doll's yarn hair.

Roksana set the folded wedding gown on the bed and sat on the floor. "Your sister?"

Matrona nodded, turning the doll over once, twice, in her hands. The doll had been made for her younger sister. Mother must have finished it just before her sister disappeared, a mystery no one in the village had ever solved. A newborn babe, only three days old, cannot merely walk away or become lost in the wood, and no wrongdoers had stolen her, unless someone had found a way to hide a growing child in their small village, undiscovered for twenty years. Esfir had simply vanished, or so Matrona had been told. She had been six years old at the time.

Matrona studied the doll. Her mother would have put it into the chest when it became clear Esfir wasn't coming home. The carefully sewn toy had never been used, yet it still showed signs of age—fading in the dress, stiffness to the thread that held the patterned pieces of its body together. Matrona blinked at the sadness of it, this doll that had lived her entire existence inside a wooden box, never to be played with, forced to be content with what destiny her maker had given her.

Lifting her head, Matrona glanced at the wooden walls of her parents' bedroom, a sluggish thought transforming it. The room itself became a giant chest at the end of a giant bed, the floorboards beneath the rag rug morphed into fingers that held her just as she held this doll.

Your foolish imagination is playing tricks on you again, she thought to herself. It was exactly what her mother would have said to her. She returned the doll to the box.

"I've never seen knit socks so small." Roksana reached into the nearly empty chest to retrieve a pair. Her other hand went to her belly. "Did you wear these?"

Matrona shrugged. "I couldn't possibly remember if I did." She gathered her finds, restored the piece of satin to cover the doll and the other remaining contents, and returned the lid to the chest. "I'll have to be very careful pressing the wrinkles from this dress."

"I'll help you when the time comes." Roksana stood and brushed off the skirt of her *sarafan*. "But don't even think of handling it after muddying up with those cows."

Matrona laughed. "You sound like my mother."

Roksana sobered. "Not funny."

Picking up the pile of wedding items, Matrona gestured to the bedroom door with a tilt of her chin, and Roksana hurried ahead to open it for her. Voices ahead drew her attention, though they were too quiet for her to make out. Curiosity beckoned her toward them.

The wooden walls of the modest front room were decorated with a few pieces of framed embroidery and a simple weaving of the Virgin Mary. Her father's writing table was pushed into the corner, her mother's old wicker chair near it. The brick stove sat cool in the opposite corner, touched by a glint of late-morning sunlight from the window—sunlight interrupted by the shoulder of their visitor, Feodor Popov.

It was not a childish thrill that filled Matrona at the sight of her betrothed, but rather a wave of self-consciousness, of wondering, *Why me?* and *What will he be like?* Theirs would be a slow-burning romance, if there was to be romance at all. Deep down, she prayed there would be.

He was speaking to her father, who looked up and noticed her first, followed by her mother. Realizing she still held the wedding clothes, Matrona flushed and quickly shoved the marriage things into Roksana's arms. Her friend, God bless her, wordlessly hurried back down the hall to Matrona's small room to hide the items away.

Again Matrona tucked those short hairs behind her ears and straightened her bodice. Before she could speak, Feodor noticed her parents' line of sight and turned around. The sunlight made his pale hair appear lighter and slightly red, which made his blue eyes bluer and his dark brows darker. Feodor was tall but slight of frame, and he stood with an erectness that looked almost painful.

"Ah, Matrona." He gave her a slight smile and stiff nod of his head. It was then that Matrona noticed the ceramic jug in his hand and the weighted satchel in her father's. Feodor was here for an exchange.

"Three pounds of beef today," he said in answer to her unspoken question.

"Yes, Matrona." Her mother's sharp eyes focused on her. A few wisps of dark hair peeked out from her mother's head scarf. "Fetch some milk for the Popovs. Don't leave dear Feodor waiting." She took the jug from Feodor's hand and hurried across the room in small steps. "Best of the cream, now," she said a little quieter as she shoved the vessel into Matrona's arms. It was unremarkable other than the depiction of a rearing white horse on its front.

"Yes, Mama." Matrona took the jug and stepped into the small back hallway that opened to the yard where the milk cows were stabled. The door was cracked open to let in the sweet morning air. Two layers of rug covered the floor, their tight braids stained with soil from outside. Multiple shelves lined the hallway, some stacked with tools, some with the barrels that held the milk. In a cellar the milk would last a few days, but there was never a need to store it there. Matrona's family was the only one in the village that kept milking cows, and these barrels were always empty by sunset, even with the evening milking.

Holding Feodor's jug against one hip, Matrona tapped the barrel to let the milk flow. It poured so easily, taking the shape of the spout as it would take the shape of the jug, doing as she wanted without complaint, without hiccup. It splattered against the bottom of the jug, wetting her sleeve with a few drops. Less than a mouthful dared to splash away.

Coolness on her hip pulled her attention down to a growing stain on her dress. She pinched her breath against her tongue—the jug was leaking. After fumbling to cork the barrel's bunghole, she scrambled about the shelves to search for another vessel. She found an empty pail, shook her mother's charm from it—bad luck to carry an empty pail about—and dumped the collected milk into it. Clicking her tongue, Matrona grabbed a rag and scrubbed her red skirt. It would dry clear, but stiff. She'd need to wash it tonight.

Feeling her parents' impatience as a worm wriggling against the back of her neck, Matrona filled the milk pail and finished it with cream from the top of the barrel before carrying it with practiced balance back into the front room, the handle of the damaged jug looped through her free fingers.

"My apologies, Feodor," she said, interrupting whatever conversation the trio had been wrapped in, "but your jug is leaking."

Feodor sighed. "I'm not surprised. It's been repaired too many times to count."

Frowning through his long beard, Matrona's father folded his arms. "I'm not one to question the work of a Maysak, but it may need to be replaced."

Her mother's eyes brightened. "Oh yes, it should be. Look at those cracks! And don't worry yourself, Feodor. Matrona will see you a new one right away. Won't you, Matrona? My daughter looks after her own."

She punctuated the statement with another sharp glare.

Breathing in a sigh that desperately wanted to escape her lips, Matrona set the pail down. "But of course, if you wish it, Feodor."

A smile spread on Feodor's mouth, but it did not show his teeth. "That would do well for me. I can see already the dedicated wife you will be."

Matrona smiled; her mother beamed. With a slight curtsy, Matrona said, "If you'll excuse me," and slipped out of the house, the conversation between betrothed and parents resuming before she'd even shut the door. A busy day she'd have, for her father would certainly push her to finish the chores despite the time it would take to procure a new jug. She'd likely be the one to fetch it once it was kilned, as well.

Outside, she allowed a sigh to pass through her lips. It mixed with the warm breeze as she started down the dirt path that wound through the village, making her way to the pottery. The late-morning sun twinkled between the leaves of the oaks and aspens that formed the nearby wood, dotted occasionally with twisting hornbeams and thick linden trees. The wild grasses grew thick between the trees and the other *izbas* that housed Matrona's neighbors, scenting the air with green. Roksana's voice called out her name, and she turned to see her friend taking a fork in the path behind Matrona, heading toward her own home. Matrona offered an apologetic wave. With the distraction of the jug, she'd forgotten Roksana was in her room.

As Matrona passed the cooper and the path that led to the glade where the children so liked to play, she heard faint peals of laughter echoing from the wood. She walked around the Grankins' small potato farm and the knitting shop owned by the Demidov family. The church bell rang; Alena Zotov, Roksana's mother-in-law, must have been starting her women's scripture meeting.

The path stretched long and straight for a ways after that, and Matrona lifted her eyes when the tradesman's home came into view. Though it had sat in its little nook against the wood all her life, Matrona never tired of admiring it.

Slava Barinov's home was by far the grandest in the village, and most certainly the brightest. Its yellow siding was heavily trimmed in blue, complemented by blue shutters and blue cornices. Twisting columns of wood held up a small, ornate portico over the door, and the two steps leading to it were vivid red brick, perhaps purchased during one of Slava's expeditions. The *nalichniki* around the attic windows, for the home stood two stories, curled about themselves like bubbling candy. Small blue tiles scaled the roof, making it look almost dragonlike. The edges of the tiles glimmered in the sunlight. Matrona almost expected the portico to rise from the earth and turn to look at her, blinking at her with sleepy glass eyes, but the home remained rooted as it was built, and within a few breaths, Matrona had left it behind.

Matrona's path soon curved around the second half of the village, for Slava's home sat at its midpoint. It wasn't until she saw the smoke puffing from the pottery's chimney that her stomach clenched within her, and her fingers grew clammy around the cracked jug's handle.

She pressed fingertips into her belly in an attempt to calm it and raised her chin a little higher to convince herself of her nonchalance. The Maysaks were a large family who ran both the brewery and the pottery, and more than one of its sons molded clay for the village. It was frequently Viktor who ran the pottery while his sisters tended to old Mad Olia, their mother. It would be Viktor she'd see, she assured herself, and the exchange would be brief. Before she knew it, she'd be on her way home to do her chores and speak soft words to Feodor in exchange for his—and her mother's—favor.

The pottery sat behind the Maysak *izba*, where Afon Maysak, head of the household, sipped at a bottle of some sort of spirits, as he always did. Pulling her eyes from him, Matrona focused on her task. The pottery was built like a barn, with two wide doors that opened into the workshop, not so different from the barn in the cow pasture. As Matrona approached, she could feel the heat of the kiln tickling the air. The scent of clay clung to her nostrils and the back of her throat.

Viktor was there as expected, his hands gloved as he shoved a long-handled paddle into the kiln burning in the back of the shop. Yet so was *he*. Her eyes easily spotted the youngest Maysak brother, Jaska, closer to the front of the pottery, his hands and arms stained up to his elbows as he separated a mound of gray clay from a bundled chunk and threw it down onto the center of a potter's wheel. Bits of clay stained his long apron as well, and a smudge traced one side of his shaven jaw. His hair, which always looked unkempt, stuck to his temples with perspiration.

Matrona found her gaze measuring the broadness of his shoulders, and she forced herself to look away, pressing the thoughts back into the dark spots of her mind, calling herself silly and odd, even a little sick in the head. Matrona was an upright woman, and engaged to be married to a fine man. Not only that, but Jaska Maysak was seven years her junior, only nineteen years of age. She needn't have reminded herself that she used to tend him when he was a child and his mother's illness had left her bedridden. By all means, Matrona was more an elder sister to him than anything else. It was foolhardy for her to notice him the way she did. The way she had for nearly two years.

He looked up, his dark eyes finding hers, and her stomach rekindled its unease, making her too warm and light-headed.

Jaska wiped his hands off on his apron before approaching. "Matrona! I apologize for not seeing you."

She smiled—an easy, innocent smile. "I only just arrived."

He glanced at the jug in her hand. "A repair?"

She hefted the jug. "I was hoping for a remake, actually. I fear this one has been repaired too many times."

Jaska took the jug from her and turned it over in his hands. He was not as tall as Feodor, or even as tall as Viktor and his other brothers, but he had half a head on Matrona, just as her father had half a head on her mother. A good height, considering—

Stop it, for heaven's sake, she thought with a frown.

"This is one of the Popov jugs," Jaska said.

She blinked. "Uh, yes, it is. Feodor came by to fetch milk with it just now."

He smiled, an upturning of one side of his lips that pressed a dimple into his left cheek. "I'm sure it was a mess for you. And congratulations, if it's not too late to say so."

Matrona flushed. She hoped the color would be interpreted as a reaction to the kiln's heat. "Not at all," she answered, her voice quieter. She tried to push more energy into it, but her throat had become oddly lethargic. "It's only been a short time since the agreement was made. Thank you."

He glanced at her, his dark brown eyes so very different from Feodor's pale blue. "Agreement? You make it sound so . . ." He shrugged.

Matrona folded her arms. "So what?"

That dimple re-formed. "So formal, I suppose." He patted the jug. "I'll make a duplicate; should be ready tomorrow afternoon, maybe tomorrow evening. I can bring it by when it's finished—or should I take it to the Popovs'?"

Matrona parted her lips to reply, then stood dumbly, considering. Her mother would likely want her to deliver it herself. To take credit for the effort, to bolster Feodor's affections. She swallowed and answered, "I'll come pick it up. It's no trouble."

"And it's not there," came a loud yet papery voice from behind Matrona, who turned with the sensation of needles pricking the length of her spine. Mad Olia hobbled into the workshop, her bowlegged steps uneven, her back hunched with age. A pink head scarf held back her half-gray hair, but a few locks had escaped the folds and dangled over either side of her nose. "And it's not," she repeated, brows pinched together. Her faded eyes glared at Matrona, then her youngest son. "I ought to switch your hide. There are worse punishments than being left out in the snow—"

Jaska sighed. "Mama," he began, but his sister Galina came around the corner just then and, spotting their mother, hurried over to grasp her arm.

"It's all right. Let's have something to drink," Galina murmured to the old woman, avoiding Matrona's gaze.

Olia grumbled something unintelligible before letting her daughter pull her away, back toward the house.

Jaska's gaze lingered on them a long moment, his eyes and shoulders drooping as though fatigued. He sighed and turned back to Matrona. "My apologies."

Matrona shook her head, mulling over Olia's bizarre words. "What's 'snow'?"

"I haven't the faintest idea"—Jaska shrugged—"but she prattles about it from time to time." He looked at the jug in his hands, then back at Matrona. "I'll get this ready."

Matrona nodded, offered her thanks, and left the workshop, trying to keep her pace respectable. She was anxious to put distance between herself and Jaska—as well as Mad Olia's ramblings—but it wouldn't do to appear too eager. She was levelheaded and purposeful, as always. Levelheaded and purposeful.

The heat from the pottery retreated as the village opened up to green space. Matrona imagined her flush was made of thousands of biting ants, and the soft breeze blew them off her skin as she walked, carrying them back into the wood. Her spine softened, and she fingered the end of her braid, twisting her hair around her fingers as though her hand were a loom. The sun beamed down from overhead, highlighting the milk stain on her skirt. She ran a thumbnail over its crusty edges.

Slava's home appeared on the path, with its glimmering shingles and blue shutters, the glass-inlaid windows far finer than anything the other village *izbas* had put in their frames. For a moment Matrona wondered what it would be like to be a tradesman, to own a horse and take her wagon out through the wood to other towns, cities she'd never seen, even countries. To bring back the strange and remarkable things Slava always seemed to have. But the thought left as quickly as it had come, banished so thoroughly, Matrona couldn't pin down just what her mind had been pondering.

A glint of silver caught her eye from the wild grass just off the side of the path. Stooping down, she picked up the slender item—a paintbrush with very long, very fine bristles. Its handle was tipped with silver and imprinted with an etching of chamomile flowers.

Matrona turned the instrument over in her hands, marveling at it for a moment before looking up to Slava's house. Surely it was his. Picking up her skirt, Matrona crossed the wild grass to the narrow path leading up to Slava's porch and portico. It was not the first time she'd knocked on the tradesman's door, but she was not at all a frequent visitor, and she marveled at the paint and stamped designs around the door frame before knocking thrice.

Matrona waited several seconds, but there was no answer. Hadn't she seen Slava's wagon around the back of the house? She knocked again, harder. Stared at the knotted square etched into Slava's brass door handle. Traced it. Touched it. Turned it.

The door opened onto a short front hall well lit by the windows. "Slava?" she called inside. "Tradesman?"

No answer. She needed to think quickly, for dark things dwelled in the thresholds of houses, so she couldn't linger long. Matrona glanced at the paintbrush in her hands. She could set it down on the doorstep for him to find later, yes?

As she pulled the door closed, however, she heard movement within the house, perhaps the brushing of a shoulder against a rough wall? She paused for a breath, then pushed the door open again and called, louder, "Slava? Are you home?"

No answer.

"It's Matrona Vitsin. I found a brush near the path that I believe must be yours . . ." Her voice faded as the heaviness of the quiet house pushed it toward the floor. Pressing her lips together, she moved to set down the paintbrush, but a *thump* from within stilled her hand.

She straightened. "Slava? Are you all right?" A vision of the aging tradesman filled her thoughts, of him trying to reach her and then tumbling to the floor, breathless, ill, with no one to help him. After gnawing on her lip a moment, Matrona pushed the door open and stepped inside the house.

Matrona had never entered Slava's home; he always completed his trades off the side of the path. She noted that the interior of the house was simpler than the exterior, though still fine. A staircase at the end of the hall, its banister unpolished, led to the upper floor. There were a few simple paintings on the wall, with simple frames, and Matrona wondered if Slava had painted them himself, if this paintbrush truly was his. She hadn't known the tradesman to be an artist, but then again, he kept mostly to himself.

"Slava?" she called again with urgency, rounding the corner and spying a rolltop desk. She touched its fine stenciling, wondering where Slava had found it, for she'd never seen Pavel Zotov, the carpenter and Roksana's father-in-law, craft something so fine. She passed a chest of drawers, a short table, and some embroidered chairs with high backs of a make she didn't recognize. "Slava, are you hurt?"

Perhaps he wasn't home after all. Matrona turned about once, looking for a shadow, listening for a groan, then slipped from the front room into a small kitchen. She spied across the empty room to a short hallway to her right, which dipped down with two stairs from the kitchen floor. Another rustle, deeper in the house, encouraged her to take those stairs; she tried to resist marveling at the aged but lush carpeting underfoot. A door at the end of the hallway was cracked open, spilling out a sliver of sunlight.

She pressed it open, half-expecting a bedroom, and instead got a face full of brown feathers. She shrieked and staggered back as a large bird grappled with the door frame before flitting to the opposite end of the room and finding a perch on the windowsill. Pressing a palm to her speeding heart, Matrona gawked at the creature—a red kite, perhaps? Surely such a creature hadn't gotten lost inside the house! Had Slava acquired the bird on one of his routes? The creature glared at her with a yellowed eye, and he wore a copper band around one of his legs.

Matrona's hand tightened on the paintbrush, and she took two calming breaths. This must have been what she'd heard, then, foolish bird. She took half a step away from the room, but its interior snared her attention: two tables—one large, one small—took up most of the space, and simple wooden shelves had been nailed into the walls. The glass window, where the kite perched, was too tall to be peered into from outside.

Her lips parted in surprise. Dolls. The tables and shelves all held dolls. Carved wooden dolls, round faced and slightly pear shaped, about the length of her forearm. They were painted in a variety of colors, and many wore head scarves and ornamented clothes. So many dolls. Dozens. Over a hundred, surely.

Glancing once at the watching kite, Matrona walked to the large table. She set down the paintbrush and picked up one of the dolls, its wooden body lacquered and smooth. It bore a remarkable resemblance to Zhanna Avdovin, were she twenty years younger. A coppery *kokoshnik* framed her face. The doll even had the same light curls and pursed mouth.

She set the doll down, for another caught her eye. She touched it, hesitant to pick it up, but she did, studying the face closely. Pavel. It looked exactly like the carpenter.

She set the doll down and stepped back to examine the other faces, her mouth opening wider with each one, a slow breath trickling into her lungs. Viktor, Sacha, Ilary. And there—that was Jaska, undoubtedly. And on the small table to her left, she found a doll resembling her *father*. Even the facial hair matched. Her father had not altered his beard in all the years she'd known him.

The kite clicked deep in his throat, but she ignored him and picked up her father's doll, turning it over. He had this same clothing as well, the blue *rubashka* with black trim, the matching hat. How long ago had Slava made this doll? All of them? And why?

Gooseflesh rose on Matrona's arms. She thought to search for her own doll when her thumbnail discovered a seam in the doll's center, encircling her father's round waist. It was two pieces, then? It opened?

Gripping the top and bottom of the doll with chilled fingers, Matrona pulled, though the pieces were stiff. The wood squeaked against itself as the top and bottom half twisted—

A thump outside elicited a muted shriek in Matrona's throat and an eager cry from the kite. Her gaze instantly fixed on the closest window, and the impropriety of the situation hit her like a bucketful of cold water. What was she doing, wandering around inside another villager's house like this? Touching his things, however odd or fascinating they may be?

Was Slava home?

Matrona hurriedly set down her father's doll and rushed from the room, through the kitchen and around the chest of drawers, past the stairs and out the front door. She heard the nickering of a horse behind the house, but she ran over the wild grasses and back onto the path, sprinting until she felt the wood at her back. Had he indeed returned home, Slava would not see her now.

She paused to catch her breath. Perhaps it had been foolish to run. She simply could have explained herself, couldn't she have? She'd only meant to return the brush . . .

It was those dolls . . . so strange and disarming. Matrona had never seen their like before. If Slava had made a habit of creating them, why hadn't he ever shared his work, even at the annual fair? Were they meant to be secret? What lay inside them?

Wiping sweat from her brow, Matrona hurried down the path, wondering if Feodor still awaited her at the house. She prayed she hadn't dawdled too badly, for her frazzled thoughts could not bear a scolding. *You must be levelheaded and purposeful,* she reminded herself. The jug would be made, she would do her chores, and she would forget about the odd collection inside Slava Barinov's house.

Chapter 2

Matrona's quick pace left her flushed and breathless by the time she reached her family's *izba*. Feodor stood just outside the door, likely on his way home. Matrona forced her legs to slow and her spine to straighten. She tucked those stubborn stray hairs behind her ears.

Feodor looked up and cocked one of his thick brows. "You've made good time."

"I tried to be swift," she replied. She took deep, slow breaths to quiet her nerves. While she'd not seen a doll for Feodor on the tables, there had been so many, and all the ones she'd inspected had borne a likeness to someone in the village. She suspected he had one, too. Did its outfit match the shirt and vest he wore now, or perhaps the gray *rubashka* he often favored?

"'He who hurries his footsteps errs,'" he said, quoting the Good Book.

They met on the path, Feodor leaning his weight onto one lean leg, taking a moment to look over her. His gaze felt like a cool breeze against naked skin, and Matrona tried not to shiver beneath it. Instead, she studied him back.

He was a fairly handsome man. While he did not have a strong jaw, he possessed full lips and a good nose. His brows were thick, and Roksana had teased her that their children would have the thickest eyebrows in the village, for Matrona's own brows were dark and bold beneath her forehead. He had a narrow torso and waist, and his hips jutted to one side due to how he stood.

Her gaze returned to his face, to his lips. Feodor had not yet kissed her—his proposal had only been accompanied by a chaste kiss on the back of her hand. But Feodor was a reserved and modest man. Still, Matrona wondered when he *would* kiss her. Not now—the timing didn't feel right, somehow. Perhaps at the altar. Surely by their wedding night. How strange to think of kissing a man and then giving herself to him only moments later. It sent moth wings up her arms and over her shoulders.

Matrona cleared her throat. "There are places where the Good Book commends haste." She spoke softly, an effort to keep her defense mild. "It should be ready tomorrow. The jug," she specified, clasping her hands together before her. She *did* look forward to learning to love Feodor—truly she did—but it would be so much easier to love him if he would love her first. Then again, perhaps he did, and simply chose not to show it. She had a hard time reading him—his conservative stances and cool blue eyes hid his thoughts.

The image of Jaska's clay-stained hands on that cracked jug, turning it over with knowledge and a strange fondness, perhaps, burrowed into her mind. She blinked twice, snuffing it out like a wax-drowned candlewick.

"Your father," Feodor said, dismissing the comment about the jug, "is he well?"

Matrona cocked her head. "Yes, of course. He was this morning. You saw him."

A nod. "I did, but he seemed tense as I was leaving. Stressed, perhaps." He rubbed his chin. "I suppose it cannot be helped, with all he has to do and only a daughter to support him. Do see that he's relieved today, hm?"

"I shall."

Feodor offered her another closed-lip smile, another nod, and stepped off the path, heading southward toward his home. Matrona watched him go, measuring his stride, noting the cleanliness of his hands. Though he was a butcher, Matrona had never seen a drop of blood on him.

Despite herself, her mind wandered from blood to clay upon entering her home.

"There's chores to be done." Her mother didn't look up from the brick oven and the growing fire in its belly. As though Matrona had forgotten. As though she ever forgot.

"Yes, Mama," she replied, passing through the front room, down the hallway, and out the door to the small pasture that lay beyond the house. She liked to pretend it was larger and more verdant, with full fields of grass instead of weed-spotted dirt, but today the whitewashed fence surrounding the land seemed especially close. She saw her father out with one of the cows, checking its ears. He turned suddenly and smacked an open palm against the wooden fence multiple times, then shook his head. Matrona's lips parted. Stressed, indeed.

Leaving him be, she strode into the barn to finish churning the butter she had started that morning, before her mother had called her in to visit with Roksana and sort through the wedding chest. She pulled up a three-legged stool and began pumping the churn's handle, her arms and shoulders well acquainted with the exercise. Her thoughts danced over the wedding dress she would wear and its matching headdress. The memory of Esfir's forgotten rag doll surfaced, and her mind easily slid back to Slava's dolls.

She very much wanted to ask the tradesman about the figures, but how could she broach the subject? The window in that strange room was too high set for her to pretend she'd seen through in passing.

More than anything, she wanted to return to that room and see the faces of the other dolls. To find her own, her mother's, Feodor's. To open them and see what treasures lay inside, if any. How long would it take a man to carve and paint such figures? How long had Slava spent crafting them?

Her arms strained, but Matrona churned steadily, pushing past the ache, letting her thoughts settle into the quiet between beats. *Never again,* she thought with a frown. That was the most likely outcome. She'd never get a chance to study the dolls, not unless she could figure out a way to persuade Slava to display them without revealing her secret. She would have to think on it more.

The butter was stubborn, and by the time it was ready to salt, her back promised soreness in the morning. She stretched out her limbs in the privacy of the barn, then set about milking the cows. By the time she'd finished the evening milking—usually her father's job—prepared cream for tomorrow's butter, and set the rest of the milk in barrels, her mother had produced cabbage and potatoes on the table. There was also pork butt, courtesy of Feodor.

As Matrona washed her hands in a pail, her mother asked, "Is your father not with you?"

Matrona shook water from her fingers and wiped them on her skirt as she peered outside. "He wasn't in the pasture . . ." She hadn't seen him since that afternoon, she realized.

A knock on the door called their attention. Her mother sniffed. "Now who could that be?"

Slava's name passed through Matrona's mind, quickening her pulse. Wringing her hands, she followed her mother back to the front room, only to discover it was not a knock on the door they'd heard, but a knock on the wall beside the brick oven. By her father's forehead.

"Papa?" Matrona asked, gawking at her father's body. His hands were pressed against the wall, and he was banging his head repeatedly against it, none too gently.

"Good heavens, Marlen!" her mother exclaimed, rushing up to him. She took his elbow, and Matrona's father stopped the banging at once, pulling away from the wall, his expression dazed. Matrona hurried to him and pressed a palm to his red forehead, then to the side of his neck. No fever.

"What's wrong?" Matrona asked.

Her father shook his head, his beard brushing across his chest. "I just . . . I just can't think my words."

"What are you rambling about?" her mother asked. "Think your words? You're sounding like Mad Olia Maysak, you are!"

"Don't contrary me to that woman!" he shouted with a raised finger, which caused Matrona's mother to drop her hand from his arm. Matrona's pulse sped quicker. Her father so seldom raised his voice, and never to his wife.

"Papa, please," Matrona tried. "You mean, don't *compare* you . . . ?"

Her father scratched his ears and shook his head. "Let's eat. Eat. Let's eat, and I'll feel wall again."

"Well again," Matrona whispered, and her mother turned to her with lips cinched tight as a barley bag. Sighing, Matrona quieted and led the way to the table, feeling powerless.

Dinner passed in general silence, minus a few grunts from Matrona's father, who held his fork in a fisted hand almost like a babe would and seemed to have a hard time swallowing. Throughout the meal, Matrona's mother kept shooting pointed glares at her, silent warnings not to speak. In return, Matrona mouthed, *Doctor?* but her mother simply shook her head. After her father retired early, leaving them to the dishes, her mother said, "He'll be fine in the morning."

He was not.

Chapter 3

Matrona watched her father as villagers came to the house to retrieve milk for their breakfasts. He seemed . . . itchy, the way he twitched and scratched or occasionally rubbed himself against the wall. Because he refused to stay abed, her mother tried to keep him to the back of the house where he wouldn't be seen. His hands lost their dexterity, leaving him unable to complete the evening milking, which settled the bulk of the work on Matrona. He spoke little, and when he did talk, his words were garbled. At lunch, he refused to eat, instead choosing to stand at the fence on the far edge of the pasture, staring off into the wood like an injured stag that knew a hunter lurked just beyond those trees.

It was then, standing at the back of the house while wringing a cheesecloth, that Matrona thought of it. *Slava.*

It was an absurd notion, she knew, but the memory of the trades-man's house nagged at her. Had her father not been well yesterday morning? Had he not spoken to Feodor with perfect intelligence? Feodor had noticed his erratic behavior first, had told Matrona of it as soon as she returned from her uninvited visit to Slava's blue-and-yellow home. After she'd seen the dolls. After she'd tried to open her father's.

She worried her lip, straining to remember. She hadn't opened the doll, but she'd twisted the two pieces before fleeing. Still, what could the wooden simulacrum possibly have to do with her father? Surely Slava Barinov didn't perform witchcraft. Surely *she* hadn't, through his dolls.

And yet it was the only explanation Matrona had. The only thing that had changed around the same time her father had.

She needed to go back.

Matrona stepped inside and washed her hands, scrubbing the scent of old milk from beneath her nails. She heard her mother in the front room, making an exchange with another villager, so she returned to the pasture and slipped through the back gate. It would be impossible to explain—her mother, who always chided her for her imagination, would never believe such a wild story. She barely believed it herself. The chores could wait an hour.

Matrona weaved around another house before turning onto the dirt path that stretched across the village, following it with unsure steps. She passed Pavel Zotov on the way and nodded to him. When the trades-man's ornate house finally came into view, it no longer reminded her of the slumbering body of a great beast, but a block of unchipped granite, hard and unyielding. Invisible ants began to tickle Matrona's chest.

A quick glance assured her that the tradesman's horse and wagon rested near the edge of the wood. Surely he was home. But how to explain herself?

As Matrona took the two brick steps to the porch, she settled on honesty as the best approach. So what if Slava thought poorly of her? She only interacted with him when he wanted some cream or butter, which was not too often.

She lifted her hand to knock on the painted door, but it swung open before her knuckles could connect.

Slava Barinov stood before her.

He wasn't a tall man, and while age had paled his trimmed beard and stripped the hair from the top of his head, he stood with a straight back and level shoulders. Crinkles edged the corners of his eyes, and long wrinkles drew down the cheeks on either side of his broad-bridged nose. He wore a simple shirt and trousers that contrasted with the vivacity of his house.

"I—" Matrona began.

"I thought it was you." His blue eyes narrowed ever so slightly while they surveyed her up and down. "Come in."

He stepped aside. Words tangling in her throat, Matrona passed him into the short hallway, looking around the home. Slava shut the door, and Matrona managed to say, "Thought it was me, Slava Nikolayevich?" She hoped the formal address would ease the tension.

The old man turned toward her, a gray eyebrow raised. "And how do you know my father's name was Nikolay?"

Matrona swallowed. "I heard Feodor Popov refer to you as such."

Slava hummed deep in his throat and nodded once before passing by her and moving into the front room. "So you did. But you do not use the patronymic with any others in the village, do you? So you must not use it with me. Understood?"

Matrona nodded.

He gestured for her to follow him, and she did so silently, her feet light and her lips pressed shut. Already she knew where Slava was leading her. She followed him past the chest of drawers, through the kitchen, and down the small hallway to the room filled with dolls. The red kite rested in the far corner, on a small wooden perch Matrona hadn't noticed before. Turning his head, he watched her with a single yellowed eye.

She hesitated in the doorway, but Slava beckoned to her. "Come. Pamyat won't harm you."

Pamyat, she wondered, crossing the threshold. *Memory? What a peculiar name for a bird.*

The dolls were all there, filling up the two tables in the center of the room, and the short shelves nailed into the walls. They were exactly as she remembered them, wooden pear-shaped dolls, intricately painted to look like the villagers, all with fine seams around their middles. Matrona glanced over them, looking for more familiar faces. There, near the Jaska doll, was Olia Maysak. And behind them rested the entire Letov family.

Slava stepped toward the smaller table on the left and picked up a doll with a blue *rubashka* and a long beard, the top half of the long shirt mismatched with the bottom half. Her father's doll.

"Sir—" Matrona began.

"Slava. Address me as you would the others," he reminded her. "I thought that only someone in Marlen Vitsin's brood would take interest in his doll, and he has little enough family. Though your mother is a snoop, I thought it would be you. Hoped it would be."

He looked over the twisted doll with a strange sort of fondness, holding it across both palms as if testing the weight of it.

Matrona eyed him, waiting for him to say more. The seconds weighed heavy on her shoulders. "Slava, Tradesman," she interrupted, "you *hoped* I would come into your house unannounced and play with your dolls?"

Slava chuckled. "Play with them, did you?"

"I—I . . . didn't have a better word." She flushed.

Pamyat shifted on his perch.

Slava nodded, and Matrona watched his hands on her father's doll. "I hoped it would be you and not your mother, for you are still young, Matrona. Your mother is not, and as you can see, neither am I.

"These dolls need a caretaker," he continued, gesturing to the rest of the room. "I made each one, and I've looked after them all. Yours included."

He pointed to a doll on the edge of the small table to the left, and Matrona gaped at the sight of her own face, her gray eyes carefully pricked with lashes, her long braid of black hair slung over her left shoulder, just as it lay now. The doll wore a red *sarafan* similar to the one she'd donned yesterday, with a matching *kokoshnik*. Matrona stepped toward it, but hesitated, eyeing Slava. What did it mean?

"I'm sure we can arrange to keep them safe," she tried.

But Slava shook his head and let out a long breath, weariness settling onto him like an iron cloak. In the corner, Pamyat ruffled his feathers. "You do not understand."

Matrona did not reply.

Slava turned her father's doll over in his hands and scanned his similar creations. "They are connected, these dolls and the people in this village. You know that, don't you, Matrona? That is why you came back."

Matrona's mouth went dry. "I—I came to return a paintbrush—"

"No one else in the village has seen this room . . . at least none of whom I'm aware," he continued. "If someone else *has* come, they did a much better job of covering their tracks." His eyes twinkled, but his voice was a little too cool to be jesting. He held up the doll in his hands so Matrona could again see how its halves didn't align. It felt as if the floor of the room had tilted, making Slava's end higher than hers, as if his body grew until it pressed against the walls and ceiling, while hers shrank into the grooves of the floorboards.

Hugging herself to banish a sudden chill in her chest, Matrona retreated two steps. "My father has been acting strangely. Unwell. Not at all himself. It began after I . . . looked at your dolls."

"Hmm," Slava grumbled in agreement. "Because the doll is connected to him, and you have altered it. But perhaps it's a blessing that you've seen this place. I need a replacement, and choosing one has proved . . . difficult." He rubbed his fingers over his beard. "This makes it easier." He chuckled. "I wouldn't have thought you bold enough to enter . . . but it's my fault for not locking the door."

His words tickled in Matrona's ears. "Lock? What's a lock?"

Pamyat clicked deep in his throat.

"Never mind that." Slava waved his hand. A simple dismissal— Matrona was so very used to that. "I will not be here forever, no matter what I do. You will care for the dolls in my absence, Matrona. You will watch over them, guard them, and create them."

The feathers on Pamyat's neck rose. The kite lowered his head, his marble-round eyes focused on Matrona.

Create? Her thoughts repeated, and she took another step back, eyeing the kite. Her shoulder hit one of the shelves stacked with dolls. "I know nothing of woodworking—"

"It doesn't matter. I will teach you."

"Slava, Tradesman," she tried, sounding out each word carefully, working to not let her voice quake, "I am a simple dairymaid, soon to be married. I cannot take on a new trade—"

"You can, and you will," he interrupted, blue eyes sharpening. He held up her father's doll so that the painted eyes looked directly into hers. "You've stumbled on something greater than yourself, Matrona. My life's work. I need you, and you will comply, for I cannot trust you if you don't."

Matrona eyed the open door. He was mad. She couldn't—

Pamyat shrieked, the noise amplified by the close walls. Matrona nearly choked on her own tongue.

"I'll not set him right," Slava added, and the words pulled her attention back to his face. Back to the doll he held. Slava grasped the upper and lower halves in his large, calloused hands, but did not twist them one way or another. Instead, he said, "I'll not set him right, and I'll see that you don't, either. He'll not be well unless he's straightened out, don't you see?"

Matrona's tongue traced the backs of her teeth, seeking moisture, finding none. She nodded. She understood.

Slava smiled. "Good." Then, with a sharp, squeaking twist, he shifted the halves of the doll. Matrona yelped, but Slava had only righted the halves so that her father's shirt buttons fell in a single, even row and his sleeves connected flawlessly with his pale-painted hands.

Slava set the doll on the table, then shifted backward to select Matrona's doll.

"Please don't," she whispered.

"Oh, I won't do anything." Slava's tone was so casual, she could hardly believe he'd just threatened her with her father's well-being, however mystical in nature. "This, *you* must do. You cannot understand me and my creations without finding your center, Matrona."

The chill in her chest abated somewhat. "My center?"

He held the doll out to her, and Matrona stared into the glazed face of her miniature.

"You must open your doll."

Chapter 4

The tips of Matrona's fingers tingled on the verge of numbness as she took her doll from Slava's hands. In the moment it seemed heavier than her father's, yet also too small, too fragile. A caricature of her face looked up at her, unblinking. Two salmon-colored circles highlighted her cheeks. The red *kokoshnik*, she realized, was one she had worn to fairs and church services as an adolescent and had since disposed of. The painted eyelashes were so fine, Matrona could not comprehend how any hand, especially old Slava's, could have painted them.

Instantly Matrona thought of her father's crazed behavior, all due to his doll's misalignment. If such a small thing could cause a grown man to stutter and speak nonsense and bang his head against walls, what could opening this doll do to *her*?

Again she glanced toward the door, keeping her eyes down in hopes that Slava would not notice. She could outrun him, couldn't she? Take the doll and flee into the wood? She did not know the way to any other villages or towns, but surely she'd find one eventually . . .

She eyed the kite, wondering how well trained he was. Did Slava use him to hunt?

But the bird was hardly her biggest worry. She remembered how her father's doll had looked cradled in Slava's hands, its body little more than an eggshell. She couldn't run off with both, not now. And what of her mother's doll? Roksana's? Feodor's?

"Please," she begged, daring to look up at Slava's face. While not unkind, it was tired, calculating. A face she didn't feel confident trusting. "I don't . . . I don't understand why . . ."

Slava nodded, the faintest smile touching his lips. He selected a doll seemingly at random—Jaska Maysak's doll. Matrona stared at it, drawn to its dark eyes. It was well dressed, not in a potter's apron, but in simple slacks and a gray shirt. The paint used for his face and hands was a smidge darker than that of the surrounding dolls, and several shades darker than Matrona's own. Somehow Slava had even mastered the unkemptness of the potter's hair. Oddly, the image of Jaska looked older than he was at present. When had Slava painted this likeness?

"Do you know how these work?" he asked, giving Jaska's doll a small shake. Something rattled within.

Matrona shook her head.

"They come from a distant island. To get there, you have to travel far over land and across a sliver of sea," Slava explained. "A narrow isle steeped in tradition and war, full of a studious and honor-bound people. I went there long ago, on one of my journeys, and found something similar to this in a small hut." He turned Jaska over, his fingers crossing the potter's clothes like spider legs. Matrona quelled the sudden desire to snatch the doll away. "I could sense the dolls' magical properties immediately. It requires expert craftsmanship to create them, and I learned all I could.

"You see, inside every doll is another doll," he said, and Matrona felt the skin between her eyebrows crinkle. "And inside that doll is another doll, and another. However many the maker wishes to create. Your doll, Matrona, is actually five dolls, each hollowed out to fit the next. They all are," he added, gesturing to the others.

Matrona glanced down at her miniature and rubbed the pad of her thumb along the seam. She gave it a gentle shake. Whatever lay nestled inside was large and had little room for movement. Another doll? Did it also bear her likeness? *How strange.*

"To understand what I need you to learn, you need to separate yourself from the rest of the village," Slava explained. Matrona's head snapped up, her stomach sinking, and the old man had the audacity to chuckle at her. "You will still *be* here, if that is your worry. It is . . ." He waved his hand in a circular motion before her, and Matrona could see him picking through his thoughts the way her father so often did, searching for perhaps the sweetest or tamest words to explain something she couldn't possibly fathom.

Heat prickled beneath her skin, and before she could cage the words, she said, "I'm sure I'll understand you if you speak bluntly, Tradesman."

He raised an eyebrow. "Yes, I'm sure you will, Dairymaid," and he smiled at the foolish nickname. "But there are some things I cannot merely *explain*, which is why you must open the dolls. *But—*" He added the last word hastily and set down Jaska's doll without taking his eyes from her. "You *must not* open all of your dolls at once. Are you listening carefully, Matrona Vitsin? You must open them one at a time, slowly, and under my supervision, or else there will be grave consequences."

The kite watched her with both eyes.

Matrona stiffened, her fingers clutching her doll as though they were talons. "What sort of consequences?"

"You will see, if you are foolish." Bitterness leaked into his voice. He looked over the large table, but Matrona could not determine which doll had caught his attention. Seconds later, his gaze returned to her. "You must also promise not to tell another soul about the dolls. Give me your word, on your honor, not to speak of it."

Matrona bit her lip.

Slava's gaze darkened. "You know what I can do. I did not intend to threaten, Matrona, but it is easier than the alternative. This is for the good of the village, as you will learn."

She found enough moisture in her mouth to say, "You would have me swear it? But the Good Book—"

Slava grumbled. "You must swear it, regardless of God."

Regardless of God. It was near blasphemy. Still, the memories of her father's condition forced her to bob her head.

It was enough for Slava. "Very good. You will open your doll now, just one, and place it on the table." He gestured to the empty spot on the leftmost tabletop. "Then you will return to me in three days' time to open the next. Understood?"

Again, she nodded, her hands sweating against the glazed paint of the doll, her dress too hot against her skin. *Just open it,* she told herself. *Open it and leave.* How desperately her lungs ached for fresh air.

She twisted the two pieces a hair's breadth. "What will happen?"

"You will be unharmed." Slava folded his arms. "The rest will soon become apparent."

The kite nodded his narrow head as if in agreement. The movement made his beak look longer.

Closing her eyes, Matrona held her breath and wrenched the doll open.

Nothing happened. She didn't feel crazed. She didn't feel different at all. Opening her eyes, she glanced down at the doll in her hands. Sure enough, inside the outer shell was another doll identical to the first, wearing the same clothes and expression. Matrona set the open halves of the larger doll on a sliver of free space on the large table and studied the smaller doll in her hand.

"Close it and place it on the table," Slava instructed.

Matrona did so, her gaze lingering on her likeness.

"Three days," he reminded her. "I will be waiting for you."

Matrona nodded mutely. When Slava seemed to have no further words for her, she turned and let herself out of the house, happy to be done with it.

She took two full breaths once the familiar dirt path appeared underfoot, then shook out her arms until her shoulders relaxed. Glancing behind her to the tradesman's house, she wondered if it had all been some sort of ruse. Had Slava merely used her gullibility to frighten her? She felt no different.

Perhaps she wouldn't know the truth until she saw her father.

She passed the children's glade in the wood and saw Alena Zotov coming the opposite way with the cooper's wife beside her, both carrying baskets to be filled by other village craftsmen. Matrona moved to wave, but the shadows on Alena's face stilled her hand. The woman's features only darkened as she drew nearer. The cooper's wife, too, narrowed her eyes at Matrona, then turned and whispered something into Alena's ear. Alena's stare did not break from Matrona's, and a scowl formed on the other woman's lips. She nodded slightly, agreeing to whatever the cooper's wife had told her.

They did not make space on the path, forcing Matrona to step onto the tromped grass beside it. Alena had never looked at her so coldly before. Neither of the women had.

They passed, sniffing as they went, and Matrona caught the words "—indecent. I feel sorry for—" and then they were gone.

Matrona watched after them, tucking back those short, stray hairs. Surely the scowls weren't meant for her. Had someone else in the village treated them poorly before they came this way? Was all well at Roksana's home?

Matrona shook herself. *Father. Find father.* She needed to ensure he was well, and that Slava was not playing some strange game with her. Picking up her skirt, Matrona returned to the path and quickened her step.

As the west side of the village came into view, so did the other villagers. Perhaps Matrona imagined it, but they all seemed to be scowling at her. The cobbler's daughter gaped with a wide *O* expression to her mouth, and old Irena Kalagin shouted out, "I was sick for three days, you wretched girl!"

Matrona's heart retreated until it hit her spine, and she quivered with its every beat. "I'm sorry," she said too quietly. "What—?"

But Irena simply spat on the ground before turning back to her laundry.

Taking a deep breath to still her nerves, Matrona focused on the path beneath her and hurried toward her house, nearly at a run, avoiding the eyes of her other neighbors. Their gaze made her feel naked, and she without a clue as to where her clothes had gone.

Slava's words, *"The rest will soon become apparent,"* echoed against her skull as the scents of the dairy farm wafted over her.

She glanced up to the safe haven of her *izba* and opened the door, letting out a long breath as she pushed it closed with her heel. Her mother looked up from the brick oven and hurried toward her.

"Mama," Matrona said, breathless, "the strangest thing—"

Her mother's open palm cracked against Matrona's cheek.

The force turned her head and pounded in her ears. Eyes watering, Matrona blinked rapidly and touched the tender bruise forming beneath her eye. She turned toward her mother, noticing the hardness in her eyes and the prominent vein drawn down her forehead.

"You dare to humiliate me and the Popovs with such a scandal?" her mother snapped. "By the saints, he's practically a child!"

Matrona's stomach sank into her hips, her heart plopping atop it. They had to be weighing down her lungs, for she found it difficult to breathe. "Wh-What?"

"And a *Maysak*," her mother spat, throwing her hands up into the air and plodding back to the brick oven to check on whatever cooked there. "His mother is a madwoman and his father a drunk!"

Matrona's skin turned cold, and she leaned back against the door to keep from falling over. Her fingers trembled. "Y-You know . . ." *about . . . Jaska?*

"About your filthy yearnings for Mad Olia's youngest? Everyone knows," she spat again. "I did not raise my daughter to have such indecent thoughts. And toward a *Maysak*!"

Matrona slid down the length of the door until her rump smacked against the floor. She pinched herself, but this was no dream. The beats of her pulse bled into one another, leaving her light-headed.

Her mother picked up a wooden spoon and threw it against the front of the brick oven. "Your father is in a rage over it. I can't imagine what Feodor will say, let alone his parents!" She spun back toward Matrona, fire inside her skin. "Get up. You think *now* is a time for rest? And I *knew* the cheese that made everyone sick two years past was your doing. I *knew* it, reckless girl!"

Irena's hard words surfaced in her mind. *"I was sick for three days,"* she'd said. The food poisoning. Yes, that had been her fault. She'd sensed the milk was turning wrong, but the demand had been so high . . . She hadn't told a soul—not about that, and certainly not about Jaska.

If Feodor cancelled the marriage, she'd be trapped inside this *izba* forever, barely esteemed higher than the rag rugs.

A murky image of her doll surfaced in her mind. *It can't be.*

The back door to the *izba* slammed shut, and her father stomped in, brow furrowed. When he noticed Matrona, his bearded lips pulled into a deep frown. "You have a great deal of explaining to do. How will we show our faces at church?"

No slurred words. No twitching. Only anger. Yet Matrona could find no peace in his apparent recovery.

"Well?" pushed her mother.

"I—I never . . ." Matrona shook her head, and her mother stormed forward to grab Matrona's sleeve and haul her upright. "I—I didn't mean for the cheese to go bad . . ." Her face flushed, and tears stung her eyes. "I never . . . Jaska, I never acted on—"

"It barely makes a difference!" her mother shouted. "The things you think about that *potter*—"

Think *about the potter?* Matrona wondered, her bones feeling as hollow as flutes. How could her mother possibly know her *thoughts?*

They bubbled up inside her, scraps of past and buried flights of fancy about the youngest Maysak. The times she'd measured his shoulders—his hips—with her eyes. How she'd imagined strolling in the wood with him, wondered about the taste of his mouth, and—

"God help me," she murmured.

"He wants nothing to do with you," her mother snapped.

Her father shook his head. "Just . . . go to your room until we can sort this out. I can't fathom what the Popovs . . ."

He didn't finish the sentiment. He didn't need to. Matrona balled her hands into white-knuckled fists and rushed past her parents, hurtling down the hallway to her small room. Once inside, she shut the door behind her, and only then did she let the tears fall. She wiped at them, but that only wet her hands and wrists.

Were all her secrets known, then? Every little sin that had ever crossed her mind, every sour thought toward her parents or other villagers? But they didn't know about the dolls . . . Surely they couldn't. No one had asked about the dolls.

She thought of Jaska, and her cheeks burned as surely as if someone had sliced open hot peppers and rubbed them on her face. Even before Feodor, she'd never shared her thoughts about the potter with anyone. Not even Roksana knew about Jaska. Matrona never spoke of him or the Maysaks unless someone else mentioned the family first . . .

Was this the reason for the cross looks Alena Zotov and the cooper's wife had given her? Because they knew she was a twenty-six-year-old betrothed woman who harbored desires for a younger man—a boy, he was practically a *boy*—in the dark shadows of her thoughts?

Could they hear what she was thinking right now? A passage from the Good Book bubbled up in her thoughts: *"Neither is there any creature that is not manifest in his sight: but all things are naked and opened unto the eyes of him with whom we have to do."*

Matrona collapsed onto her bed and smothered her head with her pillow until her body craved breath. Did her fellow men suddenly possess the eyes of God? Her mind sought out any other secrets she'd buried over the years. Did the villagers now know about the triangle of moles on her left hip? The time she'd lied for Roksana so her friend could visit the granger? What of the test she'd cheated on in school some fifteen years ago? Did they know about that, too?

Shooting up to her knees, Matrona grabbed her tear-spotted pillow and threw it against the wall. She'd spent her whole life trying to do what was right. Trying to keep her parents smiling enough that hard words would never leave their lips. Trying to be good. Even so, she could bear the whole village's censure—she was sure she could bear it—were it not for the gossip about Jaska.

She wiped her sleeves across her eyes. There was a reason she was twenty-six and unwed. There was not an abundance of bachelors in the village, and she had stayed away from them as a maiden should. As her father had always wanted her to. Only an occasional smile or nod of her head. She had chosen her words to any possible match with care to ensure they could not be misconstrued. Yet she would be punished for this? Who among her family, her neighbors, had *not* harbored indecent thoughts?

She collapsed back onto her mattress, biting her tongue to control the urge to weep, wishing she could sleep and wake up to a normal world without secrets and without dolls. She did not sleep. Matrona never napped during the day—there was too much to do. Too much required of her.

The walls of her room pressed into her, the slivers in their wood picking apart the rhythm of her breathing.

Spitting Slava's name like a curse, Matrona pushed herself off her mattress and stepped back into the hall. She heard the mumbling voices of her parents talking in the front room, but she slipped through the kitchen and out the back door to the cow pasture. Work would pull the strain from her body. Work would clear her thoughts. Work would make her sleep.

Matrona churned butter with a vigor that would have surprised her had her mind been present enough to realize it. She lost herself in the familiar pain of her arms and shoulders. She muddied the bottom of her *sarafan*, hauling hay into the cow troughs and mucking out their tie stalls. She rubbed her hands raw twisting cheesecloths.

She was separating the curds from the whey when a familiar voice spoke her name, startling her from her work.

"Feodor." She kept her focus on the curds. Rude of her, yes, but she just couldn't—

"I've been speaking to your parents." His voice sounded deeper than usual, flatter. "I must say . . . you have shocked us all."

"I didn't do so willingly." She scrambled for something clever to say, but the sudden exposure had left her empty.

Feodor scoffed. "I should hope not. The entire village is whispering about you and that Maysak boy. You've dragged my family's name through the mud as well."

"Do they also talk of the dolls?"

His brow furrowed as if she'd spouted gibberish. "What dolls?"

So that secret had been preserved, no doubt by some sorcery of Slava's. Matrona crushed the curds in her hand, took a deep breath, and let the cheesecloth fall to her worktable. Turning around, she bowed her head. "Please forgive me, and do not hold it against my parents."

The words felt like sand in her mouth, and her blood seemed to pump the wrong direction through her veins. Her head spun, and an ache formed behind her eyes. Did he have to confront her *now*? Could Feodor not allot her one day to process her humiliation?

Could he not understand?

"I suppose I should not." From the corner of her eye, she saw him fold his arms. He was silent for a long moment, then sighed and said, "I don't know what to do with you, Matrona. Hide you and myself away until the gossipmongers find something better to talk about? I need to sort out my own . . . feelings on the matter."

Matrona lifted her eyes to meet his, but Feodor stared at an unknown spot on the wall behind her. Feeling daring, Matrona asked, "Then you will not break the engagement?"

"I have not decided," he answered, too quickly, as though he had been waiting for the opportunity to say it. To let her know what a disappointment she'd become to him. His gaze finally met hers. "You know I value tradition, chastity—"

"I am not unchaste."

"—the subjection of a woman to her husband," he added, his lip curving downward. "You are well dispositioned and know how to hold your tongue and please your family. You strive to follow the Good Book. That is what drew me to you, Matrona. To know of these"—he scowled—"*fancies*—"

"Matrona!" sang a new voice, Roksana's, and the loudness of it was jarring. "Matrona, are you here? You never told me—"

Roksana appeared in the doorway to the barn and stopped short, her eyes open and round as she took in Feodor and Matrona, who undoubtedly looked a mess. "Oh, excuse me." She offered a small curtsy. "I didn't think—"

Feodor waved her apology away with a limp hand. "I have nothing else to say, only thoughts to think. Good day, Roksana."

Roksana nodded, and Feodor pushed past her. Matrona picked at the cheese under her nails. She ached to tell her dear friend to leave her be, just for now. To give her time to sort through this strange mess that had been laid upon her lap. But the words wouldn't come, and then it was too late.

"Matrona." Roksana glanced back at Feodor before stepping into the barn, guarding her full belly with her hands. "Oh, he must be livid. What did you tell him?"

Matrona shrugged and turned back to the cheesecloth.

"I'm sure you can mend it," Roksana added, stepping up to the worktable, her own dark braids swinging over her shoulders. "I'm in terrible trouble with Luka, I hope you know. He had no idea the granger and I used to fancy each other, though I'm not sure why he cares so much. It was before Luka and I even noticed each other."

"Of course he does." Matrona squeezed the cheesecloth, milky water streaming over her sore knuckles.

"But *Matrona*," Roksana urged, leaning against the worktable to better see her face. "You told me you had no fancy for anyone, and that Feodor—"

"Roksana," Matrona pleaded.

"You always were good at keeping secrets."

Not anymore, I'm not, she thought, untwisting the cheesecloth and dumping the crushed curds into a bowl. Her eyes burned, but they stayed dry.

"His father—Feodor's, that is—is raving mad," Roksana continued. "He was in my papa's shop when we found out—"

"And how did you find out?" Matrona snapped. How had any of them found out?

Roksana paused, blinking, her forehead slowly crinkling above her eyes. "I don't know . . . Where are you going?"

Matrona was nearly to the door, wiping her hands on the dingy apron tied around her hips. She hastily loosened its strings and let it fall to the barn floor. She didn't answer Roksana, only continued walking. Searching for some sort of respite. How she itched to go to Slava's house, walk straight into that room of the nesting dolls, and choose one at random. Open that first layer and spill someone else's secrets for the village hens. Surely there were darker truths than her own to occupy her neighbors.

How cruel that would be.

She pushed through the nearest gate and exited the pasture, her strides long and quick. She wound around the back of the land, but still managed to catch sight of Pavel Zotov across the way. His eyes lingered on her too long, like hot stones burning her skin. So she changed direction once more, toward the quiet homes of her neighbors. Their yards were empty, which encouraged her. This route was the way to Feodor's butchery, but she would not go there. Her goal was simply to go *away*, where the ill- and well-meaning alike couldn't find her.

Only, as she neared one of the less trodden paths toward her betrothed's properties, she *did* see another person on the route, coming from the opposite way. Matrona froze, her throat instantly knotting into a hard lump. Jaska.

When he looked up, he stopped midstride, and she saw the recently kilned jug in his right hand.

Her body turned cold and stiff as the terrible truth dawned on her. He must know, too, just as all the others did. She could see it in his eyes, despite the long space between them.

The air felt too thick. It crushed her lungs from within. The urge to run was overpowering. The wood stretched to her right with its promise of hiding her, of absorbing her humiliation among its trees. But she was no hunter, and if she ran, it would only confirm the truth of the secrets everyone whispered about. How much more embarrassment could she withstand?

He started toward her, and a sharp panic pierced her from neck to navel. She stepped off the path and hurried, nearly running but not quite, through the village. North. Her braid whipped her back as she went, and her nails dug into her palms. By the time she reached the church, her lungs blazed like two oil lamps.

Resting a hand against one of the church's outer log walls, she took a moment to catch her breath and wipe perspiration from her forehead. A couple passed by, and Matrona slipped around the building's corner to avoid being seen. She could not handle another accusing gaze, not right now.

She looked up at the church, a cross-wall structure with *prirub*. Two of its three roofs were conical in shape, and from those two stretched short wooden spires that ended in simple crucifixes, carved by Pavel. The church was probably the second-finest building in the village, after Slava's dragon house. It should not be so—she'd heard others whisper the same—but she was not about to petition the tradesman to donate his glass-and-blue tiles to decorate the house of the Lord.

Letting her fingers trail across its walls, Matrona circled around the church until she reached the front door. She peeked in—the space within was empty. Thanking the saints, she stepped inside and sat on one of the backless benches, huddling against the wall, hoping to meld with the shadows. There was a simple altar near the front, along with a pedestal that held the village's only copy of the Good Book, a thin volume with a leather cover. Matrona had thumbed through it once. To her it felt the Book should be longer. Some of its passages left off mid-sentence, while some parables finished without conclusion. As though whoever bound it had pulled out words . . . But of course that was nonsense.

Elbows on knees, she cradled her face in her hands and offered up a weak semblance of a prayer. She wasn't sure what to pray for, or if she should address one of the saints or God himself. Strength to withstand Slava's spell? Mercy from her fellows? Would God heed her, a woman who lusted after a man to whom she was not betrothed, and who had willingly sworn an oath to . . . What was Slava? A sorcerer?

A chill in her bones made her shiver, but she stayed on the bench until her nerves calmed and her thoughts reordered themselves. Until the sun set just enough that she could walk home in relative privacy and begin counting the days until Slava unleashed his next terror.

Chapter 5

Matrona's parents were so distracted by her perceived scandal and the question of how to amend their relationship with the Popovs that they did not notice her late return, if—indeed—they'd noticed her departure.

Matrona slept uneasily, her mind torn between the airing of her most private thoughts and the consequences that would follow. When she did sleep, she dreamed of Jaska, which made her head feel packed with clay come dawn.

Even distracted parents would never forgive shirked chores, so Matrona set to the cows early, partitioning the milk for the villagers, making the butter and cheese, and watering the animals in the crispness of morning. Her mother prepared breakfast, which Matrona ate before wordlessly excusing herself back to the pasture. When she'd completed the bulk of her work, she let herself through the gate and walked toward the western wood while the air still held some crispness, away from the homes of the other villagers. She let the greenery and the birdsong clear her thoughts. Dewy grass licked at her shoes. The scent of fresh lumber tickled her nose—someone must have been chopping upwind. Sighing, she let go of the momentary peace and made her way back to her *izba*.

Her mother was standing outside when she returned home. There was such fury on her face, Matrona nearly cowed when her mother came near and snatched Matrona's wrist.

"Foolish girl," she spat, dragging Matrona around the *izba*, to the pasture's front gate. "Hurry up and make yourself decent."

"What's wrong?" Matrona asked as the gate swung open.

"Oleg and Feodor Popov are here, that's what! And you're nowhere to be found, out dallying without the chores done—"

"The chores are done, Mama."

Her mother rolled her eyes and hurried Matrona to the back of the house. "We'll see about that, but not right now. Fix your hair and change your dress." They passed into the short hallway stocked with milk jugs, and Matrona lightened her feet to sneak by the front room, where the guests would be, and to her bedroom.

Worrying her lip, Matrona pulled off her milk-spotted dress with its soiled hem and traded it for the red *sarafan*. She took out her small hand mirror—one of the imports Slava had sold in the market years ago—and checked her hair. It didn't look amiss, so she merely licked her fingertips and smoothed back the short, stray hairs over her ears, then pinched her cheeks to redden them. If she didn't pinch them, surely her mother would, and none too delicately.

Matrona angled the mirror to see the faint line of a bruise on her left cheek where her mother had struck her. She frowned. Only noticeable if one looked for it.

As soon as she finished her grooming, Matrona stepped into the hallway. Her mother ushered her into the front room.

The air stretching between the log walls was warmed from the brick oven, and her father, Feodor, and Feodor's father, Oleg, sat on the nicest rag rug the family owned. It measured about nine feet in diameter and was woven with pinks, blues, reds, and yellows. The men had propped themselves up on pillows and were sharing a small pitcher of mint kvass.

Feodor noticed Matrona and offered one of his tight-lipped smiles. It startled her at first but, finding her senses, she offered a small smile in return. Perhaps this talk—these negotiations—had gone well.

Matrona couldn't help but wonder if the Popov men drank kvass after a good bargain on cattle.

Her father glanced up and grinned. "Ah, Matrona, there you are." He set his mug down, stood, and smoothed his beard. "She works so hard to see to the needs of her family and the village. And not a spot on her. Graceful hands make graceful work."

Neither Matrona nor her mother corrected him.

Feodor stood, too, and stooped to help up his father. Oleg Popov did not set down his kvass, and a few drops splashed onto the rug.

"I see that." The bottom of Oleg's thin white beard brushed the rim of his cup. "A girl trying very hard to become a woman, indeed."

Trying to become a woman? Matrona thought, raising an eyebrow. She looked at her father, who did not return her gaze. Had that been part of the discussion? Playing off her now-public faults as the whims of a child? A child who could simply be righted by marriage?

She glanced to Feodor, who folded his arms across his chest and nodded in agreement with her father. Matrona took a deep breath. *No, this is good. If my parents can salvage my reputation and solidify this engagement, we'll all be the better for it.* It was a more decent excuse than anything Matrona could have come up with.

Oleg downed the rest of his drink and handed the mug to Feodor before striking his fist against his chest in a show of honor and offering the same hand to Matrona's father. "Let's keep out of sight for a bit before moving forward with the planning. She *is* easy on the eyes, once you look long enough."

He smiled at Matrona. Matrona wasn't sure if she offered one back.

Feodor gathered the mugs from the rug and crossed the room, offering them to Matrona's mother, who beamed happily at him before running the dishes to the kitchen. To Matrona, he held out his hand. Though still unsure of the situation, she placed her fingers in his.

"I'm glad to see this sorted out," he said, though surely he knew Matrona had no idea what had been discussed in her absence. She swallowed the questions spinning in her brain, letting them die in her stomach. If the marriage was on, then all was as it should be, and she could relax. Feodor bent over her hand, but Matrona felt only the puff of warm breath before he stood back up and returned to his father, whom he escorted to the door.

She rubbed the back of her hand as the Popovs left. Why had he pantomimed kissing it without completing the act? She smelled her hands but detected no sourness from unscrubbed milk. If he had truly forgiven her, wouldn't he have pressed his full lips to her flesh?

Matrona found herself wishing that Feodor would kiss her. Truly kiss her. Not here, in front of their parents, but somewhere. She wished that he would meet her on the path behind his butcher shop or leave her a letter requesting a rendezvous in the wood. She tried to imagine it: standing in the shadows of an oak grove under a purple sky, crickets singing in the evening's warmth, and Feodor's arms encircling her. Perhaps he would whisper something against her ear, something meant only for her, something that revealed a hidden aspect to his character. Then he would kiss her, and Matrona would feel new possibility bloom within herself. Feel like the wood had opened a little wider to make a special place just for her—a place situated in the crooks of Feodor's arms.

The door shut, and Matrona blinked the vision away. There was still time. Time to be held, to be kissed, to be loved. She and Feodor had their whole lives ahead of them. Years to grow into love. And surely a husband would be as eager to grow as his wife, yes?

Years? You have two days, she realized. Two days until Slava would make her open the second doll. What if Feodor didn't stay after the next round of revelations?

But what more could the village possibly learn about her?

Her mother returned from the kitchen. "Now, Matrona—"

"Do we need bread for dinner?" Matrona asked, chancing the interruption. "I can start the bread and wash the cups."

Her mother seemed pleased, which trickled relief like cool water over Matrona's skin. "Yes, that will do nicely."

Matrona offered a minute curtsy before heading into the kitchen, her thoughts full of twilit woods and painted dolls.

❆

Matrona wondered if she would see Slava Barinov before his three-day deadline, but the tradesman did not come to pick up his share of milk. He seldom did. Perhaps cheese and butter weren't kind to his tongue, or his gut.

By the time the third day arrived, Matrona's public humiliation had somewhat abated; the older a rumor grew, the less excitement it elicited from wagging tongues. She had taken time to mull over Slava's words, tone, and demeanor in the doll room, and it left her with a sour stomach. The way his aging forehead wrinkled when he told her a *must*. The way he left her no choice in the matter. The way he held her father's doll in his hands—her father, who had always been kinder than her mother, and whose heart hadn't been so damaged after the loss of Esfir.

But Slava had her doll, too, and answers to her questions. So later that afternoon, when her father was away to collect potatoes from the Grankins and her mother was busying her hands hanging laundry, Matrona took the well-worn path to the center of the village. She made her way to the bright blue-and-yellow house, where a simple paintbrush had brought her so much grief . . . and enlivened her with an almost childish curiosity.

Slava answered the door after her first knock. He had been expecting her.

"Good." He spoke first. "Come."

Matrona followed him silently down the hall, tracing the now-familiar path to the sunlit room of dolls. Their eyes all seemed to watch her, each pair set in a face she recognized. A clicking of talons on the floor revealed Pamyat, who boosted himself to his perch with two flaps of his long wings.

"Tell me how they know," Matrona said as Slava reached for her doll, kept in the same place at the edge of the left table. No wonder he'd noticed her earlier trespass—he kept everything in this room in such strict order. The paintbrush alone would have given her away.

Slava clasped her doll by its head and lifted it from the others, turning it toward her with narrowed eyes. A small smile stretched his lips and deepened the wrinkles under his eyes. "Ah, I forget about these things. I never have the opportunity to discuss them."

"Never?" Matrona asked. She tried to think of whom Slava associated with, but no names rose to mind.

"I have never needed to. Only one other has noticed the mass revelations, among other things, and she does not have the liberty to discuss it."

His smile faded, and Matrona's bones grew cold.

She croaked, "Who?"

"You would not notice the suddenness of others knowing, if your eyes had not been opened," he said, ignoring the second question and rattling her doll in his hand. "You will see more, as you must, before you replace me as keeper. Have you kept your word?"

Matrona swallowed and nodded. *Who else knows, and why can't she speak of it?*

Then, *What did Slava do to her . . . ?*

Her eyes shifted to Pamyat. She shivered.

"Good." He glanced over the other dolls. "I have not heard any mention of us on the tongues of our friends in the village, so I believe you."

"You assume me dishonest." Matrona let disapproval flavor her words. Her body warmed. "I'm sure you've heard plenty of other things from our *friends*."

Slava smiled, and Matrona flushed despite herself. "The Maysak boy is especially interesting."

Matrona folded her arms across her chest.

"Your secrets are mild compared to those that could be shared." Slava held out her doll, and Matrona took it and held it tightly between her hands. "Open it," he ordered.

Matrona licked her lips. "You could not have offered so much as a warning, Tradesman? Do you know what it nearly cost me for that knowledge to be made public? What it still costs me?"

Slava shrugged, which angered Matrona all the more. "A few cold glances and whispers. They will pass."

"My betrothal—"

"Is still intact. I spoke with Oleg Popov just this morning. Now open your doll."

Her hands trembled around the glossed wood. Her heartbeat quickened. "What will happen this time?"

His pale eyes hardened. "It does not matter."

"You say it so easily! Open your own doll, Tradesman, and let us see what *you* are hiding."

She snapped her lips shut the moment the words left her mouth, and she retreated into the shelves. So loose was her tongue before this man. Her mother would have slapped her again for such insolence.

Slava glowered, and in the corner Pamyat hissed his own disapproval. "You think this is the worst the world has to offer you? That *I* have to offer you? You're fooling yourself, Matrona Vitsin." His hand reached for her father's doll.

"I will open it." Matrona meant to sound strong, but the statement was a strained whisper. Fingers slick with perspiration, Matrona gritted her teeth and turned the second doll on its seam, then let out a long breath and pulled the two halves apart.

Inside was a third doll, painted like the rest, though the details in its dress were much simpler than they'd been in the first two layers.

Matrona stared at it, expecting . . . She wasn't sure. But nothing changed about her, mentally or physically. Nothing altered within the room. Nothing happened at all, save for the slight steadying of her breaths.

Slava nodded, once. "Good, good. I'm glad it is you, Matrona."

She didn't understand the sentiment.

"Return in three days," he continued as he reached out a hand. When Matrona didn't give him the doll, he pried the pieces from her fingers—both the inner doll and the two pieces of the second layer—saying nothing as he carefully reassembled them and placed them back on the table.

"Tradesman."

He glanced at her from beneath an arched eyebrow.

Matrona took a steadying breath before speaking. "You say, 'Return in three days.' Why? If you insist on my pursuit of . . . this"—she gestured to the dolls—"against my will, why not open the doll yourself? Why have me come here?"

He turned toward her, lip quirking. "Because I will never open the dolls. Not again. I will see this done right. To replace me, you must be wholly independent. You must learn it on your own."

Not again? "Learn what? Sorcery?"

"Three days," Slava repeated, and turned back to his dolls.

Willing her unsteady heart and bubbling frustration to calm, Matrona fled the room while Slava's back still faced her, relief bolstering her when she reached the front door.

She stepped outside and stumbled when a sudden heaviness struck her body, as though a cartload of leathers had been draped over her.

She took another step and gasped, pulse quickening. Tumbled beyond the portico and landed on her knees as voices assaulted her mind.

So many years of practice, yet you still milk so slowly. What good are ugly, chapped hands if they can't be useful?

No one will ask for your hand. You're too ugly, too boring.

Your jaw looks like your father's.

What kind of a woman fancies a potter boy, and one she used to tend as a child? What a horrible person you are, a vagrant!

You've ruined a day's work with your clumsiness!

You deserve that beating and another one, too.

You're useless.

You're vile.

You stupid, stupid girl.

Images of all her failures flashed before her eyes, memories she had forgotten. Broken ceramics, spilled milk, crooked stitches, misused words. Tears pooled in her eyes, pushed out by cold fingers in her mind. All the bitterness and sorrow she'd swallowed in her twenty-six years of life surfaced at once, and the bleak thoughts wrapped around her like an endless serpent, wickedly familiar.

She recognized the loudest voice in her head as her own.

Something in the assaulting darkness registered the grass under her fingers and the sun at the back of her head. She struggled to breathe, blinking wetness from her eyes. More and more of the ugliness bubbled up from deep in her core: *You're a coward.* There had been a spider in the barn, and she'd been too scared to go inside. *You're slow.* She hadn't kept up with the others in the glade. *You clumsy oaf!* She'd spilled dinner over her dress. None of them were her parents' words. All her own. So many of them. So many.

It sucked her downward toward the cool grass. She folded over herself, shuddering against the consuming odium—

"Matrona?"

A tiny bit of her mind registered the voice. *No, Slava, leave me alone.*

You don't deserve to replace Slava.

Get up. You're pathetic. How can anyone stand you?

"Matrona?"

Not Slava's voice. A hand settled on her shoulder, the sensation jarring. Matrona blinked, seeing the grass, wishing only to curl over it and disappear into the earth.

If only Esfir had lived, then your parents could have a useful daughter.

The hand shook her. Its mate found her other shoulder. "Matrona, what's wrong? Are you sick?"

She tried to blink back the tears and shadows blurring her vision. Found strength to lift her head.

Jaska Maysak looked at her.

Tense energy flooded her back and limbs, quickening her heart, making the criticisms in her skull bounce back and forth with painful speed. *Pathetic. Unchaste. Childish.*

Words caught in her throat, and she merely shook her head like a crazed woman, trying to sort out where she was, what she was doing.

Slava's house. *You look foolish.* The dolls. *No one wants you here.* Three days. *Just lie down and die.* She needed to get home.

The hands left, and the shadows pushed inward, pulsing against her forehead. But the grip returned, this time under her arms, hauling her upward. Heat flushed her skin. *You're a disgrace!*

"Matrona." Jaska's voice was soft and level. "Can you walk? Are you hurt?"

"I . . ." She struggled to orient herself, struggled not to lean against the potter. Someone was going to see. Feodor . . . Her head felt full of nails, and a hammer pounded the points deeper with every heaving breath. She winced and pressed a palm between her eyes. "I'm not . . . hurt . . ."

You should be.

The Maysaks' donkey stood on the dirt path, a narrow wagon tied to it.

A warm breeze—no, Jaska's sigh—wafted against her hair. "Your parents aren't going to like this."

The ground beneath her gave way, and the brief sensation of falling startled Matrona almost to her senses. Jaska's strong arms around her shoulders and under her knees sent gooseflesh over her skin. The dark voice inside her pounced—*You're sick*—shredding Matrona's gut with its blades. When he set her down in the wagon, Matrona tried to utter an apology, but she wasn't sure if it passed her lips.

Everyone will see you. Feodor will leave you. You'll be a burden to your parents all their lives, and only Mad Olia Maysak will tolerate your company.

Foolish, foolish girl.

❄

Matrona lay on a tear-wet pillow and could barely remember how she'd gotten to her own bed. Her body was made of lead, save for the soft spots of her joints and head where nails pounded and pounded, never set. Her stomach squirmed and gurgled, and she slept on and off—she knew because her dreams were filled with monsters and twisting black clouds in a deep and unfamiliar sky.

She started to fight back, but whatever she'd unleashed in Slava's house was stronger.

A rag rug has more use than you. Look at you. Pathetic.

Matrona pushed against it: *Leave me alone.*

It didn't. It turned and came back, showing her even more memories of past mistakes, of embarrassing moments, of failed schoolwork. A trove of them.

I was young, Matrona shot at it.

You were stupid, and you still are. Do you ever even try?

Distantly she heard her parents address her in turn, her mother more often than her father. Fists on the door. Demands for chores, questions about what was wrong. The pressure inside her head made her sweat, and when a steady hand rapped against her bedroom door during the afternoon, Matrona thought someone had finally sent for the doctor.

The old door opened on creaking hinges, and Roksana's voice rang through the air. "Matrona? Look at you! Like you've been trapped in a pillory under the sun all day."

Matrona rubbed her fingers over her temples—they were starting to bruise, she'd done it so many times. Her back ached from her mattress, and she pushed herself upward.

You don't deserve her friendship, the persistent voice murmured.

"What are you doing here?" Matrona asked when the voice repeated itself.

The mattress shifted when Roksana sat on its edge, setting a bag down beside her. "The children are out of school for the day. Darya Avdovin mentioned you were ill—among other things—and I was concerned that maybe the stress . . ."

Roksana shrugged; Matrona moaned and buried her face into her pillow.

Even the children gossip about you. Matrona wasn't sure if the thought was hers or something brought on by that deplorable doll.

"And how would Darya know?" Matrona spoke into her pillow, squeezing her eyes shut as a sharp pain shot up her jaw and into her crown. The girl wasn't yet ten years old.

"Well, she said her grandmother came by for milk this morning. There wasn't butter to be had, and your mother complained it was because you're ill—"

You leave all the work to your parents. You've never pulled your weight, the voice rattled.

Matrona spoke just to hear something other than the incessant insults. "Roksana." She pulled back from the pillow. She blinked green-and-blue spots from her vision, and her friend's frown replaced them. "What would you do if every terrible thing you'd ever said to yourself, even as a child, came back at once?"

"I don't know what you mean." Roksana's delicate eyebrows scrunched into nearly flat lines.

Matrona's head throbbed, and renewed pressure pushed down on her chest. She took several seconds to breathe deeply, trying to ignore the punishing sensations. "Haven't you ever seen your reflection and thought, 'Oh, I look homely today,' or perhaps reprimanded yourself from some small wrong you did as a student or a teacher?"

"Well, yes, I suppose."

"They're such little thoughts"—Matrona winced, fingers returning to her temples—"often passing as quickly as they came, or after a good night's rest. Only, imagine if all those thoughts were . . . I don't know, saved in a chest. Every single one. And every bad feeling you've ever had. Guilt over telling a lie, or shame from doing something wrong. All of it inside this chest. And then suddenly you're in the room with the chest, and it opens, but someone's jammed the door and you can't get out—"

"You're rambling, Matrona." Roksana clicked her tongue and resituated her heavy body, trying to get comfortable. "You sound almost poetic, in a sad, strange way."

"Just imagine it, Roksana!" Matrona cried, her hands jerking away from her temples and slamming fists into her pillow, making her friend jump. "Imagine how it would make you feel. What would you do, trapped with all of it around you?" Tears wet her eyes, and she blinked rapidly to banish them, her eyes still sore from the night's weeping. "Tell me what to do."

Roksana's frown deepened, and she stood from the bed, returning her bag to her shoulder. "You're not trapped in a room with some devil's chest." The distance in her voice made Matrona's stomach squeeze, made a harmony of voices in her head sing, *Stupid, stupid, stupid.* "What's wrong with you lately? First you embarrass yourself, and Feodor, no less, and now you're wasting away in your room, talking about chests and jammed doors. You sound like Mad Olia Maysak."

"I'm *not* mad," Matrona spat. She prayed it was true.

Roksana sighed. "Get some rest, then, and find me when you're better." She shrugged and turned about, leaving the room with the door cracked open. Matrona heard Roksana say something to someone in the hallway; then her footsteps faded in the direction of the front door.

Matrona's abdomen panged as the cursed doll spell erupted inside her again, bubbling up shame and loathing that could not be assigned to any one happenstance or memory. She curled over her pillow, swallowing, trying not to sick up, again.

Her door opened with enough force to bang into the wall behind it, and her mother said, "There's a bath ready for you in my room; go get into it and clean yourself up. Your father just returned from his errands and said Feodor means to see you, and I'll not have you looking like this after all the mending we had to do for you!"

Matrona pressed a clammy palm to her forehead. "Please, Mama, I don't feel well."

"Neither do I, but I'm up and about. Get up before I pull your hair."

Stomach clenching, Matrona released her pillow and slid off the bed, shaking her head at the dark whispers in her ears. Once in the hallway, her mother snatched her by the elbow and yanked her into the other bedroom, where she practically ripped off Matrona's clothes—the same she'd worn to Slava's home the day before—and dunked her into the basin of river-cold water.

Matrona gasped, the shock of the cold clearing her head. "It's not warm," she gasped, more air than voice.

"Only because you dallied," her mother snapped, shoving Matrona's head forward and dragging lye over her neck. "Can you wash up, or must I do that, too?"

Matrona reached up a trembling hand and took the lye. Her mother left, slamming the bedroom door behind her.

❄

"You must resolve this." Feodor paced the length of the front room, moving back and forth before the brick oven, his hands clasped behind his back. His shirt was wrinkled around the waist and elbows. The evening sun trickled through a window, casting the shadow of the half-open shutter over the floor. Matrona's parents were in the pasture, milking the cows.

"I have been very patient with you," Feodor continued, glancing Matrona's way as he walked back and forth, back and forth. Matrona felt the glance more than she saw it. Feodor had been pacing for nearly half an hour, lecturing her thoroughly enough that his disapproving voice had replaced the mocking one inside her head. It left her body limp and heavy, as though ink flowed through her veins, instead of blood, smudging her insides with darkness. He'd begun to repeat himself, and Matrona's tongue was too heavy to ask him to stop. He continued, "I don't understand the enigma you've become this week, Matrona. For heaven's sake, I thought we were past this."

Unseen cords wrapped around Matrona's shoulders and tried to pull her toward the ground. She fought against them. Though a full day had passed since her last visit to Slava's house, the urge to curl up into a ball and let the earth suck her up had not lessened. Her head continued to ache—more so if she focused on it—and the dismal thoughts running through her brain had long since begun to repeat themselves, much as Feodor was doing now.

The comparison made her stomach turn, but perhaps that was just hunger. This bizarre depression had consumed her appetite as well.

"I'll be well in a couple of days," Matrona murmured, cradling her forehead in her hands. Surely she would recover by Slava's next deadline, else he could expect nothing from her. The voice inside her attacked again. *Is that the kind of posture you choose to take before your future husband? Can you not bear it and smile for his sake?*

She bit the inside of her cheek and shot back, *Can he not bear a smile for mine?*

She tried to straighten, to pull up the corners of her mouth, but they were so heavy, and the effort made her bones throb.

Feodor's footsteps paused. "Stop this *now*, Matrona."

The order ran down the back of her neck like sharpened fingernails. She gritted her teeth. "I *am* trying. I am merely not well."

Feodor's toe tapped against the floorboards, and the echo carried in the silence of the room. "I'll send for the doctor."

And then Feodor left, too.

Matrona dragged herself back to her bed and lay there, trying to sleep. But while the desperation stretching inside her made her weary, it also kept her alert. She tried to let it roll over her, water off a lark's feathers, but the effort made her body ache all the more.

Her father came in at some point to lecture her, but his voice dropped as pebbles in a bottomless well. He gave up, for Matrona *did* fall asleep, and by the time she awoke to twilight, her father was gone.

❄

Feodor did summon the doctor to the Vitsins', which Matrona might have found endearing were she in a sound state of mind. And she tried to appear sound, for fear that the doctor would declare her mad. Maybe she *was* mad.

The doctor checked her for ailments, trying to diagnose hurts that had no physical cause. He claimed her in good health, so with heavy hands Matrona tied an apron about her neck and waist and forced herself outside. If the sunshine would not help, then perhaps work would. She could not let this darkness paralyze her.

Matrona breathed deeply as she walked to the barn, shivering despite the cloudless day, trying to imagine her skin opening up and drinking in the late-morning light. Her thoughts had calmed, at the very least, leaving her head foggy and lined with cobwebs. The headache pounding behind her eyes persisted. Sitting at the butter churn,

Matrona plunged the handle up and down in time to the beat within her throbbing skull, hoping the exercise would unravel the tautness across her shoulders and back.

It didn't.

She churned for a long time, trying to breathe through Slava's spell, though this morning the smell of the cream turned her stomach. If the hateful voice in her head had ceased its prattling, then soon the rest would wear off as well, yes? Matrona tried to grasp that glimmer of hope. She could pretend to be well until true relief came, and if it did not, she would drag her leaden body to Slava's and demand an antidote . . . Yet she feared what future torments he had in store for her. Removing the second doll had produced a worse effect than removing the first. This doll attacked her from within, and she still didn't understand *why*.

A knock sounded between beats of the plunger hitting the base of the churn, and Matrona looked up, blinking back shadows and webs to see the person in the doorway. It took her too long to recognize him, and when she did, a sliver from the plunger handle bit into her index finger.

Jaska.

She blinked again and rubbed her wrist over her eyes.

"I'm sorry to intrude." Jaska's voice seemed to skim along the sides of her neck. It was pitched lower than Feodor's, yet not as deep as her father's. "I tried to come sooner—"

Matrona dropped her wrist and looked at him as he approached. She shook her head, trying to loosen some sense in it. "For . . . for milk? I'm sorry, our production has been . . . low—"

He offered her an expression that was half-frown, half-smile. "I meant to see *you*, Matrona. You were so ill, and I hadn't heard any news of your recovery." He shrugged. "I'm afraid your mother was not happy to see me either time."

Her mind strained like a thorn-caught cricket wing, and she gritted her teeth, forcing it to work faster. Either time? When he dropped her off, and . . . he'd come again? Yesterday?

She felt a flush creep up her neck, but the voice in her head, the one that had been hounding her since she'd opened that second doll, remained blissfully silent.

Matrona released the plunger and sat back, moving both hands to the sore muscles of her shoulders. "I'm . . . fine. I will be."

"You don't look well." Jaska lingered by the worktable. He had a few clay stains on his rolled-up sleeves, but his hands were clean. "Have you seen the doctor?"

Matrona scoffed. "Yes, I have, and I fear he thinks me dramatic." She touched a new, pulsing pain in the center of her forehead.

"You should rest."

Matrona shook her head. Maybe she would have laughed, were her lungs not so heavy. "I've rested too much." She tried to remember the time, an impossible task when she could not even recall the day of the week. Wasn't Slava's third day tomorrow?

She couldn't see Slava. She *wouldn't* see him. This humiliation, this torment, these threats—it would be her undoing. Slava couldn't possibly reprimand her without telling others of the dolls, and they would laugh at him. He would twist her father's doll, maybe her mother's . . . but if Matrona acted like she didn't care, if she played aloof, he would have to set them back to rights. He couldn't skew every person in the village. Or perhaps she could steal them . . .

If I go back, he'll make me open the next doll, she thought, pressing her palms into her eyes. Slava had not used force, yet, but who was to say he would not? It wouldn't be the first time another had raised a hand against her—

"Matrona? Are you all right? Do you need something to drink?"

Matrona dropped her hands, blinking spots of color from her vision, and saw that Jaska was much closer now, crouched on the other side of the butter churn. She wanted to slump over that half-formed butter and weep.

"I can't go back," she whispered, a sob slicing through the sentence. She pressed a knuckle against her lips and shook her head. What would Slava do if she told?

Jaska's brows lowered, narrowing his dark eyes. "Go back where?"

Matrona shook her head again. "Maybe I should rest." She stood from her three-legged stool. It toppled over behind her, and she wavered, blood rushing from her head.

"Slava's house?" Jaska stood up beside her.

Matrona froze. Eyed him. Did he know? Heart racing, she searched his face, hoping for an answer.

He licked his lips. "That's where I found you, Matrona," he said, as though she had forgotten. He spoke with deliberate enunciation. Much the way he spoke to his mad mother. "Did he feed you something strange? What were you doing there?"

He didn't know. No one knew. Matrona closed her eyes for a moment, letting the dizziness subside before she opened them again. She pressed a hand to the wall and leaned into it. "Just a visit," she managed.

Jaska's eyebrows eased a fraction. "Let me help you to the house," he offered, turning slightly so Matrona could take his elbow.

Matrona stared at that elbow, the gray sleeve of his shirt pushed up around the crook of it. No one else had offered her support, had they? Her father hadn't offered to lift her from bed; her mother hadn't helped her climb into the cold bath. Feodor rarely touched her, and even Roksana . . .

"I don't think anyone is home," he added, "if you're worried about—"

"Have you ever wanted to . . . escape?"

Jaska's proffered elbow drooped. "What?"

"Escape. Leave." She peered out the back doors of the barn, beyond the pasture, to the tree tips of the wood to the south. She could open no more dolls if she merely disappeared, the way Esfir had. The humiliation would become moot if she surrounded herself with new people in a new village. Perhaps she'd even find a man better suited to her than Feodor, if God had such a plan for her. Running would cast her as a terrible daughter, especially after Esfir, but if this was the only way to protect her family from Slava's game . . .

"The village?" Jaska's voice sounded softer.

She nodded.

"Are you unhappy here?" he asked, but closed his mouth awkwardly around the last word. Rubbed his jaw. He was a witness to Matrona's struggles, just as every other person within the walls of the wood was.

"I've never left. Not once." Matrona turned her attention to a loose thread on her sleeve. "I wonder if I were . . . what it would be like."

"I've wondered myself." A dry chuckle escaped his throat. "I thought to, once, with Kostya."

Her eyes met his. "To leave?" A cool pang of something like sadness plucked within her.

He nodded, once. "A couple years ago, when Mama was especially bad, and my father . . ." He didn't finish the statement. "We headed south. Didn't tell anyone. Strapped our packs on and ventured through the wood. We walked maybe half a day before we turned back."

"Why?"

Jaska's forehead crinkled as he thought. "I'm not sure. I just . . . felt compelled to go home. We both did. Wouldn't do to leave the care of our parents to Galina and Viktor, besides."

Matrona's gaze fell to the butter churn. South. What lay south? Or north, or east, or west? Only Slava would know. No one else ever left the village.

Would he search for her if she left, or would he choose someone else?

"Matrona!" Her mother's distant voice formed the name, perhaps from inside the house. She must have just returned home. Matrona's skin prickled, and she pushed her heavy body off the wall.

Jaska frowned, glancing behind him, though he would not see the house from where he stood in the barn. "I should go. I have no desire to cause more trouble for you."

Matrona nodded. "Please. Out the back gate."

He took one step toward the back doors of the barn before hesitating and looking back at Matrona with dark, calculating eyes. But Matrona's mother called out to her again, and he turned away, quickening his steps, disappearing into the day.

The ache in her back and head drummed a steady rhythm of encouragement. She could leave. Stow away in another village until things calmed down and Slava moved on. Then she could come home, if she wanted. Feodor might even wait for her.

Matrona hurried out the front of the barn and made it halfway across the pasture before her mother appeared at the back door. South. She would go south, as Kostya and Jaska once had. She'd seen Slava's wagon head south before, so there had to be something in that direction. Perhaps she could find the wagon tracks and follow them.

Matrona glanced over her shoulder, but Jaska hadn't left so much as a shadow in his wake. She frowned, but held to her conviction.

Tomorrow morning, she would go.

Chapter 6

In the shadows of night, the darkness reared up with a blistering vengeance.

Ugly, filthy girl. The slick voice stirred her from restless sleep.

Her mother's voice murmured, *My other daughter would have worked harder. My other daughter would not have embarrassed me so. She would not leave when life grew difficult.*

A child's voice cried, *I'm not pretty like the other girls. My brow is too thick and my cheeks too wide. I'll never be pretty like them.*

Matrona sat up in bed, shivering with a chill she couldn't feel. "Stop," she whispered.

Who would kiss such worked hands? The low, feminine voice crooned. The tone lightened, mimicking her own voice: *All I'm good for is milking cows and beating rugs.*

"Stop," she repeated again, louder. Serpents coiled around her chest, thinning her air. Her head pounded, and her palms went slick with perspiration.

Useless.

Vulgar.

Coward.

Vagrant.

Clumsy.

The way you look at him—

I cannot help how I feel! Matrona shouted back, her thoughts piercing the oily venom far better than her own voice did. *I cannot change the leaning of my heart any more than I can move the sun in the sky!*

The darkness stirred and lashed out once more. *Stupid girl. You never get anything right. Remember all your failings? Your struggle with arithmetic. Your clumsiness with the milk. Cream, spilled every—*

Enough! she shouted, wincing against the stabbing in her forehead. The muscles in her legs and abdomen tightened like sinew drying in the sun. *I was a child, and I tried my best! I learned it! And I cannot be held accountable for every misstep. Be gone!*

Aloud, she said, "You will not have power over me."

The voices shifted, reverting to her mother's. *You have humiliated me before the village—*

Matrona did not let the words finish. *I am a good and virtuous woman.*

The darkness sneered. *You are—*

I am a good and virtuous woman, Matrona repeated, clutching fistfuls of blanket in her hands. *I have strived to be good all my life, and I have succeeded. You cannot take that from me.*

A glimmer of warmth sparked in her heart, loosening the serpents, and Matrona realized she believed it. She believed her counterattacks. She *had* strived to be wholesome and upright, since she was a little girl. Not because her mother demanded it, not to impress her father, but because that was who she wanted to be.

The darkness hissed, and when it addressed her again, it did so in the young child's voice. *You are—*

"I am beautiful," she whispered, and the storming shadows dissipated into clouds of ash, drifting away from her thoughts like the remnants of a bad dream.

Matrona took in a deep, shuddering breath and opened her eyes, searching her moonlit room. She listened, waited, but the voices did not return.

A smile pulled on her lips. She wiped tears from her eyes, rested her head on her pillow, and fell into the most peaceful slumber she'd ever had.

❄

The third day, Matrona awoke with bones of iron instead of lead, a headache that tapped instead of pounded, and clear vision that only spotted when she moved too quickly. She headed out to the pasture early to do her chores, before her parents had awoken for the day, though the neighbors' cock had already crowed twice. If she finished the work before she left, her parents wouldn't have reason to seek her out until she was miles away.

Despite the lightness of her heart, her hands trembled as she milked the first cow.

She stared into the pail, watching shots of milk splatter against its base and sides, puddling where she directed it, slowly taking the shape of the bucket. Unable to form itself. Unable to escape.

The third day. Slava would be expecting her.

She squeezed the teats harder, and the cow turned her head to eye her with one heavily lashed brown orb. Matrona rested her head against the coarse fur as her hands moved up and down in their familiar rhythm, building on callouses she'd developed as a child. Matrona breathed in the crispness of the morning and the scent of the pasture that clung to the cow's hide. Her mind had been quiet since waking, its detrimental thoughts unheard as she washed and dressed and milked. Still, she couldn't go back to Slava's abode. Wouldn't.

Slava cared deeply about the dolls, didn't he? That was why he made them, why he kept them, and why, for some reason, he wanted Matrona to watch over them in his stead. Surely he wouldn't destroy the dolls for the sake of bending her to his will. He might twist a few in anger, but eventually he would give up, wouldn't he?

Matrona leaned back, listening to the rhythm of falling milk. "I don't know what he'll do," she whispered, and the cow turned back to her feed.

She milked in contemplation until the right side of the cow went dry, then moved her pail to the left. Not for the first time, Matrona tried to imagine her lost sister working beside her. She'd be about Jaska's age. Matrona wondered if Esfir would have the same black hair Matrona did, or if it would be lighter, more like her father's. A strong jaw or a slim one. Surely she'd wear the strong Vitsin brow.

What would it have been like to have Esfir's companionship throughout childhood and adolescence? To have someone else draw her parents' attention, especially her mother's? Matrona couldn't help but wonder if these recent events would have happened had Esfir not mysteriously vanished from her cradle.

The milk stopped, and Matrona leaned back against a sore spine. If putting distance between herself and the tradesman didn't resolve the situation, then perhaps Feodor could intervene. The Popov family was well respected and held sway over many in the village. Of course, she would need to tell Feodor about the dolls, and she wasn't sure he'd believe her.

Her hand trembled as she picked up the full pail and carried it to a clean, empty barrel. She glanced back at the barn's open doors, picturing Jaska between them, remembering the way he'd stood before her as she held the churn in her hands. His proffered elbow and his soft words, so different from . . .

She blinked hard. *Feodor.* Jaska didn't matter. She'd humiliated herself enough for one lifetime, hadn't she?

Her father came out to tend the small herd, pausing for a moment to watch her work, then nodding his approval when she met his eyes.

The subtle gesture felt like warm tea on a tight stomach after two days under the thumb of that unyielding darkness. Hopefully he would still look at her kindly when she returned from her journey. She would have to come up with a story to explain her absence. Yet it could be a long while before she returned home—only time would tell.

When her father left, Matrona quickly distributed milk and cream and hurried to her room to gather her things. Her mother had taken to the laundry, and so Matrona helped herself to the kitchen stores, choosing that which would last the longest in her pack, enough for a few days. She pulled on her sturdiest shoes and vacated through the pasture, trying to keep her walk casual, though her muscles itched to run.

She followed the path toward the butchery, where it would turn south toward the wood. The grasses made Slava's wagon tracks hard to find, but she thought she saw their direction and traced them into the wood, to a wide place between the trees. Uneven patches of wild grass gave way to moss, clover, and old, trampled foliage. She filled herself with several deep breaths to calm her nerves as she moved farther and farther from the village. Usually only the hunters delved into the wood, but Matrona had played among the roots and trunks as a child. It was not long, however, before she surpassed the distance she'd dared to travel in her youth.

Oddly, the aspens grew tightly together, forcing her to choose a path around them. She hesitated a brief moment, for no wagon would be able to pass between them, and there was no other route the tradesman could have taken. Had she guessed his entry point wrong? She worried her lip as she picked her way through sun and shadow, pack bouncing against her back. She thought of the glares of the village women, her mother's open palm against her cheek, and the dark swirl of her own self-loathing. The memories propelled her forward.

After another mile, the trunks loosened, and Matrona paused by a crooked hornbeam to catch her breath, resting her hands on her knees.

The wood was absent of the sound of people; only the soft noises of busy insects and hungry birds greeted her. There was nothing to fear here, especially while sunlight still infiltrated the canopy formed by the trees. The earth beneath her feet was relatively flat, veined with brooks and goatsbeard. Were she to venture deep enough into the wood, she'd likely see a stray sika deer or a wild ass, perhaps even a pig, but nothing that would harm her. Still, were the trees to break for a road, she would thank every saint she could name.

So she walked, savoring the absence of people, focusing on the sounds of life around her—songbirds and grouse, shrews and red squirrels. She walked with her arms folded at first, but the exercise loosed them, and soon Matrona found herself picking her way over fallen branches and large stones, careful with her balance. She paused once more to gain her bearings—and was surprised to see that she was just outside a familiar glade with foot-crushed grass and a tall, triangular boulder in its center.

She paused, glancing behind her. No, that couldn't be right. This looked like the children's glade, on the other side of the village. The north side, and she had walked southward. There was no way she could have circumvented the village to arrive here. Then how . . . ?

She trudged forward, through the glade—it had to be one that looked similar, for Matrona's route had never faltered, else the direction of the sun would have warned her. The symphony of insects hushed a little, and the noises of people milling about and working pricked her ears. She held her breath as the wood opened up to the village. The north side.

She'd walked a straight line, yet somehow managed to loop around to the opposite side of the village.

Her thoughts instantly turned to Slava.

But I'm not the first to delve into these woods. The game hunters frequented these trees far more often than Matrona did. They would have noticed the strange—what to call it?—*loop* from one side of the village to the other. Jaska and Kostya would have noticed it. Jaska would have said something.

Unless . . .

Matrona touched her stomach, the place where the seam would have been were she one of Slava's wooden dolls. Slava had said she would separate herself from the village. Did that mean she could see this loop when others couldn't?

Knees buckling, Matrona dropped to the forest floor and stared up at the sun. It all connected. There was no other explanation. Which meant one thing.

Matrona would never be able to escape.

Chapter 7

Matrona would not give in to Slava's demands. If she could not run from the village, she would hide within it.

Fatigue dug at her body as she passed through the children's glade. She ate a bit of cheese to assuage her hunger.

Her mind reeled. What would Slava do when evening came and went and the night stretched long and she still did not approach his door? Would he come for her in her own *izba*? What excuses could he possibly make to her parents?

Could she claim sanctuary at the church? Yet it would only be a matter of time before her own hunger drove her out.

As Matrona passed by the candle maker's home, something on the path froze her feet in their steps.

Slava.

He approached her family's *izba* from the main path. He strode with purpose, a towel slung over his shoulder, perhaps from whatever work had been occupying him before this jaunt. Like a mouse, Matrona skittered around the corner of the candle maker's home, her neck flushing. Her pulse beat in her ears. Slava did not look her way. She drew in a shaky breath.

The appearance of the tradesman solidified in Matrona's mind what she had already suspected—if she would not go to him, he would come to her.

Running her hands over her braid, Matrona took in her surroundings. The Demidov *izba* sat a short ways from her, and Lenore Demidov squinted at her from the window. Matrona pushed off from her hiding place and bolted west, daring to cross the path behind Slava before stowing behind another *izba*.

Roksana. She'd go to Roksana's. Her mother would give her an earful for missing a visit from the most important man in town, but she would rather face Toma Vitsin than Slava Barinov.

The sun beat down as she hurried, and her lungs seemed unable to pull in enough air to sustain her once the Zotov *izba* came into sight. She forced steadiness into her pace, again checking over her shoulder as she approached the front door. Blotting her forehead with the edge of her sleeve, she knocked and waited. Knocked again.

Licking her lips, Matrona walked around the *izba* to the small workshop behind it, drawn to the beating of hammer against nail. Roksana, however, was not within. Only her father-in-law, Pavel, who glanced up the same moment Matrona glanced in.

"Matrona." He picked a nail out of a heavy leather satchel hanging from his belt. A faded depiction of a rearing stallion marked the bag's front. He'd only just begun nailing together planks of wood, but Matrona thought he might be making a headboard. "Roksana is with the midwife today. Unless you needed something made?"

"I . . . No, Pavel. Do you know when she'll return?"

Pavel set his hammer down on his work and pulled a measuring stick from a pocket at the back of his pants. "I'm not sure, but you'll find her there."

Matrona nodded her thanks and backed away from the workshop. The midwife didn't live far from Slava's home. She was so old that most of her patients visited her for routine checkups, instead of the other way around. That *izba* would offer her no sanctuary.

Matrona glanced up at the sun. Slava—and her mother—would have discovered she was missing by now. Surely the tradesman had returned home.

However, as Matrona came around the Zotov *izba*, she saw someone heading up the main path. The gray beard, the broad back, and the towel still slung over his shoulders instantly identified him as the tradesman.

A yelp suffocated in Matrona's throat as she flashed back behind the *izba*, her blood pounding enough to make her dizzy. Their village was so small; it was no secret that Roksana and Matrona were close friends.

He knew exactly where to look for her next.

Mouth dry, Matrona ran straight into the wood, keeping the Zotov *izba* at her back. She was breathless by the first tree. Her legs grew light as she ran over the uneven forest floor, passing a narrow brook and ducking beneath tree limbs that all looked similar to one another. She ran until her chest and thighs ached, until the energy left her stride.

She slowed, pulling at her collar to relieve the heat building beneath her dress. Turning around, Matrona searched for Slava, but he wasn't there. Only the quick skittering of a gray shrew as it scrabbled across the forest floor. That and . . . the sound of a blacksmith's hammer?

Picking her way carefully, Matrona moved in as much of a straight line as she could. Before long, other noises of the village reached her ears: the beating of a staff against rug, the creaking of a bellows, the occasional crowing of a rooster.

She focused on the bellows and hammer, then the steam churning from the brewery behind the smithy. The two buildings were on the east side of the village, not far from the pottery. But she had entered the western wood.

She looked over her shoulder, but there was no obvious point at which the wood had changed. *Just as it is with the south-and-north woods.*

The strange loop surrounded them. Matrona suddenly felt wooden and hollow, as if Slava's fingers were encompassing her, pressing. Suffocating. The enchanted wood swallowed the village whole?

Matrona paused at the edge of the east wood, placing a hand on a twisted hornbeam. How was she ever to leave? How did *Slava* leave? There had to be a way, for she had seen him set off with his empty wagon and return with it loaded with goods. Was there a break in this eternal perimeter, or would she have to pry the answer from Slava himself?

Slava. Matrona rubbed gooseflesh from her arms. If only her mind were still comforted by the blissful peace of ignorance.

Shying a step back into the wood, she searched for Slava, but this corner of the village was empty save for a couple of children. She worried her lip. Turned toward the hornbeam and knocked her knuckles against it, half-expecting the trunk to turn to smoke beneath her touch. But no, the wood remained solid.

"What are your secrets, Tradesman?" she whispered, stepping away from the tree and over the grass that cushioned the village from its surrounding forest. *You know mine, but when will I learn yours?*

She shuddered and crossed her arms over her chest. *Hopefully never.*

Her run had made her weary. She walked slowly, contemplating where she should go next. What to do? She was so weary, even her senses grew exhausted.

"Matrona!" yelled a man's voice, and Matrona startled from her thoughts long enough to see Boris Ishutin, the granger that Roksana had favored years ago, tugging two goats behind him on lengths of rope. He waved an arm. "Slava is looking for you!"

Matrona froze, and Boris turned his back to her, looking down a footpath. Matrona recognized Slava immediately and choked on her own tongue.

He'd seen her run into the wood. He'd known it would spit her out here.

Matrona fled farther into the village as Boris—the fool!—shouted to Slava. Her legs protested the new exercise, but Matrona pushed them, fleeing behind a shop, looping around an *izba*. Slava must have seen her—there was no way he hadn't. Matrona's heart grew too large for her chest. She couldn't breathe.

The scent of smoke strangled her gasping breaths even more. The pottery, just ahead. Squeezing her hands into fists, Matrona ran into it, thanking Saint Michael when she saw Jaska repairing a pottery wheel. The only other occupant was Mad Olia, who sat in an old chair against the right wall, gently rocking herself.

"Jaska," Matrona called, a hoarse half whisper.

Jaska glanced up from his work and, upon seeing Matrona, stood so abruptly, he scraped his shoulder against the edge of the wheel. He winced but replied, "What's wrong?"

"Please." She rushed to his side. She'd never stepped so far into the pottery before. "Slava is looking for me. I can't face him. I don't know what he'll—"

"Slava?" Jaska's dark eyes glanced between Matrona and the wide opening to the pottery. His hand on her elbow cut off her words. "Come with me." He pulled her toward a narrow door near the kiln and tugged her through it as her name rang through the pottery, carried on the rich baritone of the tradesman.

Chapter 8

The fresh air in the narrow space between the pottery and the Maysak house struck Matrona with a strange chill. Slava's voice rang in her ears. Had he seen her flee through this door, or only toward the pottery?

Words bubbled up her throat—*We have to move quickly, he's just around the corner, I'm so sorry*—but within half a breath's time, Jaska pulled her around the nearest corner of his home and to the cellar doors. He pulled one open and stepped onto the narrow wooden stairs leading into the darkness below. One tug on Matrona's elbow was all the encouragement she needed to follow him. She winced at the loudness of the door shutting behind them. Darkness flooded her vision, reminding her too much of the second doll.

She almost tripped at the bottom of the stairs, but Jaska steadied her, and once her feet found the dirt floor of the cold cellar, a few words finally made it to her lips. "I'm so sorry."

"What does Slava want?" Jaska asked. He still held her elbow, and in the coolness of the cellar, she could feel the heat wafting from his skin the way it would from a kiln. Sunlight trickled through small spaces between the planks of the cellar doors, none wider than half a finger, and her eyes began to adjust to the shadows.

"I . . ." Her tongue turned leaden in her mouth. The secrets danced within her, pressing, begging for escape. "You wouldn't believe me."

Jaska shook his head, turning from her for a moment, walking to the nearest stone wall and back. The Maysaks were a large family, but their cellar was no bigger than anyone else's. The scents of mice and mildew hung in the air, and the muffled noises of people and birds occasionally filtered in through the cracks in the doors.

Matrona felt his eyes on her before she saw the faint glint of choked sunlight in them. "You'd be surprised. Believe me, I can keep a secret."

She shook her head. "It's not a matter of trust, Jaska! He threatened to—"

Some of the sunlight snuffed out as a body approached the cellar door. Matrona froze, but Jaska grabbed her hand and tugged her to the back of the small space, opening the door to a closet Matrona hadn't noticed. He thrust her in gracelessly just as the cellar doors creaked open, then shoved his way in behind her and pulled the door shut, careful not to let it close too loudly.

The closet was just wide enough to fit Matrona's shoulders, and just short enough to force Jaska to bend his head down ever so slightly. He pressed his face to the doors, peering through the crack between them. The faintest sigh passed from his lips. Matrona held her breath, trying not to think of his arm pressing against her arm or his feet spaced between hers. Only a few more inches and they'd be body to body.

Chiding herself without words, she listened. The steps coming down the stairs were not heavy enough to be Slava's. A few jars shuffled on a set of shelves, and then the feet returned up the stairs. The light between the closet doors vanished as the cellar was shut once more.

"My father," Jaska whispered, and Matrona relaxed into the corners of the closet. A dim slice of light illuminated his grim expression, and she wondered if Afon had just retrieved a bottle of kvass. Matrona knew little of the relationship between Jaska and his father, but the man had never been around on the occasions she'd watched the younger Maysaks.

Still, Jaska didn't open the closet doors. His eyes lingered at the crack. "I'm sure Slava saw us," he continued. "What does he want with you?"

Matrona pinched her lips together, too many words boiling in her throat.

"Matrona," he whispered. "What happened that day, at his house?"

"Dolls," she croaked.

He pulled back, smacking the back of his head on the closet ceiling. "What?"

"Dolls," she repeated. "The tradesman's house is full of dolls." She knew she sounded mad, but if anyone could tolerate madness in the village, it was a man who had been raised alongside it. "He has a room full of them. Wooden dolls, only with smaller dolls nesting inside them. They're painted to look like us—the villagers. I have one, you have one, my father has one. So many dolls. All of us are in there."

He shifted in the darkness, and she wished he would stoop enough for the sliver of light to reveal his reaction.

She swallowed and steadied herself. "I returned a paintbrush. I saw them, all of them. Tried to open my father's and left. He acted so strangely after that. And I went back. I went back to his house"—she was breathless—"and he told me I had to replace him. Slava. That *I* had to take care of his dolls because I had seen them. Because he was old. They're connected to us, Jaska."

The way she issued his name made it sound like a desperate cry. Jaska held very still, listening. Matrona straightened as best she could.

He tried to lift an arm, but there wasn't space, so he dropped it. "I don't understand."

"They're connected to us, somehow," she whispered, suddenly aware of the silence settling in the cellar. "Witchcraft . . . I don't understand it. But he made me open my doll. After I removed the first layer, everyone knew my . . . secrets."

Her face burned, and she thanked the darkness, though the close walls made the air sweltering. Steeling herself, she asked, "How did you know, Jaska? Who told you those parts of my . . . thoughts?"

He went so still, he could have been a carving. Even his breaths barely registered to Matrona's ears. "I . . ." He paused. "I'm not sure."

"Everyone knew instantly." Words flowed from her like water. "And three days later, I opened the second doll, and it brought up such *darkness* inside of me. Torture rolling around my head, torture I put there from the time I learned to think." She couldn't explain it any other way. "It hit me right before you found me. And it's been three days. He told me I had to come back after three days, but *I don't want to go back.*"

She leaned against the closet's back wall, ignoring the splinters poking through her dress. "It sounds mad," she whispered, "but it's true. It's all true."

The quiet between them grew stale.

Matrona pushed against the closet door until it opened. She couldn't do this without seeing his face. Without knowing if he thought her mad. The cellar air felt cool when she stepped out. She eyed the cellar doors, listening.

Jaska stepped out as well and closed the closet doors. "I've heard worse." A weak smile touched his lips. "And no one else believes you?"

"I've told no one else. He forbade it."

Jaska drew a long breath through his nose and released slowly through his mouth. "I don't know Slava well." It seemed as if he wanted to say more, but any further words died in a low sound in his throat. "These . . . dolls," he spoke carefully, "they're why he wants you?"

She nodded.

"As what? An apprentice? To take over this sorcery?"

The word *sorcery* prickled the back of Matrona's neck and sent a new burst of energy through her weary limbs. She tried to study the shadows of the young man's face. "You believe me?"

"I don't have a reason not to."

For a moment, Matrona tried to imagine those words on the lips of her mother, or Feodor. It was impossible to envision it. "But it's so far-fetched."

"Not if you pay attention."

"What do you mean?"

Jaska shrugged, hesitated. "Have you ever noticed . . . how *content* everyone is?"

Matrona's lips parted slightly. She thought of her mother, her father . . . Feodor pacing in her front room, lecturing her for the suffering to which Slava had subjected her. "I can't say I have."

"They are." He rubbed the back of his head with a hand. Noticing the glove over his fingers, he pulled it off, then did the same with its match. "So . . . complacent. Or how everyone is born here, and everyone stays. There's no . . . mingling with other towns, save for the goods Slava brings from them." He, too, eyed the cellar doors. "Aside from your sister's disappearance . . . nothing bad ever happens."

"What do you mean?" Matrona wrung her fingers. "What sort of 'bad' things would happen, Jaska?"

The potter pulled away from the closet, shaking his head. "I don't know." He paused. "Things my mother says."

Matrona frowned. Mad Olia had a lot to say, and most of it was nonsensical, if it could be understood at all. Like bad poetry spoken underwater. *But,* Matrona conceded, *were she* my *mother, I would try to make sense of it.*

The cellar doors creaked again, and Matrona's hands tightened into fists as she waited for the doors to open. They didn't. A trick of the wind, perhaps.

"I don't trust him," Jaska murmured after a long moment.

"Slava?"

"Mm."

"Why? Because of what I said?"

He shook his head again, watching the cracks between the cellar doors. "Because he's . . . different."

"Different how?"

"Look at him, Matrona. Listen to how he talks. He's different."

"I hadn't spoken to him much before . . . this," she confessed. "But yes, he is. Dragon house and all."

He turned from the crack. "Dragon house?"

Matrona flushed. "It looks like . . . Never mind. He's a sorcerer, he has to be. If only you could see the dolls—"

"I'm not surprised. Makes me wonder about the others."

Her spine stiffened. "Others?"

Jaska didn't answer.

"Who else do you not trust?" *Who else should I not trust?*

He shrugged and leaned onto one leg, tilting his shoulders. "I don't know."

"Jaska—"

"Pavel." The name struck her chest like a hammer. But there was nothing off about Pavel. Matrona knew him well. "Ole—" he continued, but the name cut clean between his teeth. Still, Matrona had heard enough of it.

"Oleg?" she repeated, skin heating. "Oleg Popov?"

Jaska ran a hand through his unkempt hair. "I didn't mean to say it."

"What is there not to trust about Oleg?" Her betrothed's father? Her heart raced.

"I don't know. Intuition. I have no good reason to suspect him of anything, Matrona."

"But then why—"

"The horses, I guess."

She paused, stared at him. "Horses?"

"He and Pavel have both asked me to paint white horses on their pottery. Both have white horses in their homes. Dozens of them. I've asked why, and neither will answer beyond admitting to a fondness for them. I don't know. I thought it was strange."

"That two men happen to like horses?"

"White horses, specifically? I've never even seen a white horse."

She licked her lips, listening to the cellar doors in the silence that fell between them.

Jaska shook his head. "Like I said, I have no reason."

Matrona pursed her lips.

After a long moment, a soft chuckle sounded in the potter's throat.

"What's funny?"

He glanced at her. "The excuse. I used to say that to you when you stayed over. You'd ask why I misbehaved, and I'd say I had no reason."

The memory surfaced easily in Matrona's mind, and she felt her chest flush at the reminder of how young Jaska was, and how foolish her own mind could be.

Jaska looked around the cellar, but didn't move toward its doors. "What if you went, Matrona?"

The words struck her like the point of an awl. "Pardon?"

"If you went to Slava. Opened the . . . third? Doll."

Matrona shook her head. "I . . . I can't. He'll break me. If only you knew what opening those dolls meant . . ."

"I have an idea," he murmured. "How many layers are there?"

Matrona paused, stretching her mind to remember. He'd said there were five, hadn't he?

She didn't speak the number, but Jaska continued, "What can he do that's worse than what he's already done?"

"I can think of a few things." She was being too easy with her tongue. Her mother would have shared hard words for the comment, but Jaska was unruffled.

"He'll hurt you?"

Matrona pondered. "I . . . I don't think Slava would physically harm me." Such a thing was unheard of, outside of parental discipline.

Would the tradesman dare do anything that would leave a mark? Something Matrona could use to accuse him? Or would his attacks be solely supernatural?

Good heavens, was this what her life had become?

"I . . . ," she began, but realized she didn't know how to finish the sentence.

"Think about it," Jaska whispered. "But not for . . . my sake. Don't you want to know what it all means?" Though the shadows hid parts of his face, Matrona felt the stiffness that hardened the air around them, reminding her, *He knows*.

Before the embarrassment could solidify around her, putting her in a cage, Jaska said, "Let me take a look around, see if he's gone. You're welcome to hide as long as you want. I'll let you know what I find."

Matrona nodded, unsure if Jaska could see it. He crossed the cellar in a few long strides, took the stairs two at a time, and pushed open the rightmost cellar door.

The sunlight it let into Matrona's chilly sanctuary was blinding.

❄

There was little time left to decide.

Matrona had spent most of the day walking the strange loop of the wood, evading Slava. It would be dark soon. She certainly couldn't stay in the Maysaks' cellar overnight.

She sat on the second-to-last stair, weariness washing over her. She helped herself to some bread from her pack as she mulled over her options.

It was impossible to leave the wood, and in the clarity of her solitude, she accepted that she could not hide from Slava forever. What more could happen if she opened another doll? She couldn't fathom anything worse than the secrets and the darkness, and her mother had always groaned that Matrona had too much imagination.

Jaska couldn't understand, not fully. He hadn't held the dolls in his hands, hadn't seen the changes one little twist created in her father. He hadn't borne the humiliation of a hundred spilled secrets or the belittlement of years of self-doubt and failures. And yet he was the only one who knew of her forced arrangement with the tradesman. He might, Matrona realized, be the only person in the village who would ever believe such an implausible tale. Matrona wondered if that was due to the stories she used to tell him when he was a boy, thanks to the very imagination that seemed to be failing her now.

Her cheeks heated a little at the thought. A boy. Mercy in heaven, what must Jaska think of her, knowing the way she'd ogled him in the past? Knowing the imprudence of her feelings?

How kind of him to help her anyway . . .

But Slava couldn't know that she'd betrayed her unspoken oath to keep the dolls secret. He could never know.

And so Matrona would give him no reason to suspect her.

Grabbing a fistful of her skirt, Matrona stood and hiked up the stairs, pushing her shoulder into the cellar door to open it. The sky began to tint pink as the sun crawled toward its wooded bed. Matrona realized that this ritual, too, was caught in an endless loop.

She hurried from the cellar before anyone could see her departure. Her parents would certainly be wondering after her by now, and she had to reveal herself to them before they started alerting the neighbors and causing more trouble. Her mind spun a story as she hurried to her *izba*. She dropped the pack inside the pasture gate before stepping inside, lest she raise even more suspicion.

"Where on God's earth have you *been*?" her mother spat. She had been drying dishes, and threw the towel into the air hard enough for it to strike the ceiling. "You're not married yet, Matrona, and this disrespect is unacceptable! And the tradesman! Slava Barinov, of all people, came by looking for *you*, and I had to fumble my words trying not to look like an utter fool—"

"I spoke with Slava." It felt oddly invigorating to cut off her mother. "We had a long conversation. He's trading for some cows soon and wanted my opinion on what he should look for. I apologize for my delay, but he was insistent."

The lie slid off her tongue so easily, it was startling—not only to Matrona, but to her mother as well.

"Slava asked *you* for breeding advice?" Her mother's voice was incredulous, her eyes calculating. "Why not ask your father? Or me, for that matter?" She paused and rubbed at her belly. "We certainly know more."

Matrona shrugged, trying not to betray the nerves that prickled beneath her skin, down to the center of her chest. "You'll have to ask him. Are you well?"

Her mother pursed her lips and stacked plates inside the cupboard. "Must have eaten something sour while you were off on your own. Father's been feeling it, too. It will pass."

Matrona frowned as she watched her mother's hand massage her middle again. That was where the seams on the dolls were, wasn't it?

All the more reason to make haste.

"Good night, Mama."

She walked away, and her mother remained silent. Matrona slid into the darkness of her bedroom, and then out the window into the twilight.

"All right, Tradesman," she whispered. "I'm coming."

Chapter 9

Matrona had never walked the village at night. Every star in the unreachable heavens felt like an eye watching her, and the calm breeze that loosed strands of hair from her braid sounded like whispers. It reminded her all too much of her shameful walk to her *izba* after opening her first doll. She shuddered.

Keeping her spine straight and shoulders back, Matrona tried not to feel like a vagrant. She pieced together excuses should she run into anyone. Then again, whoever might see her would have explaining of their own to do, wouldn't they?

She glanced over her shoulder—she'd been doing that a lot recently. Listened to the voices of the nearby wood, the silence of the *izbas* around her, all darkened windows and cold chimneys. The air smelled different at night: earthier, cleaner. She could taste grass in the air. Crickets called after her, muting her footsteps along the worn path encircling the village.

When the path turned eastward, toward Slava's house, a muffled giggle startled Matrona. She nearly tripped over her own feet in her haste to leap off the path. It was a maiden's laugh, and Matrona's gaze followed the sound to the tiny shops to her right, where she saw two shadows dancing. Her blood heated when she realized they were a man and a woman. They shushed each other as they ran from eave to eave, oblivious of Matrona's proximity.

She thought to continue walking, but her muscles froze at the sound of a whisper from the man. Squinting, Matrona tried to draw his outline in her mind, and her stomach sank. Was that . . . Jaska?

The roving couple dashed to a new eave, and the moon cast just enough light for Matrona to see the cut of the man's hair. A long breath escaped her. Not Jaska. In fact, it looked quite a lot like his brother Kostya. Matrona pinched her lips together, forced her gaze away, and trudged up the path with renewed energy. The sooner this was over, the better.

Even in the embrace of night, Slava's house was not hard to spot. Not because of its size, its incredible decor, or the fact that, at the right angle, it looked like a dragon. No, it stood out from the shadows for the light in its window. A single candle flame, but amid a village sleeping in the dark, it blazed like the sun. Matrona fixed upon it, slowing to watch the subtle shifting of its light, before approaching the front door.

The bright colors of the home looked muted, almost gray and dull, and Matrona fancied that if she ran her hand against the siding, she could wipe off the shadows like ash from fine porcelain. Instead, she brought her knuckles toward the door. Paused, and dropped her fingers to the door handle. She stepped inside.

The air in the house was too warm—almost suffocating after her brisk walk through the cool night. It smelled faintly of kvass and strongly of smoke. Turning the corner by the stairs, she saw Slava sitting in one of his fine chairs beside that flickering candle, a glossed pipe held to his lips. Corn-silk-colored smoke passed through his nostrils as he looked up at her.

Dragon, indeed.

He pulled the pipe's stem from his lips. "I was concerned I'd have to persuade you," he said, and Matrona noticed two dolls on the table beside him—her parents'. Were their bellyaches Slava's doing? How far would he have gone, had Matrona not come?

He paused to puff twice on the mouthpiece, then let the smoke flow all at once from his lips. "I'm relieved I do not have to."

Persuade me, Matrona thought. She didn't bother to hide the frown tugging on her lips. "I'm here now, Tradesman." She emphasized his occupation. A bit of metal caught her eye—a bridle, new enough that it gleamed without blemish, beside a leather satchel, its sides expanding with the contents within. Slava must be leaving for his trades soon. Matrona wondered again how he alone managed to escape—

"Tell me about the loop," she said.

He raised a gray brow. "What loop?"

"In the wood. Walk too far south and you appear in the north. Too far west and you appear in the east."

"So you've noticed." Smoke spilled from his nostrils. "And what were you doing so deep in the wood?"

Matrona rolled her lips, trying to determine how far to extend her honesty.

Slava's face seemed to melt into his wrinkles. "I will teach you soon enough, and you will not speak of it to another soul, is that understood?"

She watched him for several long seconds through his halo of smoke. "Show me what's inside the third doll."

He smirked faintly—Matrona saw it only by the twitching of his beard. He took one more draw of his pipe before dumping its ashy contents in a bowl on a small side table. He stood, both knees popping as he did so, and took up her parents' dolls before walking back toward the kitchen and the carpeted hallway that led to the dolls. He said nothing to her, only motioned with his hand, fully expecting her to follow.

She did.

The hallway was unlit, save for the light of a lamp glowing under the door to the room of the dolls. The hall seemed much longer than

Matrona remembered, and she was oddly out of breath by the time Slava opened the door.

The hissing of the kite scared Matrona. Her shoulder slammed into the doorjamb when she jumped.

"Easy, Pamyat." Slava spoke with a grandfatherly tone, his voice worn. He set her parents back in their respective places on his tables. Matrona wondered again at his veiled desperation to have her take his place as the keeper of the dolls. He was old, yes, but seemed to be in good-enough health.

The dolls watched her enter. All their faces looked forward, as if in anticipation of her arrival. Matrona tried not to shiver under their relentless, flat stares, but her resolve could go only so far. She hoped Slava had not seen her shudder.

She stared back, her gaze jumping from face to face. There was Boris, Pavel, Oleg, Roksana, Irena, Lenore, Nastasya, Darya, herself. Slava moved for her doll, and Matrona stepped to the side, inching closer to the watching kite, to study more of the faces. She found Jaska and his siblings, Feodor, the Avdovin clan. A few of the faces took longer to recognize, for they were either younger or older versions of the people they represented. Children were depicted as adults, their faces still round in Slava's style of art. A few of the elderly were youthful, free of the wrinkles they bore in life. Matrona wondered, briefly, what had inspired Slava to draw some of the villagers old and others young.

Slava turned about, his large hands wrapped around her third doll, but Matrona did not meet his eyes. She turned, scanning the dolls on the shelves. Slava said nothing, and when Matrona's attention returned to him, she asked, "Tradesman, where is *your* doll?"

Slava's expression did not alter the slightest bit, not even a twitch of an eyebrow. "You assume I have one?" he asked.

"Everyone has one." Matrona gestured to the full tables. She could not think of a single person in her acquaintance that was not represented among the figures, and there was not a single doll she did not recognize. "But I don't see yours."

"Hmm." He lifted her doll in his hands. He removed the first two layers and presented Matrona with the third. "It is time."

Matrona folded her arms. "You will not answer me?"

He held out her doll.

Swallowing back a complaint, Matrona took the doll in her hand, looking it over. It was the length of her hand, and today she wore the red *sarafan* that matched it. She turned it over, studying its back. Ran the pad of her thumb along the seam.

"Why must I do this?" she asked, half a whisper.

"I have explained it to you."

"Have you?" she asked, feeling bold, ignoring a second hiss from Pamyat.

Slava's lips drooped. "You must find your center, Matrona. You cannot understand any of this until that is done."

Matrona took a long breath and let it out slowly. She examined the doll. "What will happen this time?"

"You will see."

"You will tell me." Her tongue was whip-like in her mouth. How her mother would fuss should she say such a thing at home. "I've endured two burdens for your sake already, tarnished my name among the villagers, and hurt my relationship with my parents. I nearly lost my engagement because—"

"You mentioned it the last time you were here," Slava cut in. "Open the doll, Matrona. You must comprehend what I have done for you before you can help the others."

Matrona's breath paused in her lungs. *Help the others?* What was wrong with them?

Slava planted his hands on his hips, making him look broader in the poor light. "How old are you now, Matrona?"

Her gaze flickered from the doll to him. "Twenty-six. Why?"

"Then perhaps nothing will happen at all." He dropped his hands. "I am weary. Open the doll before I force your hand."

She gritted her teeth together. *So much for conversation,* she thought, and clutched the head of the doll in one hand, the base in the other. Her heart sped, making her feel light headed.

"What can he do that's worse than what he's already done?" Jaska's voice whispered in her thoughts.

Squeezing her eyes shut, Matrona twisted the halves and pulled until their snug sealing opened with a faint pop. She held her breath, but as before, she felt no change overtake her. Opening her eyes, she looked down at the doll. A fourth doll sat inside it, identical to its counterparts, save for the simplified details to the clothes and *kokoshnik*. As Matrona fingered the small fourth doll, however, she noticed the third doll was different from the first two.

The inside was painted completely black.

She held the top piece toward the lamp, causing Pamyat to rustle on his perch. Entirely black, not a sliver of clean wood to be seen. The bottom half, too. She wondered at it.

Slava's hands overpowered hers and pulled the dolls away. Her signal to leave, but as she turned for the door, the tradesman said, "You will return in three days. Do not try to thwart me again, Matrona."

She glanced his way; he reassembled her doll and put it back on the table before meeting her eyes. She thought of the satchel and bridle and asked, "Will you be here in three days?"

His eyes narrowed. "If you think I will merely vanish, or give up on this, you are wrong," he continued, blue eyes piercing even in the dim room. "If you knew who I was, you would not dare to hide, to speak out of turn, or to deny me in any way."

Matrona's skin prickled into gooseflesh. Trying to steel her voice, she asked, "And who are you, Slava?"

He straightened, then snorted, the corner of his mouth turning up ever so slightly. "I am a more patient man than I once was. Three days. Good night."

Unsure of what to do, Matrona offered a simple nod and stepped from the room, following the faint guidance of the front room's candle until she reached the door. She paused, searching behind her for the tradesman, but he did not follow.

Sucking in a deep breath through her nostrils, Matrona pulled open the door and stepped out into the cool darkness of the night.

It hit her all at once. Images filled her eyes, bright despite the cover of dark. A splintered table, a heavy coat, a bowl full of thin soup. Her fingers, small, wrapped around a wooden spoon.

Her mother, younger, wearing a tattered shawl as she rubbed Matrona's numb feet.

A smell she didn't recognize—something burning, unnatural, hanging in the air. The sound of marching footsteps in the distance, like—

The sky, contorted and dark, full of thick clouds that rumbled and . . . The word dragged slowly across her mind. *Thundered.*

A muddy street scarred with wagon tracks, a strange whiteness to either side of it. Breath fogging under her chin.

Matrona blinked, and once more found herself in front of Slava's dragon house. Still, the new, startling images lingered in her mind. They were not crisp, but they were undeniable, like old drawings smeared by a careless hand. Her head ached as she tried to make sense of them. Then she remembered Mad Olia's prattling the day she'd visited the pottery to ask for a replacement jug for Feodor.

"Snow," Matrona breathed, touching both hands to her breath. "Jaska . . . I know what snow is."

The light in Slava's window extinguished. Matrona whirled around, staring at the tradesman's quiet house.

Snow. But what was the rest?

Had she traveled outside the loop before, and forgotten?

A pressure like angry, pressing fingers flared in her temples. Snow. The more she thought of it, the stronger the pain grew. She needed to get home, to sleep. When she was well rested, she'd pick apart the details of Slava's newest curse.

What did it mean? And how had Mad Olia Maysak named the cold whiteness before Matrona ever knew what it was?

She stumbled away from Slava's house. The breeze felt too cold. *Cold, like the snow.* A coldness Matrona had never felt before, and yet these strange images made her think maybe she had.

One thing was certain—tomorrow she would find Jaska and tell him that maybe, *maybe*, his mother wasn't as crazed as they believed her to be.

Chapter 10

"Have I heard of what?" her father asked, setting his water cup beside his empty breakfast plate.

"Snow," Matrona tried again, unsure of where to settle her eyes. She customarily did the respectful thing and kept them downcast, but today she felt the need to study her parents' expressions. Her father's forehead wrinkled into thick lines. Her mother watched her with a sidelong look, her brows drawn, her lips puckered.

"Sounds odd." Her father watched her, waiting for explanation.

Matrona tried a small smile. "Oh, it's this strange plant in the wood, something . . . Slava told me about when I met with him yesterday. Small with white tips."

"What are you babbling about flowers for?" her mother asked, standing from the table with a burst of energy. She scooped up her plate and cup as though they offended her. "Make use of yourself, Matrona."

"Yes, Mama." Matrona collected her dishes as well. She had risen early to do the milking, but the small barn needed cleaning, as did one of the milk barrels. There was always butter to be churned and bread to be baked.

Unfortunately, Matrona wouldn't have time to do any of it until later in the day.

She took the pail and brush outside for scrubbing, making sure her mother saw the supplies for what would be a time-consuming chore. She set them on the table in the barn, but left her apron on the rack.

Just me this time, she thought, leaning against the table, eyeing the bin of cheesecloths that needed to be laundered. The opening of the first doll had affected other people, but the last two had only affected her. Neither of her parents had experienced the same strange visions that had flitted through Matrona's mind last night. Now those visions perched in faded colors alongside her memories.

She'd dreamed strange things, too—tiny *izbas* and large gardens of half-dead plants. Steam and smoke rising from odd buildings far larger than even the tradesman's home. Blocky things with long rows of square windows. And gray—everything around them was gray. The sky, the buildings, even the broken snow that littered the ground in uneven patches.

Her temples began to throb anew, and Matrona rubbed her head, trying to ease the strangeness away. She thought to ask Slava what it meant, but he never gave her clear answers. She could only hope that, after the last doll, the puzzle would be solved.

Lowering her hands, she thought, *Find my center. What does that have to do with . . . this?* The humiliation, the darkness, and now these gray, cold images. When Slava had told her she would be separated from the village, had he meant the others would ostracize her?

She thought of Feodor. Best not to mention the snow—or any of this—to him.

Matrona pushed off the table, smoothed her dress, and hurried to the nearest pasture fence, moving carefully to keep the barn between her and the house. She skirted around the Grankins' potato farm before finding the road that cut through the village west to east. She spied Irena Kalagin—her doll had been painted to make her look younger—outside the cobbler's, chatting with Lenore Demidov. Lenore's eyes found Matrona first, and Irena's followed. Their talk quieted instantly, and Irena's face soured. Matrona averted her eyes, pretending not to notice. She may have advanced to the third doll, but not enough time had passed for the village to forget her shames.

She wondered if Slava viewed her any differently.

The village grew noisy as she reached its east side. The sounds of striking hammers, working billows, and tossed firewood cracked through the air. Boris crossed her path, carrying a yoke across his shoulders, a full bucket of water tied to either end. She hurried around him, avoiding another pair of judging eyes, and entered the pottery.

The workshop teemed with people today. Zhanna Avdovin waited in the corner with her arms folded, tapping her foot impatiently. Alena Zotov held an urn in one hand and used her other to make wide gestures as she spoke to Viktor Maysak. Behind him, Kostya—the one Matrona had seen out with one of the village girls last night—leaned sleepily over a slate, writing down instructions dictated to him by Rolan Ishutin, Boris's father. Beyond them, Galina swept the floors. In the back of the pottery, Matrona spotted Jaska dressed in a dark-viridian *kosovorotka*. It looked new, and the ends of his hair brushed its stiff collar.

Matrona glanced at the villagers around her, most of whom hadn't noticed her arrival. Of course there would be people here to witness her approach Jaska. She sighed, then remembered the door tucked away behind the kiln. Escaping out the wide doorway, Matrona hurried around the pottery, finding the door across from the basement where Jaska had hidden her just yesterday. Slipping through it, she inched into the pottery, hoping to remain unseen by the bustle of people at the front.

Jaska didn't see her; the firelight of the kiln reflected brightly in his eyes. A rag tied about his crown kept his hair back from his face. He hefted a large hook and shoved it into the kiln, sliding it around a large pot there. The sleeves of his shirt were rolled up above his elbows, and Matrona watched the lines of his forearms tense and shift as he hauled the pot from its oven.

She flushed and tucked loose hairs behind her ears. Jaska noticed her then and started ever so slightly. Attention back to the pot, he grasped it between thickly gloved hands and carried it to a stone block beside the kiln.

"Matrona." He glanced to the front of the shop. Matrona's cheeks flushed hotter—did she embarrass him, too? He passed her, moving to a small table against the wall, upon which sat three clay jugs ready for baking. He hesitated and asked, "What's wrong?"

"I spoke with Slava last night." The noise of the pottery almost swallowed her voice.

"You did?"

She nodded. "I opened the third doll."

Jaska glanced again at the front of the pottery. Picked up one of the jugs and brought it to the kiln. Glanced back at her, as though he wasn't sure where to settle his eyes.

"Nothing happened at first, but these images . . ." She struggled to make sense of them, to not sound foolish in front of the potter. "They're like . . . memories, almost."

Jaska hefted the jug into the kiln and shut its door, then wiped his forearm across the bridge of his nose. Glanced at Viktor, then at Matrona. "Maybe now isn't—"

"I know what snow is."

He dropped his arm, and for a moment he was still as a painting. Licking his lips, he reached toward Matrona, but then lowered his hand and instead gestured toward the back door. Matrona gratefully fled to it, eager to be away from onlookers.

The air outside felt blissfully cool, and she took in a deep, refreshing breath of it. Jaska shut the door and stepped around her. Pushed both hands into his hair, then grabbed the rag and pulled it off. "My mother, she talks about snow all the time. I haven't a clue . . ."

He gazed at Matrona with a strange sort of intensity—almost like Slava's, yet different. It made Matrona's stomach clench.

He asked, "What? What is it?"

She forced her body to relax. "It's cold. It's white." A new image came to her head—pale blankets of clouds, soft down floating through the air. "It falls from the sky, like rain."

Jaska turned away, paced a few steps, then turned again and leaned against the wall of the pottery. "'Falls from the sky, like rain,'" he said, not incredulous, but thoughtful. After a moment, he glanced at her. "You've seen it?"

She nodded. "I have . . . in a sense. Not with my own eyes, yet . . . it's like I did, once upon a time. A strange sort of memory. Like an old dream."

She thought the words too poetic, but Jaska merely nodded. His mouth worked for a few seconds before he managed, "My mother knows, too."

"We could ask her . . ." Matrona tried, but the words faded before she could finish them.

Jaska offered a sad sort of half smile. They both knew Olia didn't answer questions. She didn't comprehend sense at all. And yet, she knew.

"Tell me the rest," Jaska pleaded. Kostya hollered his name inside the pottery, but Jaska ignored it, shortening the distance between himself and Matrona to no more than a pace. "What else did he show you?"

Matrona looked down, in part to pull her focus from Jaska's nearness, in part to concentrate. She told him about the gray skies, the cold. The houses scattered along a muddy road, smaller and far drabber than the ones in the village. She described the snow and the large buildings puffing smoke into the air, the echoes of marching footsteps.

"I feel . . . like there's more," she continued, "but I can't quite grasp it. Like it's too far away."

Jaska was silent for a long moment. She wondered if he was processing the strangeness of her visions, or if, perhaps, he was trying to compare them to his mother's ramblings. Something inside the pottery broke, but Jaska didn't seem to hear it, and Matrona dared not disturb his silence.

She looked away, studying the grass growing between the pottery and the Maysaks' home, the basement doors, the tips of the wood beyond. A few people passed them, but none looked their way.

Then Jaska's warm hand clasped hers, and everything else fell away.

"Matrona." His voice was just above a whisper, his hand calloused and dry. His skin looked tan against hers, the nails clean and trimmed. Clay stained a few knuckles.

Her entire body became a heartbeat.

He looked squarely at her, eyes perfectly level with her own. "I want you to open my doll."

Her spine prickled, and she pulled her hand from the potter's grasp. "Jaska, no. You don't understand—"

"It doesn't matter. I'll suffer through it. I need to know what you know, see what you see. I want to know what's at the center of those dolls."

Matrona shook her head. "Then let me open the last one and tell you what I see."

She found herself thinking again about the warning Slava had given her: *"You need to separate yourself from the rest of the village."* What did it mean? Would she even be able to speak with Jaska once she finished Slava's work?

"I need to know for myself. I have . . . questions, Matrona," he pleaded, keeping his voice low, glancing up once when someone passed by. "I've felt it for a long time. These dolls . . . If what you say is true, perhaps my answers lie in Slava's home."

"You don't believe me?"

"No, I didn't mean that." He slouched a little, coming closer to her height. "I want to understand this. I want to understand *you.*"

Matrona tried to swallow a sore lump in her throat. "If Slava knows I told you—"

"That's why I'm asking you to do it. If I thought it possible, I would go myself—"

"Don't do that."

He smiled, one dimple peeking at her. "Please. Just open the first one. If I can't handle it, we can stop, right?"

"You don't understand." Matrona wrung part of her skirt in her hands. "*Everyone* will know your secrets, Jaska. *Including* Slava. He'll know we opened it."

He leaned back, a sigh passing over his lips. "And he'll know it was you."

"It couldn't be anyone else." Matrona chewed on her lip, watching Jaska's expression fall. Slava had never told her not to open the other dolls, had he? Just not to share the secret. Which, of course, she already had.

Even so, wasn't Slava's plan for her to replace him, and soon? Once that happened, *she* would be keeper of the dolls, and they would be in her stewardship. In a sense, they were already hers. Why shouldn't she open Jaska's doll?

"*Jaska!*" Kostya bellowed.

Jaska straightened, though his whole person seemed to wilt. "I have to get back inside."

"Tonight," Matrona whispered.

He looked taken aback.

"Tonight, after sunset," she clarified, "When full dark settles. I think Slava is leaving for another trip, if he hasn't already." She thought briefly of Pamyat, but the kite hadn't attacked her the first time she'd entered the room, and surely the beast was used to her by now. "I can go then, when the others won't see—"

"Let me come with you."

She nodded. "But not into the house. I won't risk that."

"Agreed." Jaska clasped her hand as though they were two men making a business deal. But the smile had returned to his face.

Heavens, he was handsome.

He released her and reached for the pottery door. "Thank you, Matrona," he said, then slid inside. Seconds later, Matrona heard Kostya shouting at him.

Matrona took a deep breath and leaned against the pottery, staring up into the blue, cloudless sky. Her fingers trembled, and she fisted her hands to still them.

One doll. It was just one doll. She'd come this far; Slava would have to be forgiving. And wouldn't it be a relief to have someone share the burden with her?

Yet as Matrona walked away from the pottery and met the scornful glare of another villager, the still-fresh memories of her humiliation bubbled to the forefront of her thoughts. Jaska would suffer that, too, and it would be her fault.

Then again, he was Jaska Maysak. Surely his secrets were light and easily dismissed. Surely he hid nothing of which to be ashamed . . .

Chapter 11

Matrona made it back to the cow pasture without so much as a glare from her mother or nod from her father. She wiped down the table and equipment in the barn, swept it out, then took to filling the villagers' dairy requests—Georgy Grankin came by for milk, Nastasya Kalagin came for cheese, and Pavel came for butter. Matrona silently wondered at Pavel as she wrapped up his butter and set it in the basket, which was already filled with potatoes from the Grankin farm. Was his appreciation for white horses so strange? She studied him as he left, trying to piece it together for herself, but Pavel was like every other man in the village, just as his doll was like every other doll.

As luck would have it, Feodor and his father came for dinner that night, an invitation Matrona's mother had neglected to tell her about until an hour before, leaving Matrona rushing to bathe and dress and make herself look proper for her soon-to-be husband. She stood behind her parents when the Popovs arrived, smiling and trying to look pretty while they exchanged formalities. By the time Feodor took any obvious notice of her, Matrona again felt like a doll—not the complicated, layered one atop the table in Slava's home, but the forgotten toy locked away inside her mother's chest, sewn for Matrona's vanished sister. Forgotten.

It made her want to touch him in a way that was not at all romantic.

Feodor and his father sat at the same side of the table as Matrona's father, and she and her mother sat opposite them. Matrona served the *shchi*, ladling the steaming soup into Oleg's bowl first, then Feodor's, her father's, her mother's, and hers last. She watched Oleg from the corner of her eye, again wondering at Jaska's words in the darkness of that cellar. Oleg was as different from Pavel as a man could be, and yet he seemed no more extraordinary than the carpenter.

Matrona sat and, when Feodor looked up from his soup, smiled at him. He returned the gesture with a nod. A nod?

"We have been discussing dates," Oleg said halfway through his bowl.

Her mother leaned forward as though Oleg were the main course. "Oh, please share. What are your thoughts?"

Feodor answered, "We believe *Pyatnitsa*, two weeks from today, would be an acceptable date. It would give us enough time for final preparations without stirring up further gossip."

Matrona's father took a sip of kvass. "Oh? And what gossip is feeding them now?"

"Why we wait," Feodor replied matter-of-factly. He seemed more interested in the food than in the conversation.

Matrona's stomach tingled as though the cabbage in her swallowed soup had grown wings and sought to escape. Two weeks!

She would open the fourth doll long before then.

"You need to separate yourself from the rest of the village."

Matrona cleared her throat as softly as she could and took a sip of water. She tried to tell herself that Slava didn't matter and that what she'd always wanted—to be seen as an adult by the rest of the village—was finally about to happen.

She thought of the hushed sound of Jaska's voice, carried on warm breath as they hid in the darkness from the tradesman.

Oleg chuckled. "You're rather pink."

Looking up from her cup, Matrona realized he'd addressed her, and nearly choked on her water.

"A blushing bride," her father joked, and Feodor smiled.

Her father continued, "What preparations? Is there anything additional you need us to do?"

"Simple things, really," Feodor answered, setting down his spoon. "Working on the house, though I suspect we'll be in my father's abode for a short time before moving in."

Matrona smiled softly to herself as she thought of her own *izba*. A good start to a marriage. To a new life.

Feodor continued, "I'm seeing it furnished as well. I hope to visit Pavel before we return home, to see the progression on the bed for Matrona."

Her smile faded, and she kept her eyes on her soup to mask it, though she needn't have—the conversation continued around her. She had been right, then—Pavel had been working on a headboard. The disappointment came from Feodor's words, *"for Matrona."*

So he did not expect them to share a bed. Such a thing was not unheard of; but even her parents shared a bed, and they did not act incredibly fond of each other, at least not when Matrona was around to play witness. Roksana and Luka certainly shared a bed.

Matrona's eyes stung, and she drank deeply of her water, blinking rapidly to prevent any tears. *It's fine,* she told herself. *We really don't know each other well, not yet. Once that happens, surely we could commission Pavel to . . .*

She glanced at her betrothed, only then noticing he and Oleg had empty bowls. Silently rising from the table, Matrona went to fetch the pork *kholodets* from the cook fire. She stepped around Feodor's chair to serve him, millimeters from brushing his shoulder. So close, and yet so distant. If her arm brushed him, would he notice? Would it send prickles up her arm the way Jaska's touch had done just that morning?

Did it matter?

She leaned in, just a little, until their sleeves brushed. Until there was the slightest pressure between his shoulder and her forearm. There, that wasn't so bad. Just a touch. Feodor didn't seem to notice, even when she set the meat on his plate.

There was nothing special about a brush of sleeves, of course. What she needed was something more. Something to make her skin tingle or her chest flutter.

Pinching her lips to keep from frowning, Matrona went on to serve her family and lastly herself before placing the pot on the brick beside the cook fire. In her mind, she prayed.

Please let him touch me before he leaves, she thought, blinking again, swallowing the soreness rising in her throat. *Let him hold my hand, kiss my cheek, anything.*

He had agreed to the marriage, even after the mishaps with Slava's doll. He was the one who had pursued the match in the first place. Didn't he *want* her?

Matrona returned to her place at the table, but found her appetite gone. She stirred the pork bits on her plate and glanced at Feodor. *Why can't you love me?*

Desperation burned her belly raw, but she wasn't going to do this, not here, not now. *Lord help me, I'm so tired of crying.*

She plastered on her best practiced smile throughout the rest of the meal, and when the Popovs took their leave, she walked them from the *izba* and onto the path. With a gentle nod, Feodor said his good-bye and headed for Pavel's carpentry, his skin never once coming in contact with hers.

Matrona drew in a shuddering breath and noticed Roksana coming down the same path, a blue *sarafan* dancing about her pregnant frame. It almost matched the shade of the darkening sky . . . which reminded Matrona of her promise to Jaska. Feodor had weighed down her thoughts so much, she'd nearly forgotten.

She had to leave soon. She had to sneak into Slava's home, again.

But what if she'd been mistaken about the satchel and bridle? What if the tradesman had merely *returned* from a trip? Surely if his horse and wagon were there, Jaska wouldn't insist on going through with their mad plan.

It suddenly occurred to her that someone could see them together in the night, just as she'd seen Jaska's brother with a village girl. She would never be able to explain it away enough to—

"Matrona!" Roksana called, a wide smile painting her mouth. She drew closer. "Feodor and Oleg at your home? For dinner? Things are going well, then?"

Matrona forced herself to focus on her dear friend, but her mind fluttered like moths near a candle. "I, uh, yes. Well."

"Don't tell me everything at once." A line formed between Roksana's eyebrows. "I've barely seen or spoken to you lately. I've been worried. Pavel tells me you came by looking for me the other day."

Matrona blinked, trying to process the new information as it piled onto the clutter of Feodor, Jaska, and Slava. Roksana, yes. To hide from Slava.

"Yes," she answered, glancing at the sky. Why was it darkening so quickly? She turned to look at the house, but neither of her parents had lingered in the doorway. "But I'm fine now."

"Fine *now*?" Roksana repeated, grasping Matrona's fingers to engage her attention. "You weren't fine before? Are you still ill?"

"No, I was just . . . visiting."

"We have time to visit now." She smiled. "Luka ran over to the Grankins', so he'll be by in a bit to fetch me—"

Matrona rubbed her forehead. "Oh, Roksana, I . . . I'm sorry. I can't talk now."

The line between her friend's brows deepened. "Why ever not? Your guests just left, and we have a lot to talk about. Do you and Feodor have a date set yet? Have you tried on the dress—"

"I have something to do. Something personal." Her tongue felt too loose. Where was that easy lying when she needed it? "Yes, we have a date. Two weeks from today. And no, I haven't tried the dress on yet."

"Not yet! What if it needs a lot of tailoring? What are you waiting for?" Roksana tipped her head to one side. "Are you sure you're feeling well?" She lifted her hand to check Matrona's forehead.

Matrona stepped back to avoid the touch. Tried to smile. "Yes, I'm fine. I'll find you tomorrow and we'll catch up. There's no school, right?"

Roksana frowned. "You've been so strange lately." She folded her arms. "You used to tell me everything."

"I will, I will!" she countered, trying to force enthusiasm into her voice. "But it's getting dark and I need . . . to do something. Please, tomorrow."

Roksana's eyes narrowed, but she nodded her consent, and Matrona took the gesture as permission to return inside, where she changed into the darkest *sarafan* she had. The palms of her hands perspired as she listened to her parents shuffle about while they prepared for bed. Matrona lit a candle and then grabbed a comb and unbraided her hair, the long black locks falling in waves over her shoulders. She plaited it in two tails, one over each shoulder, as Roksana wore hers, then found an old scarf to wear over her head. If she changed her silhouette, perhaps she would be less recognizable in the dark. She checked her pockets to ensure they were empty—it would bring bad fortune to take more out of the house than needed at night, and Matrona wanted to secure as much luck as possible.

A shifting of darkness at the window caught the corner of her eye; she turned, but saw nothing in the gap between her curtains. The wood had devoured the last wisps of twilight. Taking a deep breath to calm herself, she tugged the curtains completely closed. Then she blew out her candle, bathing herself in darkness, and slid it and a single match into her pocket.

Listening for her parents and hearing their low voices in their bedroom, Matrona slipped into the hallway. She winced when a floorboard creaked under her heel and then quickened her step, again waiting until she was in the pasture to put on her shoes. Traveling this path in stealth had become all too familiar to her.

She slinked out the gate, spying windows in the village alight with candles and lamps. One extinguished under her gaze. She kept her distance from the main path, walking just close enough to follow it. She heard two men talking to each other on a porch; one laughed heartily. Matrona eyed the sky, the slim band of light over the wood summoning the rising moon. She was late. Her steps moved in time with her heartbeat, quick and sharp.

A few more windows darkened as she pulled away from the thickest grouping of the *izbas* and moved toward the north face of the wood. Cricket song filled the quiet space between each breath. The moon peeked over the treetops, and in its light Matrona saw the edge of Slava's roof. No light emanated from his home. A good sign, yet Matrona's nerves stung her limbs like hornets.

Her steps slowed as she neared the house. What if Slava lingered inside? What if he saw her? Her mind fumbled for an excuse—

A hand on her elbow shot her heart out of her chest. She spun and smacked her open palm into her assailant's chest—

"Matrona!" the shadow whispered, letting her go. "It's me!"

Matrona stepped back, trying to catch her breath. "Jaska?"

He rubbed his chest, the rising moon glinting off his teeth. "Quite an arm you've got."

She adjusted her head scarf. "A butter churn will do that."

He chuckled deep in his throat. The sound faded. "You were right; his horse and wagon are gone. The house is empty."

"Except for the kite."

"Kite?"

"His pet." The darkness swallowed Jaska, so there was no telling if his expression changed. "How long have you been here?"

"Since twilight. I thought . . . I wondered if you'd changed your mind."

"I promised."

"You're a woman of your word." His tone softened in a way that rose gooseflesh on Matrona's arms. *Just the cool of night,* she told herself. Certainly there wasn't any hidden meaning in Jaska's words or the way he'd said them.

She swallowed, the walls of her throat feeling too thick.

Perhaps sensing her hesitation, Jaska said, "I'm sorry . . . If you tell me where the room is—"

"No, I'll go. It'll be quicker that way." Besides, she couldn't explain all the rules of the dolls to him now, and she couldn't trust him to leave everything behind exactly as he'd found it. Scanning the path behind her and finding it empty, Matrona crept toward the house, Jaska falling in step beside her.

"Will they know you're missing?" he asked. "Your parents."

"I don't know. I hope not. If they find out, I'll tell them a cow escaped or something."

She could feel his grin beside her like a flame. It gave her courage. Halting, she turned to him. "Stay here."

He nodded, stepping into a black shadow beside the house.

Matrona licked her lips. "You know what it will do, don't you?"

"Will it be the same?" he asked. "As . . . yours?"

Matrona shocked herself by not blushing at the question, at the reminder of how her most guarded secret had spread through their village like the seeds of a weed. She answered honestly. "I don't know. I assume so."

He hesitated only a second, but it was long enough for Matrona to notice. "I suppose we'll see."

She nodded, once, and hurried to Slava's front door. Every footstep in the grass sounded like shattering ceramic, and the rays of the moon, so faint and gentle, became blazing suns. She reached the portico and spun around, pulling her scarf close, searching the village for onlookers. Her breath caught at the sight of movement close to the wood, but as she stared into the darkness, she saw only the rustling of leaves in the soft breeze.

She hurried to the door. The sooner this was done, the better.

Grasping the handle, Matrona pushed the door open, smelling wood and the faint traces of Slava's cigars. She slipped into the entry hall, shutting the door behind her, the squeaking of its hinges rattling her as much as a baby's cry. She listened for movement within the house, heard none. No light peeked under any doorways or down the staircase.

She hurried through the front room, from which the satchel and bridle had been taken. The toe of her shoe caught on a chair leg, and Matrona paused just long enough to ensure the furniture was positioned exactly how Slava had left it, before cutting through the kitchen and down the carpeted hallway.

Away from the windows, Matrona pulled her candle from her pocket and tugged her sleeve around her fingers to keep the melting wax off her skin. She lit it, the bright burst of flame marring her sight with brown spots. Through the pulse thumping in her ears, she heard the rustle of feathers.

She opened the door to the room of dolls. The candlelight reflected off Pamyat's yellow eyes as the bird hunched his wings, opening his beak and hissing. The bloody skin of a rat hung from one of his talons.

"Hush," Matrona snapped at it, the word sounding like her own hiss. "Does he ever let you out of this room?"

The kite's wings didn't settle, and his beak remained open, threatening, but he stayed on his perch. Perhaps the close walls and ceiling hindered him from attacking her, but Matrona didn't want to stay long enough to test the theory.

She knew exactly where Jaska's doll lay, as Slava never moved it. She hurried over and picked it up, careful not to bump any other dolls. Her eyes looked over it quickly. Its likeness was a flat painting, and yet it looked remarkably like Jaska, down to the unkemptness of his hair.

Her gaze fluttered to the other dolls. The gloss of Nastasya Kalagin's green eyes reflected the candlelight. What secrets did she have? Or Lenore Demidov beside her, who had sneered so righteously when Matrona's own secrets spilled into the village. Would Lenore purse her lips and turn up her nose if *her* secrets became common knowledge? Pavel and Oleg had roused Jaska's suspicions. What could they have to hide?

Yet that would make her just like Slava, wouldn't it? Playing with these people as if they were the very dolls the tradesman had made them out to be, toying with them against their wills. Subjecting them to the same torment Matrona herself had suffered.

The candlelight flickered as she leaned toward the dolls. The painted face of Feodor caught her attention. Her stomach tightened as she met the doll's gaze. What did he really think of her, and of their betrothal? She could find out. All it would take was one twist, one pull. Yet as Matrona stared into the blue gaze of the doll, she wasn't sure she wanted to know.

Pamyat hissed. Matrona shook her head. Sticking the unlit end of the candle in her mouth, she grabbed both halves of Jaska's doll and popped them apart.

A moment of silence descended on the room, quieting even Pamyat.

A creak in the hallway shot a chill of terror through Matrona's spine. Slava wasn't home. He couldn't be. Had Jaska followed her in? Fumbling with the doll, she pulled the candle from her mouth and blew it out. The smoke from the wick tickled her nostrils.

She waited, listening. Heard nothing more.

Using the dim moonlight from the high window as a guide, Matrona shoved the pieces of Jaska's doll back together, lining them up as best she could, and then set the doll back in its designated place on the table. Squatting, she checked the floor for beads of wax and found none.

She peeked into the hallway, seeing nothing but ordinary shadows. She rushed back down it. When she reached the front door, she nearly threw it open in her eagerness to get outside. She stumbled onto the portico and pulled the door shut behind her.

And just like that, like a lantern lit within her mind, she knew.

All his secrets.

They sprouted in her mind like a wild garden: Playing cruel pranks on neighbors after his mother lost her mind. Crying into his pillow so his siblings wouldn't hear. Trying to persuade his mother to be sane again.

Matrona's eyes widened as more and more secrets bubbled up. Finding Nastasya Kalagin on a spread of blankets in the basement, his brother Viktor—his *married* brother, Viktor—writhing on top of her. Viktor swearing him to secrecy. Stealing sausages hanging in the butchery because Oleg Popov wouldn't give his "detestable" family their share.

Matrona rested a hand against one of the portico's twisting columns to steady herself. Small secrets, childhood fibs and the like, speckled her thoughts. Then a new flower bloomed, and Matrona caught her breath; Jaska Maysak didn't believe in God.

She pushed off the column and hurried down the steps of the porch. Jaska came to church every *Voskresen'ye*, yet it was only for show. That secret alone would ostracize him from the village. The spell of the doll held back the reasons for his disbelief, but Matrona's heart ached for him and the judgments he would face come morning.

More secrets, ones Matrona already knew—his distrust of Pavel and Oleg, of Slava.

But as Matrona came around the side of the house, the spell revealed a secret she had not been expecting.

What Jaska thought of *her*.

Chapter 12

Matrona froze in her steps as truths unfolded in her mind. She wavered on her feet.

Jaska hadn't thought anything special about her until that day all *her* secrets filled *his* head, nestling there as if he'd always known them. The day he learned Matrona Vitsin desired him and hated herself for it.

Seeing her later, on the path to the butchery, he had looked at her differently. Noticed her. Matrona was beautiful, wasn't she?

Over the last week, Jaska's thoughts had turned and turned, kneaded like bread dough, and as Matrona peered into the shadows where he hid, she *knew*.

He wanted her, too.

Air expelled from her lungs, and she struggled to breathe it back in. Her entire body felt light. Her skin tingled. Her mouth dried. Her blood . . .

A vision born of the third doll crossed her mind: *lightning*. That's how she felt. Like it flashed relentlessly inside her.

She was wanted—and by *him*, no less. She had never experienced a sensation like this.

A voice that sounded too similar to the berating voice awakened by the second doll whispered, *You marry in two weeks, you wretched girl.*

But Feodor didn't truly want her. Not like this. Not the way she so desperately needed to be wanted.

"Matrona?"

His voice sounded like pine needles caught on the wind. He shifted from the darkness, letting a sliver of moonlight catch his features.

Matrona forced breath into her lungs. They ached like a deep bruise.

"Did you find it?" he asked.

But of course—Matrona had felt nothing after opening her first doll. She'd learned of its consequences secondhand.

She stared at him without speaking. Could this be some sort of trick? Perhaps Slava had done something to Jaska's doll.

"Matrona?" he asked again.

She nodded, her neck stiff. "Yes." Her voice poured like sand from her tongue, rough and broken. She rubbed her throat with her finger-tips. "It's done."

"You're . . . sure?" He sounded unconvinced.

She worked up enough moisture to swallow. "I—I'm sure."

He didn't respond immediately, only watched her. What did he expect her to say? *Do you really feel that way?* Even if it were true, could his feelings really be genuine? And what if Matrona had misread his thoughts somehow? Would Jaska laugh at her? His denial would crush her.

Instead, she said, "I know about . . . Viktor."

He pulled back from her, breaking their gaze, and startled her by cursing. The word sounded like one of Pamyat's hisses.

Running a hand through his hair, he asked, "They'll all know, won't they?"

The sound of rustling—footsteps?—touched Matrona's ears. Likely her imagination again, but in a flash of boldness, she grabbed Jaska's hand and pulled him away from Slava's extravagant home. Only when they reached the edge of the wood did she say, "We shouldn't linger here."

Coming to her senses, she dropped Jaska's hand like a match burned through. Her insides felt like tumbling gravel. If only she could hear his thoughts *now*. What she wouldn't do for an assurance, or even a negation before her hopes climbed too high.

"What else do you know?"

The gravel sucked into her core, weighing it down, yet her lips felt as insubstantial as water when she stuttered, "I—I suppose everything."

He stepped closer to her. Matrona's skin burned like he was the sun. "What do you know?" he asked again, softer.

Her pulse was everywhere. "I know about . . . God." She closed her eyes for a moment, ready to use Jaska's curse on herself. *Jaska* was the one exposed, the one who would suffer, and her thoughts were centered entirely inward. She could not still her heart, but she managed to sort through her thoughts enough to ask, "Why don't you believe in God?"

Jaska made a sound similar to a chuckle, though Matrona detected no mirth in it. "I don't know," he answered. "I don't remember ever making the decision."

"But you don't."

Just enough moonlight peeked through the darkness to reflect off his eyes. "No. I have a hard time thinking there's a greater being looming somewhere in the heavens, apart from us, picking and choosing who to love and who to punish."

Matrona shook her head. "But God doesn't work that way."

"You don't think my mother was punished?" Jaska asked, the question barely audible, half-stolen by the breeze. "My father?"

Words piled in Matrona's mouth, but she was too exhausted to swallow them. "Your father punishes himself."

Jaska turned away.

The gravelly feeling returned. "Jaska, I didn't mean—"

"No, he does," Jaska agreed, hands on his hips. He looked back at her. Despite the darkness, Matrona thought she could feel his gaze on her face, her breasts, her stomach. "What else . . . do you know?"

She licked her lips. "Everything, I'm afraid. Just as you know my secrets."

"Tell me."

The tone of his voice bristled over her skin. *He knows I know.* The knowledge made her tremble. Hadn't she imagined herself walking through the wood with a lover?

She cleared her throat. "You and your mother, some thievery. Other . . . things."

A strong breeze made her jump.

"What will Slava do?" he asked, hushed.

Matrona shook her head. "I don't know."

"Find me if you need me. If you need anything. If he confronts you, I'll come with you—"

"Slava cannot know you asked me to open the doll, Jaska." Her voice bordered on begging. "He can't know you know. Promise me you won't do anything to let him know."

Then again, Jaska's secrets had spilled to the entire village. Had Matrona's confiding in him been leaked as well, or was that secret solely hers?

She hugged herself. "I should go home." She thought of the creaking floorboards inside Slava's home, but pushed the uneasiness away. There was enough for her to worry about without jumping at ghosts.

She turned to leave, but Jaska's voice snared her. "Matrona."

She paused.

He hesitated. "Do you love him? Feodor."

The question thickened the air between them. Feodor's name weighed like a yoke across her shoulders.

Jaska already knew her secrets. Why must he ask?

"It doesn't matter if I do or don't," she answered, offering him a smile she wasn't sure he could see. "The date is already set."

She tore herself from the shadows of Jaska's web, though unseen filaments tugged at her feet. Her heavy limbs dragged, and her chest danced with uncertainty as she followed the border of the wood to her own home.

Her parents slept soundly in their bed, dreaming of Jaska Maysak's secrets.

❄

In the dark of Matrona's room, secrets ran through her mind like briars, scratching against her thoughts every time fatigue tried to pull her asleep. Jaska. *Jaska.*

The darkness buried deep inside her stirred. She closed her eyes and tried to ignore it. To ignore everything.

When slumber settled upon her, however, she dreamed not of Jaska, but of Roksana. Roksana, her hair intricately plaited, arriving at the Zotov household to speak to Luka. Luka, who fancied Nastasya Kalagin, but fancied her less with every lie Roksana told him about Nastasya. Roksana had demeaned the other woman's character until, eventually, the only woman Luka saw was Roksana herself.

The dream flashed forward in color and speed, and Matrona saw her dear friend offering a new bottle of kvass to Oleg Popov and murmuring, "She is a fine woman who will bear strong children. The Zotov house would not forget your kindness if this betrothal were made."

Roksana, bending over a child's work and frowning at the poor answers he gave in school, then lying to his parents about his progress so he would not be thought dumb.

Childhood, adolescence, and adulthood. Matrona dreamed strange things all punctuated by Roksana, until they became a blur of imagination that settled in the corners of her mind before dawn awoke her.

❄

The slightest scent of burning porridge drew Matrona's attention to the brick oven, and she hurried over to pull the breakfast kasha off the heat before the smell could waft to her parents' noses. It looked well and fine, but upon stirring it, Matrona noticed burned porridge sticking to the bottom of the pot. Hopefully her mother wouldn't notice.

"Unthinkable," her father said as Matrona set the pot on a folded towel and grabbed a pitcher of water to fill cups. The words weren't addressed to her, but to her mother, who was setting the table. Her father leaned against the wall near his seat at the table, his arms folded against his chest.

"I've always said they are a vile family," her mother retorted, setting down a bowl almost hard enough to shatter it. She glanced once at Matrona, who pretended not to see. "With sons like that, it's no wonder Olia lost her mind."

Matrona pressed her lips together, trapping her tongue. When had it become so hard for her to swallow words? They pushed against her teeth, demanding that she come to the defense of Jaska Maysak, but she would be sentencing herself to further humiliation to do so. Already the threat of spinsterhood loomed ahead of her, though she had yet to hear Feodor's thoughts on the revelations.

"Do you love him?"

Her heart beat a little faster, her thoughts threatening to consume her yet again. Those same thoughts had made her burn the kasha and kept her awake most of the night. The revelation that Jaska cared for her.

It was too absurd to believe.

"I always thought Viktor . . . ," her father began, but whatever sentiment he intended to utter died on his lips.

"I don't feel at all bad about Nastasya, seeing how she turned out. To hell with all of them," her mother spat.

Matrona flinched, spilling water on the floor as she carried the cups to the table. "Mama!"

"It'll be no surprise to them!" her mother countered, throwing spoons for the porridge onto the table. "Can't go to heaven if it doesn't exist. Hypocrites, every one of them. Feigning worship of the good Lord and then spitting on Him when our backs are turned."

Matrona set down the cups. "I hardly think the Maysaks would spit on another's deity."

"Another's!" Her mother turned on her, jabbing a pointed index finger into Matrona's breastbone. "There is only one God, Matrona! Still my heart, what will I do with you?" Her eyes narrowed. "You stay *away* from that disgusting boy, you hear me?"

"I assure you, I have no intention of mingling with Jaska Maysak," Matrona lied, stirring the kasha.

Her father rubbed his forehead with a thumb and forefinger. "I'll visit Oleg today."

Her mother grumbled and rubbed her eyes. "It's no fault of ours this time. He'll have to be lenient. We already gave him the dairy."

Matrona nearly dropped the pot. "You did what?"

"Didn't I say we made sacrifices to keep this marriage together?" her mother snapped.

Her father said, "It's not so much as all that. Feodor will run the dairy and double his family's allotment is all."

"Double?" Matrona set the porridge on the table. "You don't just double an allotment; everyone receives the same."

"Tell that to Afon Maysak," her mother spat. "Half his brewing goes down his own throat." She turned to Matrona's father. "Yes, see Oleg. Take Matrona."

"I don't believe that will help," her father said.

Her mother turned to her. "You should bake. Something delicious, to ease the tensions. Feodor won't have forgotten your own indiscretions."

"A folly I never acted on," Matrona countered, but her heart split into fluttering pieces within its cage of ribs. *But* could *I act on it?* How it would humiliate her parents if she abandoned a strong marriage prospect for a too-young potter boy who didn't even believe in God.

Yet she could not forget how alive Jaska made her feel. The sight of his shadow by the tradesman's home, the warmth of his skin in the cellar of the pottery, the strength of his arms as they lifted her into his cart—each moment she'd spent with him had made more of an impact on her than the weeks of her engagement to Feodor.

Days. It seemed like years.

Squeezing her eyes shut, Matrona thought, *Stop it, stop it. You're making it harder for yourself, and for him. Pretend like you don't know. You'll ruin everything, knowing.*

Feodor and Jaska were so different, Matrona thought as she sat down to break her fast with her family. Feodor was an outstanding man, well disciplined and well liked among the village. Skilled with a knife and competent. Intelligent beyond his occupation. He was lean and attractive. Should Matrona open his doll, she didn't think a single foul thing would escape from it.

Yet Jaska . . . Jaska was so much more *feeling*. He was adventurous. He was bold, and he was compassionate. Matrona had always admired the way he helped his aging mother around the village, using soft words whenever she got anxious. Even the thought of him touching her made her skin tingle. Already he had touched her more than her own betrothed, and guilt ate away at Matrona's gut from the way she craved it.

It still shocked her, his disbelief in God. She believed in Him; she always had. To think He didn't exist . . . she'd be a shell empty of its nut. God was limb to her body, one she was sure she couldn't function without.

But Jaska. Jaska wasn't a heathen or a devil worshipper or whatever other names her mother had to sling at him. He was a good person, one of the best in her acquaintance, and she couldn't stop thinking about him.

Thinking about him thinking about her.

After Matrona's spoon scraped the last bits of kasha from her bowl, she stood to take her dishes to the sink. Before she left the table, however, her father said, "You fool, you don't know what you're playing with."

Matrona froze, glancing at her father, whose eyes watched her with still glassiness. She settled back onto the bench. "Pardon?"

"Did you think I wouldn't notice?"

Matrona blanched, shivers running up and down her arms. Her mother continued to eat her breakfast, as though completely unaware of the bizarre exchange.

"Papa." Matrona's words were slow and deliberate. "I don't know what you're speaking of."

"Use your brains, foolish child," her father said. "I've seen the work of your clumsy hands on Jaska Maysak's doll. How dare you defy me."

Matrona felt snow jump from her memory and pack around her. "S-Slava?"

Her father's lips moved stiffly with each word. "You will come to me. *Now.*"

Matrona's gaze darted to her mother, still eating, still unaware. "Mama?"

No response.

Her father blinked twice, then resumed his breakfast as well.

Matrona collected her dishes. Neither parent so much as glanced at her. She didn't know what bothered her more—the fact that Slava had, somehow, spoken through her father as if he were a puppet or the fact that she'd already been caught.

She set her unwashed dishes aside and left the house immediately, nearly jogging up the path that led to the tradesman's abode. None of the other villagers tried to talk to her—something that she wouldn't have noticed on an ordinary day, but now the hairs on the back of her neck bristled. She offered a quick prayer for her safety and glanced heavenward. Blinked and shielded her eyes from the sun.

The sky . . . there was a pattern to it, faint as a sleeper's breath. Curving lines like the whorl of a thumbprint. Blue against blue, but she saw it, though staring into the brightness overhead made her eyes water.

She spun slowly, taking in the sky cupped by the crowns of trees. The faint lines were almost like wood grain.

Another blink, and the pattern vanished, leaving her with watery eyes and an aching head.

Sucking in a deep breath and trying to still the trembling in her fingers, Matrona hurried along the path. Slava's home looked twice its usual size as she approached, and the door swung open before she could knock.

Slava's face was dark above his beard, his eyes bright and narrow. Yet as Matrona met the hardness of his gaze, her fear extinguished, replaced by heat that bubbled in her core.

"How dare you," Slava growled.

"How dare *you*!" Matrona snarled back. "What sorcery have you cast over my father to speak to me in such a way?"

Her mother had likened Jaska to the devil, completely unaware that the devil dwelled beside the north wood.

Slava snatched her wrist and yanked her into the house, slamming the door the moment she cleared it. She nearly tripped over her own toes.

Slava seethed. "Did you think I wouldn't know?"

"Of course you would know." Matrona matched his tone. She spun around to face him, determined to be bold, to be brash, to protect Jaska. "You never forbade it."

"I never—" Slava shook his head and balled his hands into fists as he pushed past her into the front room. "I never *forbade* it? Must I spell out every consequence to every possible indiscretion?" He whirled around and shot a glare at Matrona that would have made even her mother cower. "Don't banter with me. You waited until I was out of the house—"

"Pamyat didn't seem to mind."

Slava snorted. "That damnable bird was a monster when I caught him. So many years indoors has clipped his wings." He collapsed into his upholstered chair. "Why Jaska Maysak, hm? Wanted to see if he returned your sentiments?"

Despite the embarrassing accusation, Matrona choked on a sigh of relief. If Slava didn't know why she'd opened Jaska's doll, then he didn't know that Jaska had asked her to do it. That Matrona had indeed defied him and told another about the dolls.

It would seem that the secret was solely hers—and that the spell didn't give away secrets made after the opening of the first doll.

Matrona merely nodded. It was an answer she didn't need to defend, for Slava knew her feelings. She couldn't quell the flush that tickled her cheeks, but found herself grateful for it, for it made the lie that much more believable.

Slava dug his nails into the armrests of his chair. "How many did you open?"

"Only the first layer."

Slava watched her, his gaze lidded, his beard twitching with the movement of his lips. His fingertips relaxed before they dug again. Matrona met his stare, trying not to blink.

Slava released the armrests. "If you continue to think of this as a game, your 'suffering' will only grow worse. You try to make an enemy of me."

"All I did was return a paintbrush."

A flash of a smirk appeared on the tradesman's mouth, and then it dissipated as a puff of smoke. He straightened, breathed deeply. Matrona remained silent through it all. Finally he said, "It is good that you only opened one."

"I do listen to your warnings." Matrona let her muscles unwind. "Why do you time my visits three days apart? And why is it good that I opened only one of his dolls? Surely I've cooperated enough for you to tell me that much."

Slava watched her for an uncomfortable minute, his gaze making her wrists and ankles itch. He opened a drawer in a short, elaborately painted table beside him and retrieved a cigar, but he did not light it.

"Sit," he instructed, and Matrona stepped to the closest chair and obeyed. She dared not push Slava's patience any further. Not today.

"It is madness," he said.

Matrona waited for clarification, but when Slava did not speak, she said, "I would agree."

He shook his head. "You know that you are tied to your doll. You know it is the same for the others. But sorcery is not natural to the mind. To unleash it all at once would drive a person mad."

Matrona leaned forward, her pulse short and quick. "Literal madness? Were I to open all my dolls at once—"

"You'd lose your mind, yes. It was not something I had originally accounted for, and I've sworn to prevent any more casualties."

Matrona perked at the words. "Any *more?*" she repeated.

Then it struck her.

Snow.

"Olia," she whispered, searching the tradesman's eyes. "Mad Olia Maysak."

Slava nodded.

"Only one other has noticed . . . and she does not have the liberty to discuss it."

That's what he'd told her a few days ago. Olia knew about snow because her third doll had been opened. "She opened her dolls," Matrona voiced, "and lost herself."

"No," he corrected. "*I* opened them."

The words shocked her like the sting of a hornet. She shook her head, thinking of Jaska, of how he'd struggled to salvage his mother's mind, to no avail. Of the cruel things her mother and so many others said about Olia and her family.

She swallowed against a tight throat and whispered, "Why would you do such a horrible thing?"

Slava's gaze dropped to the floor. He leaned his elbows on his knees and clasped his thick fingers in front of him. The breaths drawn through his nose were loud in the silent room.

A long moment passed before he spoke again. "I loved her."

Of all the answers he could have given, Matrona had not expected that.

Slava cleared his throat. "I loved her, and I wanted her to love me. I wanted her to know the truth, as you know it. As you will soon know it. And so I opened her dolls, unaware of the consequences. Of the cost."

Matrona massaged gooseflesh from her arms. "But Olia is married."

"It did not matter to me."

"How can you say that?" Matrona asked before she could think to bridle the words. "Do you think you can simply dismiss a marriage made under the eyes of God?"

Slava looked up at her, and there was a sting to his gaze. His lips pulled into a grin, but it was not a friendly one. "You think yourself fit to judge me, Matrona Vitsin? You are naïve now, but you will soon follow in my footsteps. You will soon understand."

Matrona set her jaw.

Slava stood.

Scraping one last bit of boldness from her heart, Matrona said, "Afon—"

"Struggled to deal with his wife's state of mind, yes. I never thought him a suitable match for her, but I pitied him and gave him the brewery after his incessant pleading for kvass."

Slava growled deep in his throat. Matrona stared at the space between his eyes. It was the first she'd heard that Slava had managed the brewery before Afon, but that wasn't what startled her.

It was Slava's fault. Olia's madness, Afon's drunkenness. The core of the Maysaks' hardships. The reason she had tended both Jaska and Kostya when they were younger. The reason so many saw them as . . . less.

Slava had done that to them . . . because of passion?

"All for your own self-interest," she whispered.

Slava pressed his lips into a flat line and stared down Matrona with a gaze that mimicked Pamyat's. A moment passed. "Now that we've had our heart-to-heart, you will return the other doll."

Matrona furrowed her brows. "Other doll?"

"Roksana Zotov's. I know you have it."

But Matrona shook her head. "I don't have it. I didn't—"

Blood drained from her face.

Roksana's skeptical gaze as Matrona excused herself last night. The feeling of watching eyes. The rustling near the wood, the creaking in the house.

The *dream.*

"By the saints," she whispered. "She was here."

Slava raised an eyebrow.

Matrona leapt from her chair and ran for the door. "She was here!" she shouted, and burst into the sunlight.

Roksana had followed her. She'd seen Jaska. She'd seen the dolls. And she didn't know what any of it meant.

Matrona barreled down the path from Slava's home, grabbing fistfuls of her skirt to free her legs. Not the schoolhouse, not today. She would be home. She *had* to be home!

Please, God, please, she pleaded as the wind whipped a tear from her eye, *please let me be wrong.*

She ran off the path, taking the most direct route to the Zotov *izba*, oblivious to passersby, uncaring of what new rumors her behavior might start. She had to find Roksana. She had to find her before it was too late.

The *izba* came into sight, smoke puffing from its chimney. The carpentry behind it lay silent. Matrona ran up to the *izba*, not bothering to pause for the door. She burst through it, the wood slamming against the wall behind. Inside, Pavel and Roksana's father looked up from a round rug where they sat, their hands clasped in prayer.

"Roksana," Matrona huffed, shoulders heaving. "Where is Roksana?"

Roksana's father dropped his gaze. Between her breaths, Matrona heard Alena sobbing in the next room.

Darting past the men, Matrona raced down the hall to the room Roksana and Luka shared. The door was ajar.

Inside, Luka sat on the edge of their bed, his head in his hands, while Roksana lay curled up on the floor, singing softly to herself as she played with the pieces of a painted nesting doll.

Chapter 13

Opened. Every single one of them.

Roksana lay on her side, her full belly resting on a rag rug, poking her fingers into the cavities of dolls painted to look just like her.

"I will tell you fairy tales," she sang quietly, taking up the top of the third doll and spinning it on its head, "and sing you little songs. But you must slumber, with your small eyes closed. *Bayushki bayu.*"

"Roksana," Matrona whispered, and Luka looked up from the bed. Matrona took a stiff, wooden step into the room, then another, another. She dropped to Roksana's side and took the doll-half from her hand.

"Roksana?" she tried.

"The time will come," Roksana sang, "when you will learn the soldier's way of life."

"Roksana." Matrona took her friend's shoulders and tried to get her to sit upright, but Roksana squeezed her eyes shut and fought Matrona's hold as a little child would. Afraid of hurting her, Matrona pulled away. Roksana snatched the doll-half out of Matrona's hand.

Her dreams of Roksana hadn't been dreams at all; Matrona had merely been asleep when her friend opened the dolls. Most of Roksana's secrets were mild, save her lies about Nastasya to Luka. Yet no one was likely to have much sympathy for Nastasya now that they knew the truth about her and Viktor. That's what Matrona's mother had meant when she mentioned Nastasya at breakfast.

"It's no use," Luka murmured behind her, his voice low and rumbling. "She's been like that since the middle of the night. Won't come to her senses, no matter how we . . ."

His voice choked, and Luka turned away. Tried to clear it.

"Sleep now, my dear little child," Roksana sang. *"Bayushki bayu."*

Tears pooled in Matrona's eyes as Roksana started a new verse of the strange song—a song that nagged at Matrona, for its melody sounded strangely familiar. She tried to place it. Visions surfaced: Fat, falling snowflakes. An old rag rug and unpainted shutters. A little wood-burning stove in the corner.

Her head ached. What place was this?

When Luka spoke again, he startled her. "We don't know where the dolls came from. She came home late, without saying where she'd been. Had that thing in her hands. Looks just like her."

Matrona's throat constricted. She blinked, and a tear traced the length of her cheek. "It does," she croaked.

"Do you know?"

The words felt like an open palm across her face. Matrona shook her head, forcing the movements as though her neck had rusted.

But it couldn't be. This *couldn't be.*

"Roksana," Matrona tried again, pushing the name through her shaking voice. "Roksana, listen to me."

Roksana merely sang, "Sleep my angel, calmly, sweetly, *bayushki bayu."*

Matrona grabbed her friend's shoulders again, but this time she ignored Roksana's attempts to break free. Shaking her, she shouted, "Roksana Zotov, listen to me! Wake up, you hear me?"

"It's no use," Luka whispered.

"This isn't you! Roksana!"

Roksana wailed and threw her fists at Matrona, forcing her to let go. As soon as she did, Roksana collapsed to the floor and sobbed into the crook of her elbow.

"Matrona."

The voice was Pavel's. He stood in the doorway, his features long and heavy, blurred—no, that was from Matrona's tears. She wiped her sleeve across her eyes, but they were wet again a heartbeat later.

Pavel sighed. "We're waiting for the doctor."

The doctor would do nothing for them, but Matrona couldn't voice the words. She looked back to Roksana, more tears escaping her eyes.

You're going to be a mother, she thought, for her throat had swollen too much to speak the sentiment. *You can't . . . be like this. What about your baby? Luka?*

It was her fault, wasn't it? If she hadn't put off Roksana last night, if she hadn't agreed to meet Jaska. If she'd never found that paintbrush . . .

Matrona shook her head. *No.* This couldn't be it. This couldn't be Roksana's fate, to be as mad as Olia Maysak, to break her family the way Jaska's had been broken. Matrona wouldn't stand for it.

Through her blurry vision, Matrona gathered the dolls, her fingers mimicking a feeding hen as she snatched them off the rug. Eight pieces. She looked for the fifth doll, for Slava had claimed there were five, but she couldn't find it. Perhaps it was in the folds of Roksana's dress or under the bed. Matrona fumbled with the dolls she had, clicking them back together, smallest to largest, lining up Slava's delicate drawings as tears splashed over her hands. She squeezed the finished doll in her fingers. "Roksana."

Roksana hummed the strange lullaby and picked at a thread in the rug.

Pavel groaned, a raw sound that stemmed from the base of his throat. "Perhaps . . . we could ask Galina to come."

"And what has she done for her mother?" Luka scoffed, his voice cracking. "What could any of the Maysaks do?"

Not the Maysaks, Matrona thought, squeezing Roksana's doll in a crushing grip. *They're not the ones who can fix this.*

Matrona stood and fled the room, bumping her shoulder into Pavel as she went. Her ungraceful footfalls echoed in the hallway. She barely noticed Roksana's father as she flew out the door, the sunlight burning colors into her tears.

Not the Maysaks. The words repeated in her mind as she choked on a sob, running over grass, cutting the quickest path to Slava's home. She burst in through the front door, finding Slava just where she'd left him, though he had at last lit the cigar in his hand.

Matrona collapsed to her knees in front of him, offering up Roksana's doll. "Fix it," she cried. "Please, you have to fix it."

Slava's brows drew together. He put out his cigar in the center of a strangely decorated bowl atop the side table before taking the doll from Matrona's hands.

He examined it for only a second before drawing his lips into a deep frown. "It's been opened."

"Every last one." Her words were like a dying breeze.

Slava shook his head, and Matrona felt her heart dry and crumble within her.

"There's nothing that can be done. Her mind is gone."

"No!"

"If there were a cure, I would have used it." *On Olia,* he didn't say.

Matrona shook her head, studying his face, searching for . . . She didn't know. Anything to give her hope. But the tradesman's wrinkles had etched themselves deeper, and his eyes seemed sunken as he placed the doll beside his extinguished cigar, with a reverence that stabbed Matrona to her core.

"Please!" she begged, grabbing the fabric of his pants. "She's supposed to be a mother. She's my best friend. Please, you can't—"

"You did not give her the doll?"

Matrona released Slava's clothing and leaned back, the coldness returning to her limbs.

Slava nodded. "So she took it herself. Foolish girl. The damage she could have done—"

"You." Matrona stood. "Why have you made them? The dolls. Why are they *here*? What do they *mean*?"

"You are learning—"

"I don't want to *learn*, I want them gone!" Matrona shouted. Through the kitchen and down the hall, Pamyat echoed her anger. Matrona took a step back. "What have you done to us?"

"I have *saved* you!" Slava bellowed, rising from his chair. He seemed a giant, broad and tall, his presence spreading out like a sunset shadow.

"From *what*? I've seen no danger save what you keep in that room!" She thrust a pointed finger toward the kitchen. "What are you doing to us?" The sound of marching footsteps on the snow-hardened ground echoed in her head. She pressed the heels of her hands to her temples. "What have you put into my mind?"

Slava didn't respond, merely fumed like fire on wet logs.

"You did this," Matrona murmured. "You broke Roksana. You tore apart the Maysaks—"

Her hands flew from her head when Slava grabbed the collar of her dress and yanked her forward, close enough that his breath clouded over her face. "Without me," he growled, "they would be starving and destitute, torn apart by war."

Matrona blinked tears from her eyes. "War?" The word was foreign on her tongue.

Slava released her. "Get out. Wallow in your misery somewhere else." He glowered. "But return tomorrow. We are not yet finished."

Matrona scowled even as new tears formed in her eyes. Resisting the urge to spit at his feet, she turned her back on the sorcerer and fled, slamming the door in her wake.

❄

The children all fled the glade when she arrived, sobbing and red-faced, the hem of her *sarafan* stained with mud. The cadence of their new rhyme still resonated in her ears:

> *Jaska's rotted to the core*
> *For Jaska has denied the Lord*
> *His mum is mad, his dad is sad*
> *His soul is very, very bad*

It astonished her, how hungry the cruelty of children could be.

She sat on the large stone that rested just off center in the glade until her tears stopped save for an occasional sob. Then she picked herself up and limped her way through the wood, hugging herself despite the warmth of the noon hour.

It grated on her, the normalcy of the village. The unchanging birdsong, the insects' chipper cadence. Laundry still hung on lines, and smoke puffed up from a handful of chimneys as it always had, up to a sky that still bore the faint patterning of wood grain in the places where the brilliance of the sun had not burned it away. By the way her neighbors walked about, did their chores, or chatted with one another, Matrona knew Roksana's debilitation hadn't become common knowledge. Yet.

She wiped her sleeve across her eyes again, surprised at how damp it had become. Surprised that she still had tears to cry, for her body felt like a corn husk left in the sun. In her mind's eye, she imagined it baking and burning, crumbling to the path in a heap of ash to be swept away by the wind. Slava had been absolute, but Matrona couldn't accept his words. Could sorcery not unravel sorcery?

She had little direction to follow, but she had to try. Something. Anything.

"Matrona."

She looked up, her *izba* in the distance, and found Feodor not two paces from her on the path, several unplucked roosters, tied with strings, slung over his shoulder. There was a wool blanket under them, no doubt to keep his clothes clean.

She had nearly walked right past him.

"I need to talk to you," the butcher said.

Matrona nodded numbly, looking toward her home. "My father mentioned visiting."

"He has, but we are old enough to sort things for ourselves without our fathers' by-your-leave. I'm sure I don't need to enlighten you."

Matrona eyed him.

Feodor sighed. "I never could have imagined the likes of Jaska Maysak being such a thorn in my side. I considered your issue with him resolved, but now, knowing he has motivation to . . . Matrona, have you been crying?"

Gritting her teeth, Matrona wiped her eyes once more.

Feodor frowned. "Whatever is wrong? But of course, you must be just as upset—"

"Feodor." Her voice sounded too low. He stiffened, perhaps surprised at being interrupted. "I'm sorry to say that the only person I care about right now is Roksana, and I cannot pretend otherwise to ensure your satisfaction. Not now. Good day."

Picking up her skirt, Matrona trudged past him to her home. Feodor would understand shortly, once the rumors ignited.

Relieved to see both her parents out in the pasture, Matrona went to her room, collected a few trinkets, and hiked back up to the Zotovs' house.

This time she knocked, and Pavel let her in without comment.

Roksana had been moved to her bed, the headboard of which had been carved to depict a rearing stallion. The doctor examined her in much the same way he'd examined Matrona last week. Matrona waited outside the room as he spoke with Luka in a hushed voice. He left shaking his head, and Luka threw a fist into the wall before following, barely giving Matrona a second glance.

Matrona stepped into the room and climbed onto the bed beside Roksana, who stared at the ceiling with lidded eyes.

"Look at this." Matrona offered her friend an embroidered handkerchief. "You gave this to me when I turned twenty."

Roksana pushed the heels of her hands into her eyes. "All the colors, all the colors," she muttered.

"Roksana."

She shook her head and rolled onto her side, her belly pressing into Matrona. "Too big, too big. Out, out. But there's the snow. It's too cold for babies."

Biting her lower lip, Matrona set the handkerchief down and retrieved a small music box. Winding it, she let it play—a simple folk song always sung at Christmas, one of Roksana's favorites. She waited for Roksana to respond, but her friend did not seem to hear it at all.

"Babies die, too cold. Poor Esfir."

Matrona's breath caught, and when it released, it carried the name of her vanished sister. "Esfir?"

"Sleep, my beautiful good boy," she sang. "*Bayushki bayu.* Quietly the moon is looking into your cradle."

Roksana's lullaby clashed with the metallic notes of the music box. Tears sprang anew, and Matrona pressed a knuckle to her lips to stifle a sob. *It really is too late, isn't it? She won't come to herself.*

Muffled voices behind the wall. Matrona caught "don't need you in here," "only asked for her," and "wait outside" among their words. The front door shut.

A knock on the bedroom door. Matrona turned to see Galina Maysak step into the room, her shoulders hunched as though she wished to be smaller, her eyes slightly downcast as though in apology. When she looked up, her dark eyes brimmed with pity. Matrona saw no hope within their depths.

Trying to swallow and not succeeding, Matrona slid off the bed to make room for Galina. She left the handkerchief and music box, now silent, beside Roksana.

Galina nodded her thanks and approached Roksana, though she didn't touch her. "Now here, what's ailing you?"

Roksana continued to sing softly.

Galina looked to Matrona, her lips forming the smallest, saddest smile Matrona had ever beheld. "Who are you singing to sleep, Roksana?"

Roksana stopped midsentence and stared ahead for a long moment before pushing the heels of her hands into her eyes again. This time, however, she screamed.

The sound hit Matrona like a cleaver.

"All the colors!" Roksana shouted, pushing her hands into her face so hard, it had to hurt. "All the sounds! All the colors!"

The sob finally broke free, heavy and slick. Matrona rushed from the room, unable to bear the feral sounds ripping from Roksana's throat—or to stomach her own guilt. Luka barreled past her and into the bedroom. Matrona made a sharp turn toward the back door to avoid the rest of the family. She stepped outside, the smells of sun-warmed grass and wood shavings from Pavel's carpentry filling her nose.

She leaned against the side of the house and buried her face in her hands, letting another sob break free from her chest.

"It's true, then."

Matrona looked up to see Jaska before her, standing on the line of shadow cast by the eaves. He seemed a stark contrast to the blue skies and sturdy wood. Remembering the hard words muffled by Roksana's bedroom wall, Matrona realized Jaska was the one who'd been turned away at the door. He looked older, as though weights hung from his facial features. The shade cast him in tones of gray.

"The dolls," Matrona whispered. "She followed me to S-Slava's home. Found her doll. Opened it all . . . Oh, Jaska, i-it's what happened to your mother. To see it all at once is m-madness, and Roksana—"

She choked, swallowed, and drew in a shuddering breath. "Roksana is gone. They both are."

Jaska pressed his lips together, his head tilting to one side as though too heavy for his neck. Matrona choked back her sorrow, wiped her eyes with her sleeve—

She noticed the warmth on her arm first, then the light pressure from his fingertip. Looking up, she saw his face, his shoulder. Jaska pulled her to him, tentatively at first, but when Matrona didn't resist, he wrapped both arms around her and drew her close. The cotton of his *kosovorotka* was soft against her cheek. Scents of clay and wood smoke tickled her nose, but his hair smelled like angelica.

To Matrona, it was as if the breeze stilled, the birds silenced, and earth held its breath. For a moment, she felt entirely whole.

Chapter 14

Matrona sat beneath the shade of an ancient aspen at the edge of the wood east of the village, far enough into the trees to feel hidden, close enough to the village to hear the calls of the livestock. One of the tree's roots had grown up and over a large rock, resting across its surface like a sun-bathing snake. It was there Matrona made her perch and waited, watching a starling flit back and forth from branch to branch overhead, its small, quick wings breaking up beams of morning sun.

Today was the third day since Matrona had opened her third doll, and while the strange memories it had awakened in her were mild compared to dolls one and two, Matrona had determined not to return to the tradesman's home. At least, she fought to be determined. The very thought of that fourth doll hardened her stomach and softened everything else. Knowing what she now knew about Olia; seeing it play out with Roksana. The mystic idea of being "separated" from the village, as Slava had put it. She couldn't trust such simple words, not from him.

He frightened her.

She thought about her parents' dolls sitting beside Slava as he smoked in his chair. He would not go too far, would he? Despite everything, Matrona was sure he cared for the people he depicted in wood and paint, else he would not strive to make her their caretaker. The question was, whose will would bend first? Hers or Slava's?

Was it fair to let her family and neighbors suffer for the sake of that contest?

Her hand strayed up to her shoulder to work out a knot as she breathed out slowly, imagining her anxiety floating away on the wind, little seeds to take root elsewhere. She didn't know how long she could put off Slava, and truth be told, she doubted she would ever manage to turn his interest from her. The tradesman was the first reason why she lingered here in the east wood, resting within the sanctuary of its trees.

The soft steps of a man walking over clover and sloughed bark reminded her of the second.

Matrona stood and smoothed out her skirt, searching for the sound until Jaska appeared between two dwarf linden trees. He looked tired, but alert. He wore older clothes, gray with a few faint stains of clay on them. His sleeves were rolled up again, but for once his hands and arms were spotless.

Matrona tried to ignore the twitching in her chest. "I was worried you wouldn't come."

"Ignore a cryptic message left for me in the bottom of a cracked pot?" Jaska asked with a small smile. "I couldn't resist." He glanced toward the village and stepped back, masking himself behind the linden tree. Matrona didn't know whom he saw, but she slipped closer to the aspen until Jaska relaxed. It would do no good for either of them to be seen together.

"I have to show you first," Matrona said, "before you'll believe me."

"I'll believe you."

The simple words brought a smile to her face. "I know. But I'd rather show you."

She stepped away from the tree, moving deeper into the wood, and motioned for Jaska to follow her. He did so without complaint, taking long strides until he reached her side, ducking under the branch of a thorn tree as he went.

"You'll not be missed?" he asked.

Matrona scoffed. "My mother thinks I'm discussing my future with Feodor. I have all the time in the world."

Jaska frowned.

"And you?"

"Little work today. Nowhere else to go, for now."

She glanced over at him as the ground dipped and rose again. "How are you faring?"

He shrugged. "Worse than usual. The key is to wait for someone else to become a more alluring topic of conversation."

They walked a moment in silence, their footsteps almost in sync with each other.

Jaska sighed. "Viktor won't speak to me. He thinks it's all my doing . . . and I suppose it is. I don't know about his wife yet. She hasn't . . . been around. Neither has Galina, helping with the Zotovs. Put my mother in a fit last night to have me walk her to bed, instead of my sister."

"I'm sorry."

"Don't be. It's not your doing."

No, it was Slava's.

"I opened the doll," she reminded him.

He looked at her and began to speak, but a stone concealed by clover caught Matrona's toe, and she pitched over it. Jaska caught her elbows and stopped her fall. When Matrona glanced up to thank him, his dark eyes were dangerously close to hers, reminding her once more of his doll's loudest secret.

Clearing her throat, she pulled away and continued the trek eastward.

"Where are we going?" Jaska asked after another quarter mile.

"That's part of what I want you to see."

He nodded and fell silent. They moved easily together, crossing a brook, spooking a deer, passing a spiderweb strung with a few stubborn dots of dew.

"Have you heard the children's rhyme about me?" Jaska asked.

"I have, unfortunately."

Jaska wiped a hand down his face. "Kind of catchy."

"The children have a gift for meter."

Jaska laughed.

They walked farther still, talking of small things. Normally Matrona didn't notice the loop in the wood until she passed through it, but today she saw something different. Her steps slowed until they ceased altogether. Jaska paused two paces ahead of her.

"What is it?" he asked.

Matrona blinked, but yes, it was there. A strange thumbprint pattern across the trees, filling even the empty spaces between them. Identical to the one she'd seen in the sky.

Beyond it, the wood seemed to go on forever. Yet Matrona knew what would happen when they passed through it.

Licking her lips, she gestured ahead of her. "Do you see it?"

Jaska eyed her, then scanned the wood ahead of them, and Matrona knew he did not. Gesturing to a bush with yellow flowers, he asked, "The pea shrub?"

"Follow me." Matrona resisted the urge to clasp his hand and pull him through the spell he still couldn't see. She walked forward first, toward the grain across the wood. There was no sudden wind, no change in sensation whatsoever, save for the sudden absence of a pintail's cry.

Jaska followed after her, looking around as though expecting something to jump out at him. Before Matrona could ask if he noticed a difference, he looked skyward and said, "The sounds. They changed."

Relief lifted Matrona's shoulders. She'd only discovered the loops after opening her second doll, so she hadn't been sure he would sense them yet. "We're in the west wood now."

His gaze dropped to her.

"A loop of some sort. From north to south, too." She walked westward now, back through the subtle pattern. "I found it after opening my second doll."

Jaska caught up with her and paused, perhaps listening to the sudden return of the pintail's song. "What else have you 'found'?"

"There's a pattern." Matrona glanced over her shoulder. Sure enough, the faint lines wrapped through the wood as though painted on the air itself. "A pattern of lines where the loop starts, and in the sky."

Jaska looked up again, but Matrona could tell by his frown that he didn't see it. It hadn't been revealed to her until the opening of the third doll.

"I'm hiding again today." She chuckled, though there was no humor in the words. "It's the third day."

"I know."

"You're attentive." She shared a look with Jaska that threatened to make her flush, so she shifted her focus to the ground ahead of her.

"You don't want to open it?"

Her steps slowed. "Jaska, if you understood—"

"I want to." He reached out and clasped her fingers, stopping her. His brow lowered. "Why doesn't he just open it for you?"

"So I'll stay 'independent.'" A shiver traced Matrona's shoulders. "And because of your mother."

"Not again," Slava had said. It felt wrong to disclose Slava's secret to Jaska, yet it seemed just as wrong to withhold the truth.

"You said she'd opened her dolls."

But Matrona shook her head. "She didn't. Slava did."

Jaska stiffened.

"He didn't know the consequences."

Jaska's expression darkened. "He's not the one who must suffer them."

Perhaps only a broken heart, she thought.

Jaska turned away from her, pulling his fingers from hers, placing his hands on his hips. His body was tense. She stayed quiet, letting him sort through the revelation on his own. She shifted toward a tree and picked at its bark. Noticed an animal trap not far off and made a note to be aware of others on this uncharted path.

"I want you to open my second doll."

Matrona turned back to him, feeling herself pale. "It's the worst one. Jaska, I could never do that to you."

"I want to know what you know."

"All you'll know is the horrors of your own existence." She continued to walk westward. "That's the one I had opened when you found me outside his house, Jaska. It's dark and horrible."

"Do you think I won't survive it?"

Matrona frowned. "It's not a matter of survival."

His face softened. "I think it is. And I think you want to survive alone."

The accusation jarred her, forcing her to stop once more. She could have laughed. *"Survive alone."* Isn't that what she'd been doing even before Slava insinuated himself into her life? Isn't that why she pined after her lost sister, why she had jumped at the chance to marry Feodor? So she wouldn't *have* to survive alone . . .

Jaska sighed. "Matrona, when you opened my first doll—"

His words sent a cool thrill through her. There was one secret they hadn't discussed. And yet the shadows still lurking in the dark corners of her mind screamed at her, reminding her how wrong it would be for them to acknowledge the way they both felt. Her parents had sacrificed so much to keep Feodor for her, hadn't they? It had been an act of love. Love they rarely showed anymore.

"Please, Jaska." His name was just louder than a whisper.

Jaska's mouth closed so quickly, Matrona heard the snap of his teeth. He ran a hand back through his hair. "Just let me know what snow is like. Let me see it for myself. To help my mother."

Matrona looked away, blood coursing too fast, pretending to study the crooked bough of a hornbeam. "There is no saving her," she murmured. "Or Roksana. Slava said as much."

"Matrona."

"I'll open it." The promise sucked the energy from her. "But we must wait the three days. I couldn't forgive myself if you . . ."

She didn't say *went mad*, but Jaska nodded his full understanding.

"Tomorrow," he said. "Three days."

She nodded. "Then I'll only have to avoid Slava for one." He probably wouldn't do too much damage if she put him off a single day . . . yet the thought made her uneasy. "I won't be able to get to your doll otherwise. I need to be invited in."

"Won't he see?"

Matrona glanced at him, at his desperate eyes, at the stubble lining his jaw. For some reason, she was glad he didn't wear a beard.

"I'll figure out something." Oddly enough, it seemed the more Matrona stoked Slava's temper, the less afraid of it she became. Perhaps that was the secret to his undoing.

Or to hers.

They trudged through the wood again, separating when the unmarked path grew too rocky, coming back together when it smoothed.

"Not if it will endanger you," Jaska said after a stretch of silence.

Matrona had already begun to formulate a plan in her mind. She nodded almost absently. "It won't. He won't know, if I do it right."

"How will you . . . ?"

Matrona smiled at him. "I have a hunch that a bit of clumsiness can go a long way."

Jaska grinned at her, bits of sunlight from the uneven canopy spotting his hair bronze. They were close enough to hear the pounding of the blacksmith's hammer.

"Thank you," he continued, "for showing me. It makes me understand even less, but I'm glad to know. And . . . thank you for not hating me."

Matrona looked at him, surprised. "Why would I?"

Jaska snorted. "Even before the dolls, people found plenty of reasons."

She shook her head. "Jaska, I could never—"

He grabbed her before she could finish the sentiment, his hand a vise around her wrist, jerking her toward him and behind an oak. Matrona's face burned like the kiln, but Jaska's attention wasn't on her.

"Wh-What?" she croaked.

Matrona glanced around the tree. They were right on the edge of the village. She hadn't realized.

"I think you should wait here before starting home."

"Why?"

He gestured with a tilt of his head. Following his gaze, Matrona looked toward the pottery. Specifically, to a tall, lean man standing outside of it, his arms crossed over a spotless *kosovorotka*.

"Feodor?" she murmured.

"I don't think he'll be happy to see us emerging from the wood together."

A defense rose up her throat, but Matrona swallowed it. "Yes, that would be wise."

Jaska ran a hand back through his hair, and Matrona realized the habit was why it always looked unkempt. "This will be enjoyable."

"He may just need a pot—"

Jaska laughed. "Matrona, Feodor is not the kind of man that waits around for anything if he can help it. If he's here, empty-handed, he's waiting for me."

Matrona paled. She almost asked, *Why?* but there was no point. They both knew.

Jaska touched her shoulder, and Matrona hoped he couldn't feel her pulse pick up beneath her skin. "Take care." He pulled away and stepped into the village.

Matrona stared ahead for a few seconds before daring to peek back around the oak. Jaska strode toward the pottery, and Feodor's gaze fell heavily upon him. They spoke for a brief moment before stepping inside the house, not the pottery. Matrona frowned. Feodor wasn't *confronting* him, was he? They hadn't done anything . . .

Did Feodor care about her enough to snuff out possible competition? Matrona snorted. *Likely he's assuaging his own pride.*

She shook her head at the thought, but then again, strange things had been pouring into Matrona's life like milk into a cistern. A frown tugging on her lips, Matrona stepped out of the wood and followed a path at random, her fingers lingering on the prints she could still feel on her shoulder.

❄

Matrona evaded her home most of the day, skirting her parents when she could—not only did she not want an argument about how she was spending her time, but she feared Slava would turn them into living dolls again. Finding her, *speaking* to her through their mouths.

So she went to the Zotov *izba*, unsurprised to find Galina there, still working with Roksana, who hadn't improved. Matrona stayed as long as she could stand, tidying the rooms and helping Alena with dinner, despite the way the woman still glared at her. Matrona could listen to her dear friend scream only so many times before her heart couldn't bear it anymore, and she left.

Slava had called for her near dinnertime, her father said when she returned home. And as she lay in bed, her mind turned over the first three dolls: the secrets, the belligerence, and the memories. What could a fourth doll show her? And what if she didn't succeed in opening Jaska's?

What if she did, and Slava caught her?

She woke the next morning with a headache that only worsened as she milked the cows, the rhythm of splashing milk pounding into her skull. So much grief, and yet she still didn't know *why* the dolls existed in the first place, *how* their vulgar magic worked, or *what* exactly Slava wanted her to do once old age claimed him.

Resolving herself for Jaska's sake, Matrona changed into a clean blue *sarafan* and left for Slava's sleeping-dragon home midmorning. She hadn't yet reached the bend in the road when she heard her name.

Turning around, she saw Feodor heading up the path toward her. Biting down on a mindless stutter, Matrona nodded her head in greeting, silent, as she usually was around him.

Feodor glanced up the path. "Are you off to see Roksana?" he asked. "I should recommend you stay away. Madness can only beget madness."

The advice chafed at Matrona. She tried to ignore it. "No, my legs just need exercise. And Slava asked to see me. His *izba* is my destination." Best to stay with as much truth as possible. Matrona's head hurt too much to keep up with lies today.

Feodor raised an eyebrow. "Again?"

"You've been speaking with my parents." She couldn't remember discussing Slava with him.

"I am perpetually speaking with your parents." He started up the path, and Matrona walked beside him, noticing he didn't offer her his arm, or reach for her hand. Were Jaska in his place, wouldn't he have done so?

He continued, "I spoke with Jaska Maysak yesterday."

Matrona kept her eyes forward and prayed away any color that might rise to her face. Feodor didn't need to use the surname, as there was only one Jaska in the village, just as there was only one Feodor and one Matrona. Yet the addition added a sort of formality—a distance that perhaps, to Feodor, made Jaska seem more a thing than a person. People often spoke of the Maysaks that way.

"Oh? Another cracked jug?" Matrona winced at the feigned nonchalance. Of course he would expect her to know about Jaska's . . . revelations.

Feodor detected it. "Are you really unconcerned? Do you expect me to be?"

Matrona glanced to him. "Have I given you good reason to be concerned, Feodor? You know where my loyalties lie." *But do I?* she wondered—a thought that sent a cold pang through her chest.

Feodor rubbed his eyes with his thumb and forefinger. "Trouble, the lot of it."

They'd moved around the bend, and Matrona could see Slava's house lurking ahead of them. She realized she'd been clenching her fists and forced them to relax. Scraping together some courage, Matrona asked, "Why do you want to marry me?"

Feodor dropped his hand. "Pardon? That's a bold question."

"But an important one." She slowed her steps to buy herself more time. "If I may ask it," she added.

A small frown touched Feodor's mouth. "Because despite the . . . complications . . . we've experienced as of late, you are the obvious choice."

Matrona looked forward again, focusing on Slava's house, trying not to let Feodor's answer burrow too deeply. She heard the underlying meaning: *You're the best choice, given my options.* There were only a handful of eligible women Feodor could marry without leaving the village—and, of course, he couldn't do that because of the loop, and because of the spell that forbade him from noticing it.

Matrona didn't know what she had thought he would say. She knew better than to hope for a declaration of love. She half expected him to say, *Who else would I offer to? Galina Maysak?* but the next words from his mouth were, "Here we are. Take care, Matrona."

They'd reached Slava's house. Matrona, who had spent all day yesterday avoiding the tradesman, found herself eager to get inside, if only to escape Feodor's obvious indifference.

"Thank you for the escort." At least he had been both kind and direct. She offered another nod before slogging up to Slava's portico. She didn't look back as she knocked on the door.

"Come," Slava's voice called, and Matrona slipped inside. She heard Pamyat squawk in response to the door shutting, the sound especially loud. She realized why when she stepped into Slava's front room and saw the bird of prey at its center, wings raised like scythes, talons digging into the leather of a long glove protecting the tradesman's right arm.

"Easy," Slava cooed to the kite, holding up his naked left hand, palm flat and facing the bird's face. Pamyat opened his mouth to hiss, but no sound came out. Stepping lightly, Slava carried the bird to his perch, which had been moved into the far corner of the room. As soon as the kite was settled, Slava fed the bird some sort of meat from a pouch at his hip. Pamyat gobbled it up without a second thought.

For a fleeting moment, Matrona wondered if Slava had been training the bird to come after her.

"You're late," Slava remarked, pulling off the glove.

Matrona lifted her chin, casting aside any lingering thoughts of Feodor. "Did you expect me not to be?"

"No. I expected this."

"You know me so well."

"I do." His reply carried a surety that made Matrona's chin drop. "I know all of you, like my own children. Come."

He moved into the kitchen. Matrona followed with quick steps.

"You have children, Tradesman?" Matrona asked as they took the short stairs into the carpeted hallway.

"I do not. Not in the sense you're thinking, Dairymaid."

As Slava opened the door to the doll room, Matrona wondered if he thought of his dolls as children. A caterpillar-like gnawing formed in her stomach as she approached the table once more. Her eyes darted to the Jaska doll near the rightmost edge. Her skin tingled as if a carding brush had traced over it. She eyed Slava, but the man had turned his back on her to retrieve her doll.

Not enough time. Matrona held her peace, and Slava turned back, handing her the doll. She took it in both hands and pressed her lips together before unscrewing the largest doll.

"No complaints this time?" Slava asked.

She set the dual pieces of the first doll on the nearest shelf and opened the second.

"Good." Slava nodded. "You're growing."

The third doll, with its black-painted interior.

"You've accepted your fate."

The fourth doll, the length of her palm, stared up at her. *Don't hesitate,* she thought. *Earn more of his confidence.*

She twisted it, the halves squeaking loudly against each other. Pulling them apart, Matrona looked for the fifth and final doll.

It wasn't there.

Holding her breath, Matrona turned the pieces upside down, then peered inside them. Nothing. No doll, no painting, no marks of any kind.

"I don't understand." She lifted her eyes. "You told me there were five."

"There are."

She turned the pieces about to show Slava their contents. "There are only four. There should be a fifth inside." One, Matrona presumed, that didn't open.

Slava shook his head. "Put them together, separately."

"But—"

"Matrona." He eyed her, and Matrona fumbled to reinstate the fourth doll, then the third, the second, and the first. She set them next to one another on a free area of the shelf, not far from the unopened dolls of Boris and Rolan Ishutin. Largest to smallest. Four likenesses of her looking forward with soft, knowing smiles.

Matrona clenched her jaw to keep from shivering.

Slava stepped up to her, pointing his large forefinger at the largest doll. "One," he said, and moved down the line. "Two. Three. Four."

His hand came down, resting like a sack of beans on Matrona's shoulder. "Five."

Matrona pulled away from his touch. The caterpillar gnawed inside; the card brush dug in its bristles. "I don't understand."

"I think you do."

Her eyes took in the dolls, trailing down the line of them. She glanced at Slava. The dolls.

"I'm the fifth doll?" she whispered. "But it doesn't make sense."

"Not at first." Slava nodded, turning from her to the full tables. "But it will."

A sore throbbing formed in the center of Matrona's forehead. She stared at the dolls. How could it be? She certainly wouldn't fit inside any of these creations!

She touched herself, feeling skin. She was no doll.

"I will teach you to navigate outside the village soon enough," Slava continued, his words raising the fine hairs on the back of Matrona's neck. "But the craft itself is more important for you to learn."

Stiff, Matrona looked to him. In his hand he held a smooth block of wood, a little longer than Matrona's forearm. Soft linden wood, by the look of it.

"You must learn to make the dolls yourself."

Matrona swallowed against a drying throat. "Why?" she rasped. "You have all the dolls already." *Except yours.* She had scanned the shelves and tables many times, but Slava's doll, if he had one, was not in this room.

"To protect them," he answered. "Roksana Zotov will deliver any day. We must prepare a doll for her child."

The throbbing in her head spread to her temples. "But why?" she asked, picking up her fourth doll and turning it over in her hands.

151

"To keep it safe. We will carve the doll and prepare its body. Create the enchantment, and finish it once the babe is born. Paint it to match its sex and foreshadow its appearance."

"Foreshadow?"

"We will foresee what the babe will look like as an adult and paint its likeness."

Matrona turned, eyeing the dolls on the table. Was that why some dolls looked older, others younger? Had she been painted as an adult when she was but a babe?

Her gaze settled on the doll that bore a likeness to Irena Kalagin. The painted face was younger than the woman it resembled, but older than the depictions on her, Jaska's, and Feodor's dolls. A chilling realization settled into her breast.

Irena had not been a babe when Slava made her doll.

When had this sorcery started?

Slava's voice interrupted her thoughts. "We will have three days after its birth to complete it."

Matrona looked back to the doll in her hands and separated its halves with a crisp pop. "Three days."

"Or the child will vanish."

Cold enveloped her. Her tongue writhed behind her teeth, and she struggled to find speech. She managed a single name. "Esfir." Her lost sister, vanished from her cradle just after coming into the world. No trace of her since.

"You see why it is a crucial skill to learn."

A tear beaded in each of Matrona's eyes. "Why didn't you make a doll . . . for Esfir?"

"I did not understand it then. My naïveté is . . . regrettable."

"How could you not understand?" she asked, voice gaining strength. "You made dolls for every person in the village! How could you not make one for Esfir?"

She looked over the tables. She knew the faces of every single doll. How long had Slava been crafting these dolls, and why did he start? Why were there no dolls for the villagers who had lived before her time, grandparents and great-grandparents?

She looked down at the doll in her hands, staring at its hollow interior. The lines of wood grain within it.

Just like the imprint she'd seen in the sky, the wood. The pattern—it matched.

It came together then. The abstractness of it all. The wood grain had always been around her, guarded by the loop. She just couldn't see it. She *was* the fifth doll.

She was *inside the pieces she held in her hands*.

Slava had mentioned navigating outside the village. Going wherever he went when he left on his trips and brought back supplies. Beyond the loop. Supposedly Matrona could now follow him.

But the others could not.

Trapped. Her mind formed the word as though carving it in a great block of ice. *Trapped.* All of them, only their bars were patterned in wood grain and bespelled by the man before her. But for how long? How long had they been jailed inside these painted cages, and what lay beyond this village?

The doll-halves fell from her hands and struck the floor in unison.

"I can't do this," she whispered, shaking her head, backing away from the halves. "I can't do this."

Slava's face darkened instantly. "You have no choice, Matrona. I have primed and prepared you. You will learn. Or do you want Roksana to lose her child as well as her mind?"

"Mind." Three days. Matrona remembered her promise to Jaska. Jaska, who was trapped like the rest of them. Heart thudding in her chest, Matrona glanced at the potter's doll. Took another step back, letting herself sway on her ankle.

"Matrona," Slava growled.

She looked up at him. "What have you done to us?"

Then she teetered on her legs, pretending to faint, and fell toward the second table of dolls. Her elbow, then shoulder, slammed into the edge of the table. Its legs held, so she swept her arm out in her descent, knocking over a dozen dolls. Half of them tumbled onto the floor with her, including Jaska's.

"You fool girl!" Slava bellowed, rushing forward to steady the table.

In the commotion Matrona's hand shot out for Jaska's dolls. She slid the top half off his first doll as another doll tumbled from the table and struck her hip.

Clenching the second doll's hands in her fingers, she pulled on the top until it popped free. She pressed it back in place just as quickly, then returned the top half to its rightful position seconds before Slava's hand grabbed her upper arm. He hauled her upward, and Matrona tried not to gasp at the force he used.

Slava did not yell at her; his words hissed from the cracks of his teeth like steam from a kettle. "Your clumsiness could cost us *dearly*. Once a doll is damaged, there's no replacing it!"

"Then perhaps you should find someone else."

Slava scoffed and released her. "Too late for that," he muttered. Matrona tried not to tremble, but failed. She pressed herself into the corner where Pamyat usually perched, watching as Slava picked up the dolls one at a time, inspecting them before returning them to the table, Matrona's included. To Matrona's relief, another doll had twisted ever so slightly, and Slava thought nothing of it as he corrected it. Hopefully Jaska's would pass inspection as well.

Slava gathered up Jaska second to last and straightened him. Studied him. Matrona bit down on her tongue.

He placed the doll in its usual spot. Matrona swallowed a sigh.

"I'm sorry," she offered as Slava stood, his knees cracking as he did so. He pressed his knuckles into the small of his back, for once letting his age show. Closing her eyes, Matrona tried to sort through the array of thoughts spinning in her aching head. Time. She needed time.

"Give me time," she asked, soft and demure, pulling on the cloak of humility she wore with her parents. "A day or two to think. I need . . . to work this through. Then you can teach me how to make the dolls. For Roksana's baby."

Slava glared at her. "You are almost more trouble than you're worth."

"Please."

He grumbled deep in his throat. "When I come for you, you will *come*, without any more of this nonsense."

Matrona nodded. "Yes, Slava."

"Get out."

Matrona hurried past him without hesitation, up the hallway and through the rooms that had become far too familiar to her. Pamyat shrieked as she passed but did not leave his perch. She headed out the door, into the sunshine.

Nothing changed about her this time, not that she could feel. But she was free now, as free as a trapped woman could be. Tilting her head back, Matrona gazed skyward. The lines of wood grain against the sky were darker and sharper than they had been before. Was this how Slava saw the world?

Not the world, the village. There was only the village. She would never look at it or its inhabitants the same way again.

Jaska, she thought, remembering the horrors she'd faced after opening her own second doll. That darkness would be weighing down on him now, and without warning. He was suffering.

Matrona had to find him, help him, and tell him what she knew.

Chapter 15

The village changed before Matrona's eyes. Or perhaps it was her urgency that colored it differently.

In her mind's eye, Matrona saw *izbas* built of paper, people milling about them like marionettes on strings. Completely unaware of where or what they were, the villagers prattled to each other about pointless things. For if Matrona was the center of her doll, were not these people also the centers of theirs?

Yet if Matrona had truly escaped Slava's spell, why did she still see wood grain in the sky?

Confusion coiled around her heart as a serpent, making it hard to breathe. The Demidovs appeared on the path ahead of her, driving an ox to pull a wagon heavy with a plow. Matrona rushed by them, clapping shoulders with Lenore, who began to shout something after her, but the words fizzled before they finished. Matrona found herself uncaring. Lenore Demidov was just a doll. All of them were.

What if that was all Matrona had ever been?

Esfir, she reminded herself, quickening her pace. *Esfir never had a doll. She was real, before she vanished. I must be real, too.*

The serpent squeezed.

Her body was flushed with exertion by the time she reached the pottery, which stood free of customers. Viktor worked near the kiln in the back, and Kostya sat at a pottery wheel, a delicate carving knife clutched in his clay-stained hand.

"Where is Jaska?" Matrona asked.

Both brothers looked over. Viktor blinked a few times as though his vision was slow to focus. The memory of Jaska's unbidden revelation about him made Matrona's stomach flip.

Kostya eyed Matrona as well, looking too long, as though he were trying to place how he knew her. His mouth worked, as if preparing to say something unkind, but no words came.

A strange sensation filled Matrona the longer she studied him, almost like the sensation of falling mixed with the cool mist of rain. Then, all at once, she saw *beyond* Kostya. Or rather, into him. She saw his insecurities about his family as if they were freckles dotting his skin. She felt his desire for thrill seeking, which often led to late-night excursions, like the time she'd witnessed him out with one of the village girls. She saw his sorrow over the absence of caring, *present* parents in his life, which simultaneously made her appreciate her own.

It shook her, seeing all that. The effect was different from when she'd opened Jaska's doll, from when poor, dear Roksana had opened hers. Those secrets had flooded her mind all at once; these impressions filled in the more she focused on the man, and they eased the moment she looked away.

More importantly, the secrets weren't *hers*.

"I . . . ," she started, unsure of herself. Was this a symptom of opening the fourth doll? Some special doll-sight?

Was this how Slava saw *her*?

"He's not here," Kostya finally answered, not meeting her eyes. Why wouldn't he meet her eyes?

Rubbing a chill from her arms, Matrona abandoned the pottery and sprinted to the *izba* beside it. She rapped her knuckles on the door.

Creaking floors alerted her to someone's approach. Afon opened the door, a short ceramic jug in his hand. His blue eyes—Jaska had inherited his dark gaze from his mother—looked at her through a film of drink, and he lifted the jug to his mouth and took a swig. Matrona smelled the stench of alcohol when he spoke. "Whattaya want?"

That strange cooling sensation erupted within her once more. She sensed a blissful stupor within the Maysak patriarch, and beneath it a thick blanket of failure—

She averted her eyes, shivering under the force of the unwanted revelations. "I'm looking for Jaska."

Afon looked her up and down. Drank again.

"Papa," Galina's soft voice sounded from within. "Please go rest." She appeared at her father's elbow and pulled him from the doorway. He silently obliged, his legs quivering slightly with every step.

Galina filled the doorway with her body, as if eager to hide the home she lived in. Matrona looked at her and gritted her teeth, resisting the strange doll-sight. To her surprise, her mind and body cooperated, and she saw only the surface of Galina.

"Matrona." Galina paused, as though seeing her for the first time. "How can I help you? Has Roksana worsened?"

The serpent dug its fangs into Matrona's heart at the sound of Roksana's name. "No. I don't know. I'm looking for Jaska."

Galina frowned. "Feodor asked him to stay away from you." Then, lower, "He asked all of us."

"Feodor is not my husband." The word *yet* danced at the back of Matrona's tongue, but she choked it down. "Please, it's important. Where is he?"

Galina shook her head. "If he's not at the pottery, I don't know. He's not here."

"Spit at his feet!" Olia's voice boomed from a back room. "Hesse . . . and by Rhine. Kiss the mouth that curses us!"

Is that why they went mad? Matrona wondered. *Olia and Roksana. They discovered themselves too quickly. Slava's spells poisoned them.*

Galina winced at her mother's shouting. "I'm sorry, Matrona." Whether the apology was for her brother's absence or her mother's vulgarity, Matrona wasn't sure.

Matrona felt the air rush out of her. She nodded. "Thank you."

Galina had shut the door before Matrona turned away.

The walk home was too long, as though the village stretched with her every step, making minutes feel like hours on a thread-thin path. When Matrona stepped into the *izba*, struck by the heat of the brick oven, her mother's head snapped up. "You've certainly forgotten your responsibilities as of late!"

Then her mother met Matrona's eyes and paused, hands frozen midwipe on her apron.

"What is it?" Matrona asked.

Her mother cocked her head ever so slightly to the side. "I . . ." She cleared her throat and looked away, the malice draining from her face. Something else replaced it—something Matrona struggled to identify. The cooling sensation she'd experienced with the others prickled her skin, but Matrona resisted it. She did not wish to see inside her mother.

Matrona asked, "What?" and looked down at herself, searching for anything amiss.

Her mother merely shook her head. Lines broke up her forehead into rows. Her cheeks sucked in slightly, her mouth pursed, her eyes clear and downcast. Not so dissimilar from how she looked on the rare occasions when Slava came for a share of milk and cheese.

Almost like she was . . . intimidated.

"Mama," Matrona pressed, "what were you going to say?"

Her mother shook her head and busied herself with the oven. "Nothing. Busy is all."

Frowning, Matrona relaxed and studied her mother. Really *looked* at her, at the faint moles on the side of her neck and the wrinkles dipping around her eyes. The feeling of falling engulfed Matrona.

She saw hard hands in her mother's life; she'd been raised by strict parents as well. There was a survival instinct rooted deep within her heart, and Matrona wondered where it hailed from. Loss twined through every part of her mother's being. Loss for Esfir, her disappearance lacking closure. Loss for her unborn children, for were her body fit, she would have had more than two. And most surprisingly a possessiveness of Matrona herself, rooted in the desire to make sure everything went well for her, because she was to be her parents' only legacy.

Matrona stepped back, blinking the impressions away. Her mother avoided looking at her, just as Kostya had, but perhaps that was for the better. Matrona was speechless. All of that wrestled inside her mother's soul? It was *protectiveness* that caused her heavy-handedness?

Numb, Matrona moved past her mother and down the hall, trying to process the revelation. She didn't understand it. Was there something broken in Slava's spell? How did such sorrowful motivations translate into harsh actions?

Taking a deep breath, Matrona shook herself, trying to clear her mind as she slipped into her parents' room. She went to the mirror that hung near the window and inspected herself in it: light skin and light eyes, black hair and thick eyebrows, strong jaw. Nothing looked amiss. Nothing was different. So why were the others treating her as if she had become someone else? Someone . . . bigger?

She bit her lip and hugged herself. Perhaps this was what Slava had meant, being separated from the village. Would everyone see her differently, without even knowing why? Would she see all of them differently as well?

Matrona had a wrenching feeling this was only the beginning.

❄

The next day, for the first time since Matrona could remember, neither of her parents reminded her to do her chores.

Her mother, especially, had always seemed to enjoy chiding Matrona over work that needed to be done, even if it had already been finished. But the morning after Matrona opened her fourth doll, her parents showed her a strange sort of deference, which they mostly exhibited in the form of silence.

Matrona wondered at it as they ate their kasha. Both of them were quiet, heads down. Just as Matrona used to be. When had she stopped bowing her neck at breakfast?

Her appetite was slim, but Matrona worked down as much of the porridge as she could. She itched, wondering just when Slava would call on her. Wondering how much time he would give her to digest what she'd learned. Not long, if he wanted to use Roksana's coming child as a lesson.

Then there was Jaska. Murmurs of her own darkness slipped in and out of her mind as she tried to fathom what he must be experiencing. Was that why he hadn't been home yesterday? Had the agony dropped him where he stood, with no passersby to help him home? Or had his family merely lied to keep Matrona at bay?

The cows milked quickly, though it may have been Matrona's distractions that made the time pass so swiftly. Once the milk was separated and the cheese left to set, Matrona scrubbed her hands and face, smoothed her hair, and donned her newly cleaned red *sarafan*. She was going back to see the Maysaks and found herself indifferent toward what the village might have to say about it. She'd already lost Roksana; she couldn't lose Jaska, too. That strange tingling sensation rose in her every time another villager crossed her vision, and she bit down on her tongue to keep it at bay. She couldn't bear seeing into the souls of so many, not now.

Had Slava intended that to be part of her "responsibility"?

She reached the pottery. Only Kostya occupied it, so Matrona went straight to the house and knocked on the door, expecting Galina to answer.

No one came.

She knocked a second time, harder. No answer. No footsteps on the other side of the door, either. She chewed on her lip. Viktor lived in another *izba* with his wife. Galina often took Olia on walks to help her stretch her legs, and Afon . . . Afon could be anywhere.

But if Jaska's darkness was as debilitating as Matrona's, he wouldn't go far.

Stomach tight, Matrona knocked a third time. No answer. She turned the knob and called into the house. Still no answer.

She stepped inside, a flitting memory of what had happened the *last* time she entered a house uninvited bouncing about her head. The Maysak *izba* hadn't changed much since Matrona's child-tending days. The front room had a wooded smell, its log sides made of a lighter wood than those in her own *izba*. Worn furniture took up three of its four corners. Beyond that, a small kitchen and woodstove. Then bedrooms and a narrow set of stairs to the attic.

That attic had been converted into a bedroom, which Jaska and Kostya had shared as boys. Matrona wondered if that were still the case.

"Jaska?" Matrona called, walking through the house. She listened for the sound of inhabitants, or perhaps Afon snoring as he slept off his latest alcohol-induced headache. "Galina?" she tried.

The place seemed completely empty, which was strange, given the number of Maysaks who inhabited it. It could be disastrous if someone, especially Afon, discovered her roaming it, but she had to check the attic before she'd be content to look for Jaska elsewhere.

She didn't want him to be alone, as she had been.

The stairs to the attic were so steep, they were almost a ladder, and Matrona had to ball her skirt into her fists to climb them. She heard a soft groan, so she hurried up the remaining steps, nearly hitting her head on the sloping roof.

There were two low beds, one against each angled wall, both narrow with bits of straw poking out from the mattress. One simple side table between them, one half of a candlestick, a pitcher, a cup. Jaska stretched out over the leftmost bed, one elbow swung over his eyes, the other tucked next to his ribs. His hand rested on his stomach as though it pained him.

It came almost unbidden this time, showing her a layer of darkness dripping like sludge. The doll-sight pierced through it, and she saw dancing across Jaska's hair a faint loneliness that mirrored her own, a desire for truth knotted in his core. There was a drive inside him to find solutions to problems, his or others'. Deeply ingrained affection for people; disorganized thoughts. A pain for his parents that pressed on her as heavily as Kostya's had.

A trust and affection for a woman tied up with another man.

Her pulse quickened and her bones felt light enough to float.

She swallowed and whispered, "Jaska."

He startled as though waking from a deep and treacherous sleep. He sat up ever so slightly, now pressing a hand to his head. Matrona thought she could feel the pulsing pain of it in the too-warm air. She crossed the room to him, ignoring the squirming feeling in her gut that told her it was improper. The floorboards creaked under her feet. Jaska blinked his red eyes before his gaze found her. Matrona thought he looked almost relieved.

She knelt on the floor beside his bed. "Is it terrible?" she asked at the same time he said, "You opened it."

His voice was strained, and he closed his eyes again, wincing as he did so. "Yes," he answered. "Yesterday . . . was worse."

"I looked for you." She took his hand in both of hers, if only to root him to reality, to give him some sensation other than the roiling darkness that consumed his mind. "You weren't home."

"I was . . . in the wood. Setting snares. There until dark, then . . . I got lost." He chuckled once, a dry and scratchy sound. "Haven't done that . . . since I was a boy."

"I remember." It was the reason she'd been asked to tend to the Maysak children for a time. The boys had gotten lost, and it was determined someone needed to watch over them since the older children struggled to do that, work, and tend to Olia's sickness.

He swallowed, the apple of his throat bobbing with the effort. Releasing him, Matrona went to the side table and poured water into the cup there. Jaska accepted it with a weak grip and drank slowly.

Matrona set the empty cup on the floor. "It will fade."

"You shouldn't be here."

"No one is home—"

"Not anywhere with me," he clarified, pressing his fingertips into his eyes. "I'm . . . awful."

"You're not." Matrona snatched up his hand again and squeezed it. "It's just the spell."

"It's all true."

"It will pass. In a day or two, the shadows will brighten, the memories will fade, and the voice will quiet. Then you'll be yourself again."

"I don't . . . want to be."

"Be what?"

He groaned. "Myself."

"Jaska Maysak." She rose from the floor and sat on the edge of the bed, though the narrow mattress barely allowed enough space for her. "You are not awful. You are not any of the things Slava's sorcery would have you believe."

His eyelids fluttered open. A vein rose in the center of his forehead.

"You are wonderful," Matrona continued, softer now. "You are diligent. You are a dedicated son and a faithful brother. You work tirelessly in that shop to see to the needs of the village. You're patient with your father . . . and with Feodor."

Feodor's name felt strange on her tongue, tasteless and heavy. *Feodor.* She hadn't thought of him since he'd escorted her to Slava's home. Didn't *want* to think of him.

Jaska snorted. "That man's back wouldn't bend if an ox sat on it." His eyes looked a little clearer, and Matrona let a trickle of relief urge a smile onto her face.

She sought to pull him from the throes of the sorcery, to push aside the shadows lingering in his expression. "You are kind. You've been nothing but kind to me even after I opened my first doll. You've helped me more through this ordeal than anyone else."

Jaska pulled his hand from her grip and pressed it into the bed, trying to sit up. Another wince.

"You may not believe in God," Matrona went on, quieter still, "but you are faithful. You believed me. You care in a way other people do not. You're not afraid to show your heart, and it's *good*, Jaska."

She felt the warm pads of his fingers on the back of her arm, though she hadn't seen him move. The touch made no sound, yet it sent a wave of alertness through her. Jaska's gaze leveled with hers, and through that singular connection, Matrona could read his thoughts, clearer even than the memories his doll had spilled into her mind. Her pulse reverberated off the slanted walls in beats of three, and in them she heard the name again: *Fe-o-dor.*

Jaska's fingers tightened, a soft grip.

Feodor didn't love her. He couldn't give her the one thing she wanted more than anything. Even if that hadn't been true, Matrona didn't love him, and she had come to realize she never would.

Jaska pulled ever so faintly, urging her forward.

We're all just dolls anyway, she thought.

She let herself drift toward him.

Jaska's lips met hers. Shivers cascaded down the sides of her neck. His hand traced up her arm and slipped behind her braid, cradling her head, pulling her closer.

His lips were softer than she would have expected. His breath washed over her cheek as he turned his head and claimed her mouth again. Matrona eagerly gave it to him, parting her lips against his. The scents of wood smoke and angelica danced through her nose and throat.

Rough hands cupped either side of her face and pulled her back, just enough so that Jaska could rest his forehead against hers. His eyes were closed. She struggled to catch her breath.

She shouldn't be here.

She didn't want to leave.

"You make it better," Jaska murmured. "The darkness. I'm sorry." Despite the apology, he brushed her lips with a chaste kiss.

Matrona swallowed, the taste of him lingering in her mouth. "It will pass."

He opened his eyes and smiled—smiled, despite the pain she knew was flooding him. That smile made her heart beat at an exhausting pace. But it faded, and Matrona knew he was thinking it, too. Feodor.

She didn't want to think about Feodor.

"I opened the doll." Her words, spoken on a whisper, were intended as a distraction, for she didn't want to disturb the strange sort of tranquility that had settled in the sliver of space between them. "Nothing . . . terrible happened. Others behave oddly toward me, as though that first doll was never opened. As though I'm older and more deserving of respect than I am. My mother . . . she's almost submissive."

Jaska studied her eyes. "I feel nothing different. Toward you, that is."

She was relieved to hear it. "Perhaps because we've opened two of your dolls. But the *fifth* doll, Jaska. It's me. It's *us*."

Jaska leaned back and rubbed his temple with his thumb. "I don't understand."

"Neither do I. Not really. But somehow we're inside those dolls. Somehow our bodies comprise the fifth part. I think . . . I think that's why I see the wood grain in the sky, in the wood. I'm seeing the inside of the doll."

He studied her. "But they fit in our hands."

She nodded.

He shook his head. "Sorcery." He winced. "And Slava?"

"Wants me to learn how to make them. Jaska, everyone has a doll but him. He wants me to make one for Roksana and Luka's baby."

"They had it?"

"Not yet, but soon. He says the baby will disappear if we don't make the doll within a few days of its birth. I think"—her voice choked—"I think that's why my sister vanished. She didn't have a doll. Back then . . . Slava claims he didn't know."

"He didn't know the rules of his own sorcery?"

She shrugged. Jaska tensed suddenly, squeezing his eyes shut. Matrona could only wonder at what cruel things stirred inside his mind. Could she use her new doll-sight to find out?

Did she *want* to?

"What can I do for you?" she asked.

Jaska leaned against the sloping roof beside his bed and gave her a hooded look, one that seemed to say *Feodor* without any letters or sound. He took a deep breath. "Make time go faster."

"Perhaps Slava knows a way."

A quick smile tugged on his lips. "When are you supposed to go to him?"

Matrona let out a sigh. "He said he'll send for me, and I won't escape his anger if I evade him again. He's giving me time to . . . ponder. I don't know what to do." She paused. "Let me help you."

Jaska tugged on her braid and kissed her again. Despite the graveness of their situation, despite Feodor, Matrona smiled against his lips.

Downstairs a door opened.

Matrona pulled back. "Oh heavens." In her mind's eye, Feodor strode through the house, ready to condemn her, to guilt her before she could tell him—

Jaska listened for a moment before frowning. "It's my father."

"How—"

"His gait's uneven." He sighed. "We don't have a back door, but I doubt he's lucid enough to notice you."

She nodded, trying to mask the jitters running the length of her arms. "Will you be all right?"

"Eventually." An honest answer. "And Slava . . . take the power from him, Matrona."

Matrona wasn't sure what Jaska meant, but the knowledge that Afon was skulking around downstairs urged her to her feet. She crept down the stairs and then quietly closed the attic door behind her.

Afon was in the kitchen—his head against the ridge of a shelf, his back to her. She hurried by on her tiptoes, and as far as she knew, the drunkard didn't turn around.

Matrona kept her head down as she departed the house and headed, off path, into the village. Not out of embarrassment, but because she wanted a moment alone. And if someone had spotted her exiting Jaska's home, she wasn't in any mood to see narrowed eyes or hear whispers behind cupped hands. Such a thing would ruin the strange, churning feelings inside her. Yet maybe the fourth doll would prevent such gossip . . .

She headed toward the Grankins' potato farm, but stopped at the small cordwainer's shop, resting her back against its rear wall. She touched her lips, igniting a feathery feeling in her chest.

All the reasons she *shouldn't* want this had gone limp within her— the village gossip, the age difference, even her engagement. In that moment, she truly didn't care, and nothing in her small world could have restrained the grin pulling on her cheeks. A new warmth flooded her body, lingering in her veins, and she relished it. The sensation was unlike anything she'd felt before—stronger than the relief she'd felt when the agreement between her and Feodor was set, more pleasant than a holiday feast, more poignant than a church sermon, more exhilarating than a wagon of foreign goods from Slava's cart. Something

Matrona had been missing all her life had finally been found, and all the reasons she shouldn't want it simply didn't matter anymore.

Rolling her lips together, she considered Feodor. She needed to speak with him as soon as possible. There would be consequences, of course. Matrona wasn't sure how dear they would be, or if the opened fourth doll would make the involved parties more agreeable.

She pushed off the building and continued toward home, but she didn't get far before her steps slowed.

Was she really doing this? Tarnishing her family's reputation by negating a betrothal? The feathers around her heart grew heavy. Kisses weren't promises, were they? What did she expect, to marry Jaska?

Did he even want to marry her?

Her stomach twisted as she recounted the words exchanged in Jaska's room, trying to interpret them. The spell of the second doll put him under so much stress. Had it affected his behavior toward her? Yet the spells of his first and fourth dolls had revealed that he returned her affections.

"It's time," a tenor voice sounded beside her, startling her. Matrona turned to see Georgy Grankin, an empty potato sack in his hands. Sweat collared his neck and dust clung to the perspiration on his face. Her blood tingled, and she saw his desperate need to impress his father and a yearning for hard work.

"Forgive me, I didn't see you." Matrona wished the doll-sight away. "Time for what?"

"She will labor soon. The pains have already begun."

Matrona frowned and took a step away from the man. The voice was not Slava's, but Matrona recognized his cool, patronizing tone. "Must you summon me in such a vulgar way? Come for me yourself."

"I would waste time if I sought you out with my own eyes," Slava said through the farmer's mouth. "Come now, as promised."

Matrona nodded, and Georgy blinked. "Oh, Matrona," he said, then turned about, taking in his surroundings. "I was just plowing . . ."

"And thank you for coming out to see me, but my ankle is fine." She feigned a smile. "I'm clumsy today."

Georgy's brows pulled together, but he nodded before turning back for his farm.

Matrona took a deep breath. *Thank goodness Slava did not look for me earlier.* How humiliating it would have been for him to have spoken to her through Jaska.

The moment Matrona started northward for the tradesman's house, her palms began to sweat, and any lingering good feelings within her fell as ash to her feet. She tried to swallow, but her mouth had gone dry.

She had hoped Slava would give her more time. And maybe he would have, had Roksana not begun her labor pains.

Her gut clenched. The baby was coming. How much of that did Roksana comprehend? How far did the madness extend? While Matrona had spent time at the Maysaks' house when she was younger, she had never studied Olia. Galina would know more—if, indeed, the madness in the two women continued to take the same pattern—but there would be no time to ask her today.

Slava stood waiting outside his house, his thick arms folded across his thick chest, looking taller than his grand home. When he saw her, he offered a short nod and retreated into the house. Matrona followed, her steps too light, ghostly. She waited for the doll-sight to come upon her, but it didn't, not even when she stared hard at the tradesman's back and tried to beckon it. The maker of the dolls must have made himself immune to her gifted prying.

Slava moved swifter than she did, and he preceded her into the doll room. When Matrona followed him inside, she saw that the open space before Pamyat's perch had been filled with another rectangular table, unadorned. Upon it rested carving utensils, wood shavers—several things Matrona had seen in Pavel's carpentry. Three blocks of linden wood sat on its edge. Beside the table was a lathe, which would hold the wood and spin it when powered by a pedal. This must be how he shaped the dolls. It was not so different from a pottery wheel.

"The body must come first." Slava selected the topmost block of wood. He turned it over in his hands, studying the grain, pulling it closer and farther from his eyes. "Once the body is made, the spell can begin to take hold."

Matrona pressed her lips together.

Slava drew his finger across the center of the wood. "It must be linden wood, and the dolls must all be made from the same piece, or they will not fit together. If you don't make them correctly, you'll do more harm than good."

Is any of this good?

"The bottom half is always made before the top, to ensure fit. This is as much about craft as it is sorcery."

When did we become your artwork?

"I estimate the Zotov child will be born tonight, perhaps tomorrow if the labor is long. That will give us enough time to carve the wood. Then, if the child doesn't survive, we can save the doll for the next infant born in the village."

Matrona gritted her teeth. He spoke so matter-of-factly, as if the child itself was no more than a doll. No more than the unshaped wood he held in his hands.

"I will show you how to begin." Slava placed the piece of wood in the lathe, ensuring with a few pumps of the pedal that it held evenly. "Then you will practice on the other pieces. Pay close attention, for this wood is aged and treated. It is not easy to prepare, and I will not tolerate careless mistakes."

Slava selected a sharp-looking tool from the rectangular table. Matrona spoke before he returned to the lathe. "Where would it go?"

Her words were hushed. Slava raised his brow. "Hm?"

"The baby." Matrona stared at the lathe. "Roksana's baby. Where would it go without this doll?"

"Another place."

"You want me to become as you are, yet you won't tell me?" Her voice raised with each word. "Where would the babe go, Slava? Where did Esfir go, when you failed to make a doll for her?"

His face darkened, the wrinkles deepening. "You're not prepared to learn that."

"A place with snow? With gray skies and marching feet?"

Slava glowered.

"Is that it?" Matrona asked, taking one step closer to the table. "Is that where Esfir went? Did you even *try* to retrieve her, or did she freeze in the night?"

Slava's fist hit the table, shaking the tools. A block of linden wood toppled to the floor. "Do not make me compel you to finish this, Matrona!"

"These are *prisons!*" she shouted back, the words tearing up her throat. She jutted a finger to the tables of dolls. "You've caged us! Why, Slava? If this life is so much better than the alternative, why did you not give us the choice? Olia, Esfir, Roksana . . . they wouldn't have suffered if you didn't intervene. Don't you see what you're doing?"

Slava gripped the lathe with one hand, the linden block with another. Pamyat screeched behind him. "You think yourself so righteous? I will not make the doll for you. If you will not work, Roksana's child will perish. Is that what you want? You will save the babe, or it will vanish just as your sister did."

Tears stung Matrona's eyes. She shook her head. "What was it you said?" Words cracked against her tongue. "You saved us. You *saved* us. Yet now you threaten me with the death of an innocent. You threaten me by manipulating the people in the village to be your puppets."

Shadows spread over Slava's features, and he stared at her with red-veined eyes. He gripped the worktable and shoved it aside, sending a sliver of cold fear up Matrona's spine. She backed away. He advanced.

"You still do not see it," he seethed. "What I have given you. What your pathetic life would be like without my intervention. You do not understand starvation. You do not understand *death*, only the idea of it from passages in your damnable Book. You cannot fathom pain, or war, or suffering. Because *I* have spared you. I *am* your savior, Matrona. I have saved *all* of you."

Matrona's back hit the door. She swallowed. "I never asked to be saved."

Slava threw the linden block across the room. It clapped against the wall. Pamyat hissed and flapped his wings.

"You want to see it for yourself?" he spat. "I will *show* you your misery, and you will wallow in it when the blood of that baby is on *your* hands!"

"My hands are clean!" Matrona shouted, clutching them to her chest. A tear rolled down her cheek. "And I will be *free*, Slava! I will not be manipulated any longer. Do your worst, but the child's fate will be on *your* head, not mine!"

Slava's arm struck out like a serpent, his fingers fangs to ensnare her. Matrona stumbled back, out the door, narrowly missing his grip. Her shoulder struck the far wall of the hallway, and the burst of pain jolted her into action. She raced for the stairs, grabbing the skirt of her *sarafan* as she nearly tripped over it. Slava's shadow filled the space behind her, his footsteps thundering over the carpet. A whimper escaped Matrona's throat as she bounded into the kitchen.

Slava grabbed her elbow, but Matrona spun from his grasp before he could hold her. His body, a wall between the kitchen and the front room, blocked the exit.

"We don't have a back door," Jaska's voice whispered, *"but I doubt he's lucid enough to notice you."*

Slava had a back door.

Spinning on her heel, Matrona sprinted for the door, moving faster than she ever had, straining every muscle in her body.

"No!" Slava shouted after her.

Her fingers reached for the handle.

"Stop!" he bellowed, chasing her.

Matrona grabbed the handle, but the hinges stuck as though rusted in place. Crying out, she shoved her weight into the door, bruising her shoulder down to the bone.

The door opened on screeching hinges. Matrona scrambled toward the wood, and *knew*.

Chapter 16

Slava hovered over the five-legged console just off center in his small but well-furnished room, turning over the pieces of the figurine he'd acquired on a trip to Japan some years ago. Its wood was yellowed with sap and painted with the face of an old man with a long forehead. The woman who had sold it to him called it *Fukuruma*. Seven dolls in all, a number for good luck. Slava had an inkling that the craftswoman had suspected the truth—he hadn't bought the doll merely as a souvenir. He had seen the magic within it, the potential.

He had almost unlocked it.

Putting the Japanese doll down, he picked up his imitation, made of linden wood. It had to be a soft wood, and the others hadn't sparked in his hands as they ought to have. They had either cracked when he tried to carve them or were simply null once formed, useless. But *this* doll was on the cusp. He had almost finished painting it, imitating the limbless appearance of the Japanese doll, but adorning the character— this one a woman—in Russian garb: a gold *kokoshnik* and a maroon *sarafan*. Not just any woman, but Her Imperial Majesty's handmaid. The magic sparked when the doll mimicked a real person. It made Slava wonder who the old man depicted in the Japanese doll was, if he still lived.

He turned both dolls over, measuring them, nodding to himself. These would hold spells nicely, but he had to know the dolls' utmost potential before presenting them to—

A firm knock sounded on his door, four even beats.

Slava straightened and rubbed his fingers into his neck and across his beard. There were a few gray hairs in it now. How long before he turned into an old man?

"Come in," he called.

The narrow door to his chamber opened to reveal a guard in navy uniform with a red breast and gold buttons. The guard nodded once before saying, "His Imperial Majesty requests your presence in his study."

"When?"

"Now."

"I will come," Slava said, and the guard departed, leaving the door open. They always did that. With a muted sigh, Slava collected the dolls and stashed them in a mahogany chest of drawers near the window. Straightening his clothes and smoothing his beard, he made the trek through the palace to Tsar Nicholas II's study.

Light poured in through the windows lining the corridors of Alexander Palace, reflected by the newly fallen snow that encased everything outside—the grounds, the fence posts, the trees. The calendar promised winter would end soon, but recent snowfalls had been heavy and unyielding. While beautiful to behold, the relentless chill would only drive more peasants to the palace gates. Winter made even the best people desperate.

Slava reached the study, which had a single guard posted outside its door. They exchanged no words, but the guard knocked softly on the door before opening it and announcing, "The mysticist, Slava Barinov." He stood back and let Slava pass.

The study was not a terribly large room, in part because Nicholas had packed it with so much. The tsar sat behind a desk lined with picture frames, the most recent displaying his new wife. The wall beside him was packed with bookshelves, atop which sat numerous clocks telling him the times of cities across Russia and Europe. Above those hung yet more frames, some with photos, some with art.

Soft sofas and chairs crowded around the desk. Slava saw Zhakar Kharzin, the other mysticist in Nicholas's employ. He was close in age to Slava, but had been working for the royal family for far less time. As such, he fancied himself Slava's rival and had become a thorn in Slava's boot. Closer to the door sat the recently appointed minister of defense and the governor of St. Petersburg. The latter shifted uneasily in his chair, his eyes shooting back and forth between Kharzin and Slava. It was a familiar reaction—many members of the orthodoxy considered mystics to be devil workers.

Despite the announcement, the conversation within went on uninterrupted. Slava took the seat closest to the door, which had the added benefit of being farthest from Kharzin.

"Can we borrow more from France?" Nicholas asked, tapping a pen against a piece of parchment on his desk, leaving an array of ink splats in the paper's corner. He was anxious.

"Do you have more soldiers to promise them?" the minister of defense asked. "That is the only way."

"What is the point of acquiring money to pay soldiers if I'm sending them to France?"

The minister knit his fingers together and set them under his chin. "They'll only demand them should war break out. Germany seems relatively peaceful."

"For now."

"It is easy to promise soldiers that won't be used," the minister pressed.

Nicholas ran the nail of his thumb over his lips. "France aside, I can't hire more soldiers to tame these revolts if I can't pay them."

"You can," Kharzin interjected. "They will follow your orders."

Charlie N. Holmberg

Slava snorted, earning him the eyes of all four men.

Kharzin growled. "What entertains you, Barinov? Do you scoff at the power of His Imperial Majesty?"

"Don't be a fool," Slava said. "It won't take long for unpaid and unfed soldiers to join the hordes of peasants. And they'll be armed."

Nicholas nodded. "My sentiments exactly." He sighed. "Letov?"

The governor said, "We've isolated two of the revolutionaries inciting these . . . incidents. Pavel Zotov and Oleg Popov. Both from Siniy Kamen."

"You know their locations?"

"I believe so. We've discovered their use of the symbol of the white horse, hailing to the Great Martyr Saint George, which has helped us single them out. They travel frequently, gathering more pitchforks for their riots, driving the ungrateful through the snow to attack good officers."

"Majesty," said Kharzin, "perhaps we do not need to throw more soldiers at these peasant men. Allow me to venture out and take care of them my way. We have names. And, as the saying goes, once the head of the chicken is cut off . . ."

Governor Letov shivered.

"No," Nicholas dismissed the notion with a wave of his hand.

"It will be simple, clean. No different than simple assassination," Kharzin pressed, presenting both hands palm up in supplication. "If you worry about rumors with the Church, I will be clandestine."

"It is not so much your skills that worry me," Nicholas answered, "but your finesse. I have not forgotten your failure with my sister's child labor."

Kharzin scowled, but smoothed his features quickly. "Some tragedies cannot be avoided, Your Imperial Majesty."

Nicholas tapped his fingers on his desk, near the ink-stained paper, for several heartbeats. "Perhaps you are correct. But I will send Barinov to take care of these men."

Slava missed a breath.

Kharzin huffed. "That pacifist will be less successful than a rat on the street."

Slava's eyes narrowed. He did not want the task, but he had never defied Nicholas's father, and he would not defy Nicholas now. Already Kharzin bordered on insubordination, raising his voice to the tsar.

If Nicholas noticed, he didn't pay the man any attention. Turning to the governor, he said, "You have the locations?"

"Yes." Letov glanced to Slava. "I will provide them, and your mysticist may do as he pleases. I will ensure my officers leave him be should anything . . . strange . . . arise within the city."

Slava raised an eyebrow. "These men are in St. Petersburg?"

"Nearby, yes. For how long I'm unsure, but I have a man I trust watching them."

Nicholas let out a long breath and leaned back in his chair. His eyes passed over the frames sitting along the length of his desk before he said, "See it done, Barinov. I want these rebellions ended."

Slava bowed his head in acquiescence, though how to complete the emperor's bidding without betraying his own heart was another matter entirely.

❉

The solution had been in front of him all along.

After two days of contemplating the tsar's request, fearing he was waiting too long, Slava looked up from the armchair in his room and saw the answer: the dolls.

Standing, he crossed the room to the console and picked up the most recent set he'd made, popping apart the halves of the first doll and studying them. Although these revolutionaries ailed his sovereign and tore into the peace of the country, he had no desire to kill them. Life was the purest form of magic, no matter how a man squandered it, and he did not want any spilled blood on his hands, no matter how much easier it would make his task. Yet he couldn't barge into the revolutionaries' strongholds and tie them up like hogs to be carted out of Russia, either. Too far, too many resources. And to deliver them to the tsar would, again, mean certain death.

But perhaps he could exile Pavel Zotov and Oleg Popov without their ever leaving Russia.

There were spells—powerful spells—for locking things in seemingly ordinary places, the most renowned being the Greek myth of Pandora. There was also the Jewish tale of the dybbuk spirit that haunted a box, and the story of the African sky god who locked the tales of all the world within a single capsule. Perhaps Slava could do something similar. Perhaps he could simply make these revolutionaries . . . disappear.

He stroked his beard twice, then opened the next doll, and the next. Layers. A box with layers, each with its own enchantment. Yes, he could use that. But how?

He paced the room, stretching his legs, from door to window and back. To trap a man inside a dark space until his death was a crueler fate than assassination, so he would have to craft a place for each of the men to live. Or, perhaps, somewhere they could live together. Could he manage that within the confines of a doll? It would need to be sustainable, at least for the lifetimes of the revolutionaries.

How easily could they escape? The little world would have to be seamless, inescapable. But they would notice, plan. He could place a mask over their eyes.

Slava tugged on his beard. A mask, yes. Over everything. Cure them of their rebellious ways while preventing them from breaking his spell.

He returned to the console and opened the next layer of the doll. He would place a veil inside it, black and impenetrable, spelled to steal their memories of life before imprisonment. They would become docile.

Harmless citizens. Not only that, but Slava would be freeing them of responsibility. Theirs would be a pleasant, harmless life.

He peered out the window, staring down at the snow-crusted world. Smoke from the new factories churned the air in the distance. How much better these peasants' lives would be. Was it wrong to reward them with such ease? But it was better than killing them. And if something *did* go wrong . . . best to discover it with the lives of revolutionaries than with innocents.

Slava took the dolls to his desk and began planning. Pulled old books from beneath his bed to study the enchantments within them. Let them take his imagination away.

He could create a better Russia. Russia as it should be, before industrialization. A world free of war and cold, of disease and greed, of locks and thieves. And he would watch over these men, guiding them, taking the rebellion out of their hearts . . .

❄

A dark-haired man looked up from the crate in the dim room, atop which rested a dirty hand-drawn map he'd been inspecting. He wore a band on his sleeve, depicting a rearing white horse. Slava tried to mask his surprise—he'd pictured Pavel Zotov older. This man could be no more than thirty.

"Pavel Zotov?" Slava asked, and the two others in the room stiffened and looked toward the door, alarm on their faces. No one else was supposed to be here.

"Who are you?" the man asked.

"I must speak with you. I have information about the Winter Palace I think you'll want to hear."

Slava squeezed the coercion charm in his right pocket. Pavel hesitated, then nodded. Slava squeezed harder. "Alone, if you will."

Another hesitation, but Pavel nodded again. Without word or gesture, the two men departed, eyeing Slava as they went.

Slava released the charm and extended his right hand. In his left, beneath his coat, he clutched a doll.

Pavel, his forehead creased and eyes narrowed, took Slava's hand.

And was gone.

❄

Zhakar Kharzin sowed his seeds by candlelight.

"Why won't Barinov simply tell you where the revolutionaries are?" he whispered into Nicholas's ear as the tsar read yet another letter penned in Slava's hand. "If they're dead, where are their bodies? You deserve their heads on a platter."

The parchment crinkled beneath Nicholas's fingers. Through clenched teeth he said, "You disturb me, Kharzin."

"It is Barinov who disturbs you," the mysticist whispered. "What is he hiding? What has he discovered that he won't tell you?"

Nicholas didn't respond.

Kharzin leaned closer. "He's hiding the revolutionaries. He hasn't slain them as you directed. He's helping them.

"You have the power to stop it, Majesty. For now. Slava Barinov, he seeks to take that power from you . . ."

❄

Slava's trek back to Alexander Palace was a long and wearying one. Pavel Zotov's sudden disappearance had sent Oleg Popov into hiding. However, armed with spells, it hadn't been difficult for Slava to track him. The mysticist knew how to make loyal men talk, even trace the steps of a man if his departure was recent. The revolutionary had made it all the way to Pushkin before Slava caught up with him. Fortunately, the hard travel had left Oleg both fatigued and alone, so capturing him had proved simple.

Slava was pleased with himself. He'd eliminated two threats to his tsar without spilling a single drop of blood. He would not call himself a hero, but surely Nicholas would decorate him as one.

However, Slava's reception at the palace was not what he'd expected.

His troika had barely cleared the palace gates when a swarm of soldiers in bear-skin hats surrounded him, startling the horses. Slava didn't even have time to jerk back on the reins before a burly soldier grabbed Slava's coat sleeve and hauled him out of his seat. Slava's knees slammed into packed snow.

"What is the meaning of this?" he shouted, trying to right himself. One of the soldiers grabbed the tail of hair hanging down from Slava's *ushanka*, and yet another wrestled with Slava's arms, trying to get his wrists behind his back for binding.

"Slava Barinov, your plot has unfolded," said the soldier who had pulled him from the troika. "You're under arrest for treason against the crown."

"Treason!" Slava elbowed the man trying to bind him. His companion readied a rifle, leveling the butt dangerously close to Slava's forehead. "I have returned from eliminating enemies of the crown! I demand to speak to the tsar!"

The soldier snorted, his breath fogging before his mouth. "The tsar issued the order himself."

Soldiers clustered around Slava, a shifting wall of bodies. Hands hauled him to his feet and again jerked his arms backward. Slava's head spun. "Treason for what?" he asked, and when none answered, he shouted, "Tell me the accusation!"

His gaze shot to the palace, its walls glittering with sunlit ice crystals. He saw a shadow on the white stairs. Kharzin, wearing a smile.

Slava understood. It was not the first time the devil's man had spoken ill of Slava, only the first time his words had, apparently, convinced the tsar.

Slava growled. Someone tried to push his head down; Slava pushed back. *"In aethere,"* he growled, his arms shaking as he resisted binding, *"ad locum meum. Vola!"*

The magic prickled as though he'd swallowed a horsefly's nest. It didn't used to hurt, but spells didn't take kindly to growing years. The weight of the soldiers' hands vanished. Slava appeared inside the troika, grabbed his dolls, and vanished once more.

❉

He had little time.

Kharzin had poisoned the tsar's mind. It would not be possible for Slava to right that wrong now. Not when the heat of the empire bore down on him. Kharzin would expect him to try to escape, but surely he wouldn't expect Slava to linger in the palace.

He had risked appearing in his room, traveling bag in tow. It still contained soiled clothes, a half-empty water skin, and the two layered dolls painted in the likenesses of the peasant rebels. Outside, the shrill cry of whistles pierced the air.

Slava dropped to his knees at his bedside, pulling out his old spell books. They were too large and too heavy for him to take them all; Slava selected one and shoved it into his bag, mourning the loss of the others. Before sunset, Kharzin's greasy fingers would no doubt ravish their pages.

"In aethere," he began, but the Latin caught on his tongue as his eyes met the chest of drawers. The one that held the Japanese doll and his remaining supplies.

They would follow him out of St. Petersburg. Kharzin or another mysticist would catch up with Slava eventually, and if he could not cleanse the tsar's mind of lies, Slava's neck would meet a rope, if not a pike. He would run forever, or find himself banished.

Yet Slava had another option, one Kharzin did not know about. He had the dolls.

Raucous footfalls bellowed beneath him. His time was slipping away.

Rushing for the drawers, Slava wrenched them open. Two pieces of wood left, his carving utensils, a silver paintbrush. He grabbed whatever could fit into his bag and began to sing in Latin.

The door to his chamber burst open on the last syllable.

❄

Slava worked in a dark room, spinning the wood and carving, carving, carving. He cut and sanded until his fingers bled, chanted spells until his tongue dried and threatened to crack. For it would not be just him.

He would not be content spending his days with brainwashed rebels. Such a world would be a place of deep loneliness, no matter how pretty he painted it. No, he wanted more. A future, a community.

Betrayed as he'd been, by both Kharzin and the tsar, he deserved it. He cut, sanded, carved, painted.

They would thank him one day. He would save them—all of them. The peasants wanted food? Shelter? Sunshine? He'd give it to them. He would save them from the harshness of the world, and in return they would be his comrades. His community. His family.

When he was finished, half-mad from the ceaseless work, Slava carried the dolls into the village called Siniy Kamen and uttered the spells to the families there, then settled the magic onto himself.

Chapter 17

Matrona stumbled into the wood, blinded by the surge of secrets flooding her senses. She stubbed her shoe on a root; a twisting hornbeam branch snagged her braid. She tripped and weaved through the trees until she reached the children's glade and collapsed at its edge, breathing hard. Slava hadn't followed her haphazard path. No footsteps dropped behind her. In fact, there was hardly any sound at all. Even the glade was eerily absent of laughter.

The sun shined brightly in the glade, but shivers coursed up and down Matrona's body. *Russia*. The word was foreign, yet familiar. She blinked away the face of Tsar Nicholas II, of *Pavel*. Sacred heavens, Pavel! And Oleg! Revolutionaries? Rebels?

She swallowed against a dry throat and gasped for air, her heart pounding hard in her chest. The images summoned by the third doll . . . snow and thunder, marching feet and the younger face of her mother. Those *were* memories. Memories of this other place. Of *Russia*.

Pressing the palms of her hands into her eyes, Matrona took several deep breaths. The village, *this* village, existed somewhere else? Or it had, until they'd all been brought here by Slava's hand. Because of Oleg and Pavel . . . No, because of Slava. Because he had feared what the tsar's men would do to him. Because he *hadn't wanted to be alone.*

"So you took us with you," she whispered, lowering her hands, staring at the boulder in the glade as colored spots faded from her vision.

But how did *she* know? She hadn't opened Slava's doll, so why had his secrets flooded her mind? Had *he* opened it? But no, the tradesman had chased her from the doll room. Unless he had snatched up his doll before following her, he couldn't have opened it at the exact moment she'd burst out the back door. That, and Matrona had searched for the tradesman's—the mysticist's—doll several times. If he had one, she knew it did not sit with the others.

She stiffened, then clambered to her feet, looking wildly into the wood behind her. Had someone followed her into Slava's house? Found his doll and opened it? Or was this another spell entirely?

"Jaska?" she called into the wood. Only insects and starlings answered.

She stepped backward into the glade and turned around, searching for any lurking faces, straining to hear any sounds beyond the forest. Finding nothing, she gazed skyward, staring at the imprint of the wood grain against the blue. She took a few more steps, watching it, the brightness of the sun making her eyes water.

She knew where the edges of the doll were—the loops in the wood. Slava had mentioned teaching her about the loops. What did he know? How could she escape this place and go back to Russia? Back . . . *home?*

She paused, turning toward the village. If it was a doll spell that had spilled Slava's secrets to her, then the others would all know the truth, too. Her parents, the Maysaks, Feodor and Luka and Pavel . . .

Grabbing a fistful of skirt, Matrona rushed for the village, taking the well-worn path from the glade. Her thoughts raced faster than her feet. Surely Slava hadn't willingly revealed his secrets. If not him, who? And what would Pavel and Oleg do, knowing who they really were?

Matrona could finally explain Roksana's condition. Maybe, *maybe*, if she could get Roksana outside the loop, her mind would become whole again.

She slowed after the wood opened up to the village, not far from the school where Roksana taught. Smoke wafted from a few chimneys. The bleating of sheep sounded far to the east. Baked bread scented the breeze.

Matrona scanned the village, unease churning in her gut. Something was amiss, but she couldn't determine what. Clenching her fists, she walked toward the village center, casting glances in the direction of Slava's home. What should she do if he appeared? Demand he tell her the mystery of the loops, or run?

She neared Zhanna's home. Laundry hung from the clothesline. A half-filled basket of damp clothes sat unattended beneath it. The next *izba's* front door had been left open. Matrona knotted her fingers together as she approached the Grankins' potato farm. Their best labor horse was hooked up to the plow, without a driver. A stray goat slipped through the fence in search of something to eat, dragging its rope leash behind it.

Matrona paused.

She was alone.

No villagers. No Zhanna, no Georgy. She could see the Kalagin *izba* from where she stood. It appeared empty.

Stomach tightening, Matrona changed direction and followed the goat across the potato farm, leaving footprints in the plowed rows. Her family's cow pasture lay across the path. The cows chewed on cud or swatted flies with their tails. Hurrying through the gate, Matrona came around to the back door of her house and called, "Mama? Papa?"

No answer.

She hurried past the milk barrels and into the kitchen. "Mama?" The front room was empty, and she checked both bedrooms to no avail.

Her palms and the ridges of her spine began to sweat. *What have you done with them, Slava?*

Backtracking, Matrona cut through the front room toward the door. Her toe hit something, sending it rolling across the floor. A marble or a stone, she thought, but her eyes glimpsed yellow and gray.

Pausing, Matrona bent over to pick up the item and gasped.

In her hand, no longer than her pinky finger, was a wooden doll painted to look just like her mother, albeit a couple decades younger.

"Mama?" Matrona whispered. The details were vague, but she recognized her mother's face, nonetheless. She drew her thumbnail over the doll's center, searching for a seam, but she found none. This doll didn't open.

Matrona felt the weight of Slava's hand on her shoulder as though he stood in the room with her. *"Five,"* he had said.

This doll was small enough to fit inside a fourth doll . . .

She thought of the quietness that plagued her from Slava's home to hers. The empty children's glade, the bare path.

Was this . . . her *mother*? But how?

Shuddering, Matrona pocketed the doll and retraced her steps through the *izba*, slower this time, searching low instead of high. She found what she was looking for just outside the barn in the cow pasture—another small doll painted to look like her father. It was the same size as the other, and with no seam.

Her chest squeezed in on itself as she stared at the likeness of her father. Were they all like this?

Shivers traced circles along her back and shoulders as she added the second doll to her pocket. "Roksana," Matrona whispered, and she ran from the cow pasture, not even bothering to close the gate after her. The skirt of her *sarafan* billowed as she pushed herself up the path from her home. Her lungs blazed with fire by the time she arrived.

A low moan within the Zotov *izba* answered her.

"Roksana!" Matrona called, throwing open the front door. The room before her looked empty, as did the kitchen, the hallway. But Roksana lay in her bedroom, blankets pulled halfway up her round stomach. Her black hair, wavy from its braids, scattered loosely over her shoulders and pillow. She opened her eyes, looked at Matrona, then gritted her teeth as a contraction rippled up her belly.

Matrona's doll-sight flickered to life, but the only emotion she sensed in her friend was confusion.

On the floor, at the foot of the bed, lay two dolls: one painted to look like Alena and the other depicting the midwife, both younger versions of themselves. Matrona scooped them up. She bit her lip to keep it from quivering.

"Roksana." She stowed the two women in her pocket and hurried to her friend's bedside, where she took up Roksana's hand. "Are you all right?"

Roksana's head rolled to the side, and her lips formed the words of that strange lullaby. The madness still had its hold on her.

Matrona felt the weight of the midwife's doll in her pocket. If the midwife was gone, and Roksana's mother . . . who would help Roksana birth this baby? Matrona had only witnessed the birthing of calves on a few occasions. Her knowledge ended there.

"Lord help us," she breathed, and moved to the foot of the bed, where the midwife's bag of supplies rested, along with a bowl of luke-warm water and several towels. Matrona sorted through the bag, her fingers trembling.

Roksana's breath hitched. She wasn't terribly close to delivery—the contractions were too far apart.

Matrona stilled, watching her friend's chest rise and fall. Roksana and Matrona had both opened their dolls—that had to be why they were still whole, still real. The others had become the literal parts of Slava's curse.

Matrona perked. "Jaska," she whispered. Would he be whole, too? Would he be able to help?

Checking under Roksana's blanket to ensure she wasn't bleeding, Matrona whispered, "I'll be back. Breathe deeply. I'll be right back."

Roksana whimpered, but as Matrona raced out of the house, she heard her friend humming the haunting strains of her Russian lullaby.

Matrona ran across the village, again cutting through the potato farm. She found Georgy's doll in the soil behind the plow; Zhanna's in the grass beneath her clothesline. Other villagers scattered the path or the porches outside their homes. Despite her rush, Matrona could not bring herself to leave them alone. She scooped up each one she saw, until they knocked together in her pockets with her every step.

Her legs ached by the time she reached the pottery, but Matrona hurried to the Maysak house and threw open the door. She ran to the stairs in the back, climbed up to the attic.

"Jaska?" she called, but the room was empty. Huffing, muscles tingling, she approached the bed against the left wall and peeled back the covers.

Her heart fell into her stomach when she saw his doll there.

"Oh, Jaska," she whispered, picking the small likeness off the mattress. He hadn't been spared.

"It's all gone bad," mumbled a voice downstairs. "The whole of it. We'll starve!"

Matrona whipped around, her lips forming the name, *Olia*. She rushed down the stairs just in time to see the old woman walking the short hallway to the other bedrooms, pressing one hand against the wall for balance. Her eyes found Matrona, then turned away, disinterested. Matrona locked the mad woman in her gaze until the doll-sight came to life, but she sensed only what she had felt with Roksana—deep-rooted confusion.

"All gone bad," Olia continued as she stepped into the kitchen, throwing a hand into the air. "Didn't salt it, all bad now. Skin your hide."

"Olia! I know about Slava," Matrona tried, but the woman rambled on, opening and closing cupboards as she walked the perimeter of the room. Matrona licked her lips. "I know about *Russia*."

Olia paused and turned, looking at Matrona as though seeing her for the first time. For a split second, Matrona thought she saw clarity in the woman's gaze, but it vanished just as quickly. Olia shook her head. "No sheep is no socks and we'll lose our toes. No salt, no salt!"

Biting her lip, Matrona rolled Jaska's doll between her fingers. Olia tripped and cursed, drawing Matrona's eyes to a doll on the floor. Rushing forward before the woman could kick it away, she grabbed the figurine. Galina.

"At least Slava spared you from *this*," Matrona muttered to the aged woman as she tucked Galina into her pocket. Olia ignored her. She'd restarted her circuit of the kitchen, again opening and closing the cupboard doors.

Matrona helped herself to a cup of water before hurrying from the Maysak home for the second time that day. She wished desperately that she had a horse, and that she knew how to ride it. For now, urgency was her only fuel, but it was enough to get her across the village.

Roksana was mostly unchanged when Matrona returned, though her forehead had begun to perspire. After soaking a rag in the pail of water, Matrona wiped Roksana's face, then built up the fire that had burned down to embers in the brick oven in the kitchen. The sun outside the window marked late afternoon.

Matrona put water over the fire to boil—and subsequently found Luka's doll near the dining table. Exhausted, she fell into a chair to rest a moment. While her body did, her thoughts did not.

She had to return to Slava.

The muscles in her arms and neck tensed at the idea, but there was no one else save Olia, and she was as mad as ever. Leaning her elbows onto her knees, Matrona cradled her head in her hands. What if Slava refused? What if she'd retaliated against him one too many times?

Roksana's groan snaked down the hallway. Matrona jumped to her feet and hurried to her friend's side. A prayer in her heart pleaded that Roksana would not be pained enough to try to leave her bed, for the agony of labor would only worsen. Already the contractions grew closer together, and Roksana's slender fingers gripped fistfuls of her blanket.

Sorting through the midwife's things once more, Matrona found chamomile and catnip for pain and tension. She mixed them into a cup and managed to get Roksana to drink most of the medicine—the impending delivery had captured nearly all of Roksana's focus, which prevented her from rambling, or worse. After checking once more to ensure nothing had gone awry, Matrona left the *izba* and ran for the sleeping dragon.

She started shouting for Slava before she even reached the portico. "Slava!" she bellowed. "You have your wish! I'll do whatever you want, just bring them back!" She ran up the steps to the door. Pushed it open. "Slava!"

The front room was empty, as was the kitchen, as was the doll room, where Pamyat greeted her with a hiss. Matrona's worry quickly shifted into anger, which imbued her body with new strength.

"No more games!" she shouted, coming back up the hallway. "I'll make your dolls! Keep your secrets! Wash your feet if I have to!"

She reached the entry hall and called up the stairs, loud enough to crack her voice. *"Slava!"*

No answer.

Had he left? All his talk about urgency, and he'd simply left everything behind?

Setting her jaw and lifting her skirt, Matrona climbed up the stairs. Only two rooms occupied the upper floor; the first was a large bedroom simply decorated, with a low, wide bed and taupe-colored curtains over a broad window. The other was a sitting room filled with remarkable wonders—shelves that held golden eggs and a bronze inkstand, plait ornaments, plates painted with unfamiliar heraldry, and the Japanese *Fukuruma* doll from Slava's memories. The walls boasted embroidered *plashchanitsas* and paintings, as well as a small flag striped white, blue, and red. On any other day, at any other hour, the treasures would have incited awe. Now she saw only the empty spaces around them.

The tradesman was gone.

Chapter 18

The *Fukuruma* doll hit the floor.

More of the wonders spilled onto fine rugs as Matrona searched behind and under the treasures for Slava's doll. She emptied bookshelves and turned over chairs both in the sitting room and in his bedroom, then went downstairs to do the same. She lifted rugs and pillaged cupboards, even received a sharp bite from Pamyat when she searched behind his perch. She physically touched each and every doll Slava owned, ensuring none of them wore his face.

None of them did. Matrona panted, weary. There was no doll.

She went through the room again, this time cleaning up the clutter, then crawled over the floors on hands and knees, searching for a small doll. A center doll without a seam. That eluded her as well. She searched the small stable behind the house, and the yard surrounding it. No sign of the tradesman.

But he'd left his horse, so he couldn't have gone far. Where could he have hidden? The wood?

Matrona sighed and trudged back into the house. Slava wasn't the sort of man to hide. He had merely . . . vanished.

Matrona collapsed on the stairs. "Slava, I need you," she said, too tired to shout. "Roksana needs you. Please."

No answer.

Matrona spat the few curse words she knew and pulled herself up, then dragged her body back to the Zotov house. She found Roksana in the kitchen, clutching the edge of the table, making a sound between a grunt and a scream as her fingernails dug into the wood. Matrona expected Roksana to resist when she put her arms around her, but the laboring woman leaned into her instead, sobbing, and allowed Matrona to lead her back to the bed.

Roksana climbed onto the mattress on her hands and knees, breathing too fast. She cried out.

"Slow breaths," Matrona urged, hoping Roksana would understand. She pulled the tie off the end of her own braid and used it to pull back Roksana's hair. "Try to take deep breaths, or you'll faint. It won't be forever."

Getting Roksana as comfortable as possible, Matrona returned to the kitchen to boil water again—she'd left the stove too long, and the first pot of water had all gone to steam. Then she ate a piece of bread and returned to Roksana's room, where she arranged towels for the delivery.

Roksana uttered the words of her sad lullaby in the short spaces between contractions.

Matrona sang them with her.

❄

The babe's cry startled Matrona awake. Her eyes hurt from being pressed into the mattress, her backside from sitting in the wooden chair too long. Folds from Roksana's blanket had left creases in her forehead.

Roksana had labored all night, but delivered a baby boy in the hours of midmorning. All three of them were exhausted, but because Matrona feared Roksana would not nurse the baby on her own, she stayed alert and nearby.

Roksana stirred groggily as the infant wailed beside her. Matrona woke her friend with a few words and helped bring the babe to her breast. Fatigue, it seemed, helped keep the madness at bay.

That evening, while both mother and son rested, Matrona ventured back to Slava's house, finding it just as empty as before. She took the path that surrounded the village and walked it, picking up a few more dolls, adding them to the collection she now kept in one of Roksana's cloth satchels. She visited Olia, who pretended to knit while only tying knots in her yarn, then went to the butchery, where she found Oleg's doll, and the Popov *izba*, where she collected Feodor and the rest of his family.

By nightfall, it became evident to Matrona that whatever spell Slava had cast over the village would not resolve itself, and that Slava would not save her from it. She also knew she could not break it alone.

She dumped the satchel's contents onto the rag rug in the Zotovs' front room. Familiar, painted faces rolled. She found Jaska's doll, palmed it, and returned to the tradesman's home.

Though it felt like weeks, only three days had passed since Matrona had bumped into Slava's table and opened Jaska's second doll. Now there was no one to interrupt her as she sought out his likeness on the table of dolls. Even Pamyat saved his hissing. The kite was looking sick, and likely hadn't been fed since Slava's abandonment. Did the bird hunt his meals? There was no meat to be had in the house. She'd need to do something—even a creature as grumpy as Pamyat shouldn't be made to suffer.

Clasping Jaska's fifth doll in her hands, she popped open his first doll, then his second, then his third. She held the fourth in her hands. The urge to pull it apart made her fingers twitch, but she set it back down. She couldn't risk losing Jaska to the insanity of Slava's spells.

She reassembled the doll and turned about slowly, studying the rest. Starting on the far edge of the room, near the kite, she opened the first doll of each one. Pavel, Alena, Luka, Feodor, Oleg, Galina, Afon,

Viktor, Kostya, Georgy, Zhanna. Irena, Nastasya, Boris Ishutin. The Grankins, the Demidovs. Every last one until her hands threatened to blister.

Then she moved a dozen of the dolls to the floor, climbed atop the table, and pushed open the solitary window. Pamyat leapt from his perch and flapped wildly for his escape, the copper band about his leg glinting in the sunlight.

Chapter 19

The tip of the chisel stuck into the turning linden wood, leaving a crooked gash. Matrona pulled her foot off the lathe pedal and barely resisted throwing the chisel into the wall beside her. Tears burned her eyes. She hadn't blinked as she worked.

Dropping the chisel, Matrona grabbed the ruined wood and threw it onto the floor with the rest before squatting down and throwing her arms over her head. She'd tried and tried and tried, but she couldn't even get the shape of a doll correct, let alone carve out its hollows and bespell them. And how was she to paint the babe's face? All of Slava's dolls were adults. Somehow he knew what the young would look like once they aged, and he hadn't told her how. She hadn't let him.

Stupid, stupid, stupid.

Two days since Roksana's unnamed babe had been born. Slava had warned her about the third day, that without a doll, the infant would vanish just as Esfir had. Yet without the tradesman, Matrona had no way to stop it from happening. Slava had promised Roksana's baby would pay the price for Matrona's disobedience, a thought that pounded through her head again and again as she kept trying—and failing—to work the lathe. She had no way to create a functioning doll, and no way to free herself, let alone anyone else, from this bespelled prison.

She rubbed a knuckle into her eye and picked up the chisel. She was so tired. Exhausted from running about the village, from tending Roksana's child, from trying to create this doll.

She knew she'd never learn the craft that quickly. But if she didn't try, where did that leave her?

She didn't even have the pleasure of the villagers' secrets occupying her thoughts. Whatever spell had turned them into wooden miniatures had also voided the consequences of opening their dolls. Matrona would have loved to know her mother's secrets, or Feodor's. If Luka's deepest thoughts had been spilled, perhaps she would discover just what he had intended to name his son.

Sighing, Matrona trudged out of the doll room and to the nearest closet, taking up another block of wood from Slava's dwindling supply. She had to try again. And again, and again . . .

❄

Matrona failed.

❄

She hated leaving Roksana like this, weeping into her pillow, calling out Luka's name in fleeting moments of lucidity. Roksana had barely seemed to realize her babe had been born, yet even with her mind gone, she felt the infant's absence. Three days old and the boy had vanished, just as Matrona's sister had.

Roksana wouldn't eat anything, and Matrona couldn't, for her belly twisted and ached with her failure. She carried the pain with her as she departed the Zotov house for Slava's abode, Roksana's wails catching the breeze that followed her.

When she arrived at the room of dolls, she reached into her pocket and withdrew Jaska's doll.

"Please, please work," she prayed aloud, and pressed a kiss to the tiny doll's head. Then, walking around the two doll tables, her feet kicking up wood shavings from the lathe, she found the other pieces of the doll and opened them one by one, until she cracked open the seam of the fourth.

Like hers it was empty inside. Matrona didn't delay. Holding her breath, she placed the fifth doll inside, then trapped it within, making sure to line up the seams. The fourth doll went into the third, the third into the second, and the second into the first.

The moment the stitches of Jaska's shirt aligned, the seam melted beneath Matrona's fingertips, vanishing as though it had never been.

"No, wait!" Matrona cried, grappling at the dolls, trying to pull them apart. Surely she hadn't just trapped Jaska forever! "I—"

"Matrona?"

Her heart lodged in her throat at the voice. She turned around, and there he stood in the center of the room, rubbing the side of his head as though it ached, wearing the same clothes she'd seen him in before the village had turned into dolls.

Eyes filling with tears, Matrona ran to him and threw her arms around his waist, burying her face into his chest. He smelled like wood and paint.

"What's wrong?" he asked, returning the embrace. "And where . . ."

Matrona stepped back, letting Jaska take in his surroundings. His gaze fell on the tables first, then the shelves, his eyes moving with deliberate slowness. At last, he noticed the doll in Matrona's hands—solid and painted with his face.

"This is it," he said. "Slava's . . . room."

She nodded and set the doll beside the others.

Jaska rubbed his head again. "How did I get here?"

"I carried you." She bit her lip. "Let me show you."

Deep lines creased Jaska's forehead, but he allowed Matrona to take his hand and pull him from the room, up the hall, and into the kitchen.

There, on Slava's small table, rested a handful of dolls—Feodor, her parents, Galina. Jaska picked up his sister's doll and studied it.

"It doesn't open."

"They're the center dolls," she explained. "Jaska, the entire *village* is like this. Moments ago, you were one of them."

His eyes widened. Matrona started from the beginning, detailing her summons to Slava's house after her . . . visit . . . with Jaska, their argument, the revelations about Slava and Russia that had filled her mind. The dolls, Roksana and Olia, the babe, the vanishing.

"Enough time passed that I could open the rest of your dolls and assemble them whole." She paced for a moment before turning to face Jaska. She held out her hand. "Come with me."

"Where?"

"Outside. The spells started to work once I left the house."

He took her hand. She closed her fingers through his and led him out the front door and down the steps, until they stood on grass.

She studied his face. "Do you remember? The third doll should have triggered memories, like the ones I told you about. Snow, the gray skies? Your family, maybe?"

Jaska's brows drew together, and his eyes unfocused for a long moment. Sighing, he shook his head. "I don't. I'm sorry."

Matrona pressed her lips together. Her own memories were faint, whereas the visions she'd gotten from Slava had been sharp and detailed.

Her mind opened to the reason like a lotus bloom spreading its petals to the dawn. Age. Slava's visions were so clear because those events had happened when he was an adult. She had been a child, and . . .

"You were born here," she whispered.

Jaska frowned.

Matrona began pacing again. "That's what it is. My memories are old. A child's memories. That's why I have so few. But Jaska, you must have been born *here*, in this world."

"I've been in that house all my life."

Matrona nodded. "You don't remember Russia because you never lived there." Jaska had been born shortly after Esfir. Slava must have realized the trick with the dolls and infants by that time. "But your mother does. I do. It must have been . . ." She sucked in a deep breath. "Twenty years ago."

Twenty years inside the doll world. Twenty years since Russia. Since Slava fled Tsar Nicholas and the other mysticist.

She went back into the house and sat on one of the kitchen chairs, thinking.

"Matrona."

She looked across the table.

Jaska stood in the kitchen doorway and offered her a weak smile. "I need to find my mother."

She nodded. "She's still at the *izba*, last I checked. I should visit Roksana, too. She's . . . not well." Chamomile had helped her sleep through some of the grief, but it wouldn't force food down her throat or calm her broken mind.

Jaska stood and rested his hands on his hips. "Does Slava have another home? Somewhere in the wood, perhaps?"

"Not that I know of. The wood is much smaller than we once thought."

He rubbed the back of his neck. "I wonder if my mother knows. She's surprised me before." His dark gaze focused on Matrona. "I'll look, once she's taken care of. See if I can find him, or any clues."

"Or anyone else." She gestured to the dolls on the table.

Jaska nodded, but didn't leave immediately. He lingered, and Matrona's skin felt tight. The quietness of the house seemed to thicken around her.

His eyes glanced down to her lips. "I'll be back. And . . . we need to talk." He turned to go. Matrona watched him cut across the front room, then listened to his footfalls echo in the short hallway to the door.

"We need to talk." She pressed her thumb into a fluttery spot in her stomach. Swallowed. Looking at the dolls on Slava's table, she reached out and selected Feodor's. Met its painted stare for a long moment. "Even without him," she said aloud, thinking of Jaska, "all of this would change. Neither of us will be the people we were."

She certainly wasn't. To think that only weeks ago she had knelt in her parents' bedroom before her mother's chest, drawing out a wedding gown with Roksana beside her. That memory was a dream, unreal. Make-believe.

Where would she be right now had the glint of that silver paintbrush never caught her eye?

She knew Feodor could not hear her, for Jaska appeared to have no memories from his time in the spell's thrall. Still, she spoke to Feodor, if only to sort out her own thoughts.

"I've always wanted to be loved. I don't know if Esfir's passing closed my parents' hearts, or if it's just their way, but affection has always been lacking in my home. I fear it's lacking in yours as well. I can't be part of that." She sighed. "I can't sit in a bedroom all my own, sharing your name and nothing else. I can't be your . . . doll."

Frowning, she set Feodor's doll down so that it looked at her, and she studied the fine lines of its face. Her gaze shifted to the other villagers before her. She could open all their second dolls today. Then three days for the thirds, and another three for the fourths. In a week the village would be restored, all cramped into Slava's house unless she moved the dolls outside.

Her eyebrows pinched together. Slava never took the dolls outside; she could assume that much. He never so much as rearranged them from their designated spots, except perhaps to dust them or waggle them before Matrona's nose until she bent to his will. How long had they been inside that room?

Inside that house?

A cool tingling ignited between her breasts. She sat straighter, lifting her gaze from the dolls to the front room, following the invisible path Jaska had just taken. She stood and walked it. Pulled open the front door and stepped out onto the portico. Down the few steps.

She studied the house, its blue-trimmed walls and cornices, its twisting yellow columns and glassy windows.

Something Jaska had said to her days ago, something unimportant, nagged at her.

"We don't have a back door, but I doubt he's lucid enough to notice you."

She thought of the fifth dolls—the people—sitting in that room down the hall, never moved. Trapped.

Trapped inside *this house*.

Tucking the short, stray strands of black hair behind her ears, Matrona walked around the house, crisp grass crunching softly beneath her shoes. In the backyard, she examined the edge of the wood and the stable. She'd let the horse out to graze a while back, and it had wandered away. She came to the back door and the steps leading up to it.

None of the dolls' spells had taken hold until she left Slava's home. The villagers had turned into dolls the day she ran away from Slava. The moment she left his house . . . through *this* door. Every other time she'd visited, she'd come and left through the front door.

A numb heaviness settled on her chest, making it difficult to breathe. She studied the back door. Rubbed her hands together. Reached for the handle and pushed it open.

Slava Barinov greeted her.

Chapter 20

His eyes, dark and shadowed, met hers. A chair fell behind him, and Matrona started to see her father and mother stumbling toward the wall, Feodor standing on the table, and Galina sitting beside him. Matrona had left their dolls on the table. They'd been restored.

"What is this?" Feodor asked, his gaze flitting from Slava to Matrona. "Why are we—"

"*Reverto!*" Slava barked, and the four shrank before Matrona's eyes, returning to small wooden dolls in a quarter of a breath's time. Feodor and Galina fell to the table; her parents rolled across the floor.

"What have you done?!" Matrona shouted, taking a single step into Slava's home before stopping. Though it would not be safe to draw too near to the tradesman, she also did not want to linger in the threshold of his house. If any doorway housed dark beings, surely it would be Slava's.

Slava growled. "You will have to tell me exactly what you did in the *Nazad* if they are to be restored, foolish girl."

"The what?" Gritting her teeth, she stepped back into the shelter of the doorway, more willing to risk superstition than Slava's anger. "I know the truth." She clutched the frame to keep her hands from trembling. "I know what you did."

A frown deepened the wrinkles in Slava's face and made his eyes droop.

"Your house is your doll. That's how you separated yourself from us. You put us in our dolls, then put those dolls inside yours." She glanced at the small dolls on the table, then at the open door before her, and she realized something else. "The spells don't take hold until we leave the house. This place is neutral ground. It binds everything together, doesn't it?"

"So you are not as simple as you appear."

"Is that why your house is so elaborate? To be some sort of . . . ultimate doll?" She tilted her head back and looked at the ceiling. It wasn't built of logs or panels, but was a solid sheet of wood. The pattern in its grain matched that of her fourth doll . . . and that of the sky.

Slava's nostrils sucked in a long breath before he spoke. "The spells on this house are far more complex than anything you could hope to understand. These dolls are child's play in comparison." He stepped away from the fallen center dolls and closer to Matrona, then pressed a flat hand to one of the walls. "This is not simply a *doll*. It is a sanctuary. A vessel. A temple."

"A temple to yourself."

She expected Slava to glare, but he merely straightened and pulled his hand from the wall, strangely calm. "You are not incorrect."

Matrona took half a step into the house—she dared not take more, and she watched Slava with the eyes of a kite. "What would you have them do, Slava? Do you plan to restore them to their mindless existence and, once death claims you, have them come here to worship your memory?"

A chill nipped at her bones. Was Matrona the first to discover these truths, or had someone else done so before her? Had Slava merely . . . reconditioned them all?

"Death will never truly claim me if the spells are right," he said. "I will be here to watch over them always. Them, and you."

Matrona scoffed. "You think yourself immortal? The tsar didn't think so."

Now Slava did glare. Several seconds passed before he spoke. "If the spells are right. This body will not last; that much is evident. But the mind is something else entirely."

"So you intend to live on in this make-believe world in spirit, using our captivity to fuel your immortality?" Matrona asked, hardly believing the words passing between them. "You think yourself a savior, but how is that saving us?" She gestured to the dolls. "How is *this* a kindness?"

"I never should have dealt with you. Better to have left you curious than to have pulled you into my plans," Slava said, more to himself than to her, for his eyes remained fixated on the wall. "You would not have spoken of it, mousy girl that you were. And if you had, who would have believed you?"

"Jaska." Her grip on the door handle tightened. "He would have."

Slava stood tall, his body like the shadow of a great beast. "Then perhaps he did not forget as easily as I had supposed."

Her stomach dropped. Jaska? Like Matrona, had Jaska once discovered something he shouldn't have, and had his memories replaced?

She took back her half step, framing herself in the doorway once more. Slava's calm demeanor melted from him—his eyes widened, and his forehead grew tight.

"You know the truth, Matrona," he growled, advancing toward her, his hand reaching forward. "You've seen the place we hail from. Surely you recall the harsh winters, the starvation, the war. Boys too young pulled from their homes to fight battle after battle, leaving their mothers and sisters with nothing. And if the hunger didn't kill you, disease would, festering and—"

"You were never hungry," Matrona snapped. "You lived in a palace."

"I was not born into luxury!" he spat. He took another step forward. He was almost close enough to touch her. "Look beyond your own nose, you selfish girl! I can sense your thoughts, and they are foolhardy!"

Matrona swallowed, trying to moisten her tongue. She whispered, "Run back to Russia, Tradesman."

Slava's hand shot out. Matrona released the door handle and pushed herself backward, falling through the doorway. Her backside hit the ground hard, sending a sharp burst of pain up her tailbone. Her lungs sought air as if she had run one of the loops.

She looked up. The doorway stood empty, without the slightest trace of Slava Barinov.

❄

Matrona's blood thrummed beneath her skin. Her heartbeat echoed in her ears.

"The Nazad." The *backward.* That was what Slava had called this place—this backward version of the village, where Matrona's eyes saw the villagers as they really were: tiny dolls made for an old man's play. But why did Slava vanish when she entered it?

The answer lay within herself, Olia, and Roksana. They had all opened their dolls. They had been exposed to the truths of this world. Jaska, too, came into his normal being once Matrona had opened all of his dolls. But Slava . . . Slava had never opened his own doll.

She stared up at the house, unsure if it held the same layers the other dolls did, but one thing was certain. Matrona had seen Slava's secrets as soon as she had opened his back door. Perhaps that was his doll's first layer. Yet Jaska hadn't known the tradesman's secrets. Had Jaska been unable to absorb the information in his small wooden form? Was that how Slava protected himself?

The tradesman ruled over their village, but he had never exposed himself to it. In that sense, this *Nazad* was his weakness—the one place Matrona could go where he could not follow . . . for now.

She had to act before the tradesman found an escape.

Picking herself up, ignoring the dirt on her dress and beneath her fingernails, Matrona ran down the narrow space between the stable and house. Jaska's home was not too far; she had to tell him what she'd learned, then go back to the house for the—

A sharp pain split her middle. Matrona gasped and tripped over her own heel, hitting the ground knees first.

Pressing a hand against her belly, Matrona took a few deep breaths until the stitch subsided. Too much exertion, perhaps. She pushed herself onto her feet—

The pain hit again, like a knife slicing across her navel. Matrona cried out this time, her shoulder colliding with the house. The agony traveled around her torso, just above her hips and the small of her back, until a ring of fire burned through skin and muscle. Matrona pushed her legs forward, leaning against Slava's house, but the ring flared up again and again, bringing her to her knees.

A seam, she realized, and her skin paled with cold. She had handled the dolls often enough to know just where the halves split. It was the exact place that agonized her.

Somehow Slava was hurting her, using her doll against her in the true village.

Her vision doubled with the thought, and no amount of blinking or head shaking would make it relent. Was this how it was for her father when she'd twisted his doll?

Grunting, Matrona crawled forward, but every breath intensified the fire looping her middle. Her doll. She had to get her doll.

She'd nearly reached the portico when the invisible knife sliced her in half. Silent alarms screamed in her head as it dipped down to the grassy ground.

"Help," she whispered, throat parched. "Jaska. Jaska!"

But he was too far away to hear.

Saint Christopher, get me to my feet, please! she prayed. Grabbing the side of the portico, she hauled herself up, crying out with the strain. She fumbled with the door handle that kept jumping in her vision, and fell into the house, her elbow slamming into the hardwood floor. The floor seemed to swing before her eyes, so she shut them, groaning.

Slava had never hurt her before, but she had become a threat. She was going to ruin his quaint little paradise.

Roksana's face floated to the forefront of her mind. Matrona opened her eyes and pushed herself onto her knees, reaching for a wall to keep from stumbling. She thought of Olia and took a shaky step forward, then another. Esfir, vanished from her cradle, got Matrona into the front room.

She tasted blood when she bit down on a scream, her torso wrenching as though her legs were twisting one way and her shoulders another. She fell to the floor again, head spinning.

In the torrent she saw the tiny form of Roksana's child. Heard the echo of Roksana's cries.

Matrona dragged herself through the kitchen and toppled down the short steps into the hallway. Clawed her way to the doll room.

Sharpness dug into her hips like an axe striking, and Matrona found herself suddenly *waking up*—her body half in the doll room, a streak of vomit staining the carpet. Though her head weighed as if an anvil, she forced it up, trying to focus on the spinning tables of dolls before her. She searched for the red *sarafan*. Dolls hit the floor as she struggled to pull herself upright.

Ribbons of fire sliced through her, dropping her back to the floor. She was underwater, unable to swim, unable to tell up from down. She tried to reach for something to balance her, to steady her, to keep her alert—

Her hand brushed a smooth rod. She clasped it. Though her vision was a whirling blur of colors, she recognized the chisel.

As her body began to pull apart, a single thought stuck into Matrona's mind: if Slava could hurt her with her doll, maybe she could hurt him with his.

Rolling onto her back, Matrona gripped the chisel and flung it sideways. The thud of the blade striking the wall reverberated up her arm.

Her vision cleared, and the house quaked.

Matrona gasped and turned toward the wall, blinking away tears. There was a small hole in the wall where the chisel had struck.

The ring around her middle blazed again. Screaming, Matrona took the chisel in both hands and dug it into the wall, pushing the blade as far as her trembling arms could. The floor bucked beneath her, knocking more dolls to the floor. A sudden wind rammed the window, as though the chisel had attacked the air and earth and not the tradesman at all.

The ring vanished. Sucking in a deep breath, Matrona scrambled to her feet, her body little-more substantial than a rag doll. She grabbed the doll wearing her face and ran back through the house until she stumbled past the portico and fell to the ground. Her shoulders heaved with every breath. Her muscles stayed taut in anticipation of the next wave of pain. It didn't come.

Swift footsteps neared her, and a shadow blotted out the sun.

"What's wrong? What happened?" Jaska's voice engulfed her. Strong hands grabbed her shoulders, then clasped the sides of her face. "Matrona?"

She looked up into his dark eyes. Over his shoulder, she saw Olia a ways off, studying them.

"The dolls," she croaked. "We have to get them out of the house."

Jaska looked down at the doll Matrona held in her hand. He didn't question her, didn't hesitate. Springing to his feet, he dashed into the tradesman's house, returning seconds later with an armful of dolls. He dumped them onto the earth beside Matrona and darted back for the second load.

Matrona forced herself to stand and rubbed at her middle. Olia neared, a bouquet of weeds clenched in one hand.

"Stay here," Matrona rasped to the older woman. Jaska dumped more dolls beside Matrona, and when he ran back into the house, she followed. She stepped in the kitchen to pocket Feodor's, Galina's, and her parents' fifth dolls before hurrying into the doll room after Jaska and pulling more villagers from the shelves. She picked up her hem to make a bowl out of her skirt so she could carry more.

She brought them outside and dumped them beside Jaska's final load.

The village flashed gray before her eyes, dark houses caught in the torrent of a snowstorm.

Chapter 21

The vision lasted only a moment, punctuated by Olia's scream. Then all was as before, green and grassy, the sun shining in a wood-grain-patterned sky.

Jaska's face had gone pale. "Did you see . . . ?"

Matrona nodded.

Olia dropped into a crouch. "We'll lose our toes, we'll lose our toes. No sheep saved. No wool, no socks."

Jaska looked at his mother, his shoulders stiff. "Was that . . . Russia?"

Matrona shook her head. "I don't know. I don't remember enough of it."

The ground trembled under their feet, as if a great beast moved beneath it. Jaska placed a hand on Matrona's shoulder as though to steady her—or himself.

"I think Slava can still reach us through the dolls," she said once the earth had settled. "I saw him."

"You did? Where?"

She explained—the story became so simple when related through words. Shorter and easier than it had been to live it. She explained the house as a doll, the *Nazad*, the seam printing itself into her middle. Jaska paled at that last part.

"So I took the doll out, and it stopped," she finished. "And the quaking . . . it started with the chisel."

"You're all right?"

She nodded.

He licked his lips. "Will it stop?"

She shrugged, and in return the ground grumbled.

Olia stood and began looking around, reminding Matrona of a bird. Jaska let his hand fall from her shoulder. "Removing the dolls from the house didn't take us back to Russia. If we're in the dolls, and the dolls are in that house, and that house is, supposedly, in Russia—"

"Then taking them out should bring us home." Matrona gazed out to the village. "Maybe it almost did."

"That could be why we saw the snow," Jaska concluded.

She nodded. "Perhaps the spell is weakening."

Jaska knit his fingers through his hair and tugged on the locks. "So what do we do now? Wait for it to snap?"

"I don't know how the magic works. He never told me."

Matrona's vision flashed again, the sky turning gray and solid, snow spinning through the air. The wood flickered away, but Slava's bright house stood untouched. A chilled gust engulfed her, shaking her down to her bones. The change lasted half a heartbeat before the sun snuffed out the icy weather.

Matrona's pulse sped in her chest. She glanced back to Jaska, who stood wide-eyed as a dormouse. "Slava cares for himself above anyone else. His house may be the safest place for us right now, so long as we keep the dolls outside of it, where he can't influence them."

When Jaska didn't respond, she stepped up to him and put a palm on either of his cheeks, urging him to look at her.

"We'll solve this. What we can do is open the others' dolls to restore them like I restored you. They'll remember more than I do; they might have ideas that can help us. I already opened all the first layers."

"Three days for each layer, Matrona," Jaska murmured. "Will Slava find a way to strike back before we're done?"

She dropped her hands and chewed on her bottom lip. "Opening the back door was the same as opening Slava's first doll. I'm not sure how to open the others. But I believe that if Slava opens all of his dolls, the *Nazad* will cease to exist. Perhaps the village itself will unravel. I don't believe he can find us without ruining everything he's created, and he will not risk that."

"Why *does* the *Nazad* exist?"

Matrona shook her head. "I'm not sure." She pondered the question, trying to piece together the ill-fitting puzzle Slava had created. "Perhaps this is where reality and sorcery collide. A space between spells."

"And if he opened his dolls to come here, there would be nowhere left to come," Jaska said methodically, thinking. "He'd be freeing us, possibly undoing these . . . spells that he believes will prolong his life."

That gave Matrona a spark of hope. "Then we're safe." *For now,* but she didn't want to voice her doubts. "We have to stay here, in the *Nazad,* where he can't reach us. Not yet. We have to open the dolls, or the village won't remember. Three days . . . Slava set that time limit for safety, but we might be able to open them faster than that."

Jaska looked toward his mother, who appeared to be trying very hard to stomp out a bug in the grass.

"And have a town full of madmen," he said.

Though the ground beneath Matrona's feet didn't shake, she heard the rumble of the earth's movement from the south of the village. A flock of starlings flew up into the sky, and the trees bowed under a heavy gust of wind.

"Madmen, or a village in pieces," she whispered. "But we have to try. Just with one. If we lose him, we'll still have the other, and we'll know to be more careful with the rest."

"Him? You know who to open?"

She nodded. "The man most likely to understand both worlds: Pavel Zotov."

❈

Matrona ran back to the Zotov household, seeing the world flash before her one more time—the blink of gray swallowed up the *izbas* and replaced them with sparse wood, where the trees stood tall and close and naked. The heavy snow had lightened to a few flakes, carried on a breeze that rose bumps across her skin.

Matrona collected the rest of the fifth dolls in a bag and packed everything Roksana would need for the move—a change of clothes, the midwife's tonics, rags for her bleeding. Then Matrona guided her quiet, barely lucid friend back across the village to the tradesman's house. She settled Roksana down on the bed upstairs. Roksana didn't seem to recognize she had moved. Olia would stay in the front room with either Jaska or Matrona, and whoever wasn't with the two women would be just beyond the portico, guarding the dolls.

The ground shivered around the house as Jaska and Matrona opened the second dolls of every person in the village.

❈

After the first night in Slava's home, Jaska spent most of his time in the wood, searching for a door or a break in the loop. He found nothing of use, save for the doll of a hunter, caught in a bed of clover. Matrona itched to open Pavel's doll, but managed to wait two days before unscrewing doll number three—the one that would return his memories to him, were he whole.

She hadn't shared her thoughts with Jaska, but if three days was the true minimum for opening the dolls, Oleg could take Pavel's place. Perhaps it was cruel to take such a risk with a man's life, but they needed to make haste.

It seemed like a decision Slava would make, and that made her stomach turn.

"I can only hope he can receive his memories in the state he's in." There was no way of knowing, since Jaska, whom she'd also awakened in the *Nazad*, had memories of only the village. She reassembled the revolutionary's doll outside the steps by Slava's front door. "If he doesn't remember, we'll be lost."

"We'll open the others tomorrow," Jaska said. The rest of the villagers would be given the benefit of Slava's three-day rule.

Matrona nodded and rested Pavel's doll at her feet. She looked over the village, its foliage still green, its homes seemingly normal save for the lack of wood smoke haloing the chimneys.

"Matrona." There was tightness to Jaska's voice. He breathed long and slow through his nose as he, too, looked out on the village.

Matrona rolled her lips together.

He remained silent for another moment before choosing his words. "Why help me?"

Her stomach fluttered. "You know why."

"And you know my reasons. They're not there because some doll spell put them into my head."

"Jaska—"

"What I need," he began, speaking each syllable with care, "is truth. Commitment." When Matrona didn't respond, he added, "Those things tend to be absent in my life."

She kneaded her hands together. "I've never lied to you."

"Are you still for Feodor"—he waved at the dolls—"after all of this is settled?"

Her stomach eased, and she let out a breath. "No. I can't fool myself into thinking marriage with him is what I want. Not anymore."

She glanced to the pile of dolls, half-expecting Feodor's to rise above them.

Jaska's voice was smooth as butter and pitched as gently as a night breeze. "What do you want?"

She looked at him, at the intensity in his dark eyes. Dark as midnight, as river silt, as sin.

He repeated himself: "What do you want?"

Matrona shook her head. "You're as foolish as the rest of them if you don't know."

"I need to hear it."

"You, Jaska."

His lip quirked just enough to show his one-sided dimple. He leaned forward and kissed the tip of her nose; Matrona lifted her chin to kiss his lips. Despite the wrongness of everything around her, the warmth of his skin felt right.

They took in the village as though it were a sunset, as though it would change if they waited long enough, but nothing disturbed the view save for the occasional growl from beneath the soil. Matrona's thoughts gradually turned back to the dolls.

"Will we open them all?"

"Hm?"

"The fourth dolls. Most of the people here will have years of memories of Russia. They might be grateful for what Slava did, but they may also be angry. Others will be confused."

Jaska frowned and leaned back against the steps. "You're worried about a mob."

A vague memory of shouting surfaced in Matrona's mind. A cold street, her mother and herself pressed under an eave. Marching men and women in tattered clothing that almost matched the gray cast of the sky.

"Matrona?"

"What if he's right?" she asked, looking over the dolls. "What if he *did* save us?"

But Jaska shook his head. "He's wrong."

"How do you know? You have no memories of our true home."

"Because he made us forget."

He looked at her, his dark eyes clear and resolute. He held his brother Viktor's doll in his hands. "If we would have welcomed this place, he wouldn't have made us forget the other."

Matrona pulled from his gaze and peered out over the village. "I suppose you're right. I don't remember enough of Russia to know for certain. I wish I did."

Leaning over, he pressed a kiss to her temple. The contact made her shiver. The ground rumbled in response.

"They'll know the truth." He tipped his head toward Pavel's doll. "Or at least he will."

Matrona lifted the doll so that its eyes were level with her own. "I'm praying he'll have some insight."

"Even I'll pray for that."

A smile tugged on Matrona's lips. She lowered Pavel's doll, rested it against her knees. She heard Roksana singing another verse of her lullaby inside the house.

"Jaska?"

"Hm?"

"What if Russia no longer exists? What if it's *only* a memory?" She frowned, looking at the wooden caricatures of her family and friends. "What if *we* don't exist?"

Jaska was quiet a long moment. Matrona listened to his breathing.

"Then I guess he's right."

"Who?"

"Slava. If we only exist in his world, then he really is our god."

A chill spiked Matrona's heart at the sentiment. She pressed her lips together.

"Matrona?"

She shook her head. "Even if it were true, Slava is one god I will *never* believe in." She glanced to the pile of dolls. "And it will be no secret."

Chapter 22

Nothing changed in the two days that followed. The earth rumbled, even shook at times. The village flashed unpredictably, showing dark houses far smaller than the village *izbas*. Gray skies, light skies, snow spotting the ground. The images never stayed long enough for Matrona to get a good look. Through it all, the dolls remained dolls, and the mad remained mad.

Two days. Matrona was willing to risk it. She only hoped Pavel was willing, too.

She left Roksana sleeping and Olia pretending to knit and stepped outside, where Jaska guarded the dolls from both the madwomen and the supernatural. He didn't ask Matrona what she was doing—perhaps it was clear on her face. Maybe he'd even expected her.

Only two days. *Please don't be mad,* she prayed, clutching Pavel's small fifth doll in her fist. She knelt beside Jaska and picked up the carpenter's layered doll and opened the first layer. *Condemned by your people.*

Opened the second. *Condemned by yourself.*

Opened the third. *To see who you were.*

Opened the fourth. *To see who you could become. Is that the riddle, Slava?*

Like hers and Jaska's, the fourth doll's center was hollow. She slipped Pavel's fifth doll inside, then carefully pieced together the layers. Once the paint had lined up on the outermost doll, the seam vanished beneath her hands just as Jaska's had done.

Jaska started; Matrona stood and spun around, searching—

Pavel Zotov knelt just beside the portico, cradling his head in one hand. His dark hair was tied back in its customary tail, and he wore a dark *kosovorotka* and faded gray slacks. He groaned. The sensation of rain and falling tickled Matrona, and her doll-sight revealed a dusting of bewilderment in this man, a desire for freedom, and a blazing fire of leadership. There was no release of secrets from the opening of the first doll. Had the *Nazad* nullified that consequence?

Would it take away his memories, too?

"Pavel?" Matrona whispered, taking a tentative step toward him. Jaska found his feet and put a protective shoulder in front of her. "Pavel, are you . . . well?"

"Feel like someone's taken a saw to my head," he said. "I—"

He was still as an oak trunk, silent as a candle. Slowly he lifted his head, wincing against the sunlight. He looked at Jaska first, then Matrona. The village spread out before them. Slava's house behind. His knees creaked as he stood, and his eyes narrowed.

"What has he done to me?" he asked, gazing back at the village. "What has that bastard done?"

"You remember." The words were a breath of relief on her lips.

Pavel turned toward her. "Remember . . . yes, I remember. This isn't . . . How did I not know this isn't where I'm supposed to be?"

He reached out for one of the house's columns and leaned against it, again pressing a palm to his forehead. "Alena, Luka . . . he brought them, too. And Oleg. All of them . . ."

"I estimate it's been about two decades, Pavel." Matrona tried to keep her voice soft, as though it would lessen the blow of the words.

"He's trapped us inside dolls of our likenesses, starting with you. It began as an attempt to stop a revolt, but then the tsar turned on him. He made this place his refuge, it seems. Only, he trapped all of us here with him."

Pavel shook his head, winced. "How do you know this?"

"I've seen it. Slava tried to make me his protégé."

Pavel glanced to the pile of dolls for the first time. His features slackened.

Jaska said, "You may be feeling ill. We rushed your release."

"My what?"

Matrona glanced at Jaska. "Let's get you some water, and a chair. I'll explain everything."

❄

The bowl of cigar ash rattled atop the side table as the earth growled beneath the house.

Pavel waited for the grumbling to cease before speaking. "That's one of the quakes you mentioned?"

Matrona nodded.

Pavel tapped his fingers on the arm of a wicker chair. Olia occupied the plush chair Slava favored. She had tuned out the conversation, mindlessly tying lengths of yarn into various knots. Jaska had situated himself on the floor, and Matrona sat on the edge of the wooden armchair. Pavel looked at the ceiling. Matrona wondered if he was merely thinking, or if he was imagining his slumbering daughter-in-law above, or his lost grandson. Though he hadn't said as much, Matrona could see from his hardened expression that he would never forgive the tradesman for what had become of his family.

Pavel stood and glanced around the room. A frown carved his mouth as he stepped into the kitchen.

"Pavel?" Jaska asked, following him. Matrona rose from her chair and did the same.

Pavel searched through Slava's cupboard until he found a small knife block. A dry chuckle erupted from his throat when he brought it out to the table. "I made this."

Jaska held out a hand as though Pavel had become a wild boar. "It's all right, we'll—"

"I've still got my mind," Pavel snapped, pulling a knife from the block. He glanced to Matrona, and though anger toughened his brow, she saw clarity in his eyes. She nodded to Jaska, who relaxed.

Turning to the nearest wall, Pavel stabbed the knife into the wood.

Matrona gasped. Despite the sunshine that still poured down on the village, thunder boomed in the sky over the house. She stared out the window, confused. Did harming the house hurt Slava, or the village itself?

"Hmm." He ripped the blade free. He stabbed it again, and the earth bucked hard enough to throw off Matrona's balance. She collided into Jaska, who grabbed the edge of the table to stay upright.

Pavel hefted the knife a third time.

"Enough of that!" Matrona snapped. "Yes, it works. I told you as much. You'll topple the roof onto our heads with your experiments." She didn't understand the spells on the house. Was this place connected to Slava the same way Matrona's doll was to her? It didn't *look* like him, so surely the sorcery was beyond her comprehension. Yet when Matrona had stabbed the wall with the chisel, Slava's manipulation of her ceased. Because she had hurt him back, or because she had risked damaging this small world he created?

Pavel dropped the knife gracelessly onto the table. "There's no way out?"

"Not that we've found," Jaska said. "I've seen no break in the loops. No secret doorways in the patterns."

"The house is the only thing we have any effect on," Pavel concluded.

Matrona focused on the gouges left in Slava's kitchen wall. "In the doll world, we can leave the house." She stepped past Pavel and pressed her fingers to the marks. She thought she could feel the wall shudder beneath her touch. "But not in the *real* world. If we even exist there."

"A puzzle meant for scholars," Pavel spat.

"Maybe not." She pulled her hand from the injured wall. "You're correct; the house is the only thing we can affect." She swallowed. "If we cannot open Slava's doll, perhaps our only alternative is to break it."

"You want to break the house?" Jaska asked.

She nodded. "Pull down its walls, see what's truly on the other side of them." How much would it hurt Slava? Would it kill him? She shuddered, her stomach souring. She did not want the tradesman's blood on her hands. If only she understood his magic!

Pavel smiled for the first time since awakening. "I like this idea. I have tools in my shop—hammers, saws, chisels."

"Matrona." Jaska crossed the room and took both her hands in his. "I want to escape as much as you, but if taking a chisel to the wall can cause the ground to shake, what will a sledgehammer do? We could be killing ourselves."

Matrona's throat constricted at the notion.

Pavel asked, "Do you have another suggestion?"

Jaska frowned. Pressed his lips together. He was silent for several breaths—they all were. Then his shoulders slumped, and he shook his head.

"The sooner the better." Matrona hated the weakness in her voice. She could think of no other way. They couldn't unlearn what they knew, and she would never let Slava wipe her memories to keep his false peace intact. Even if Russia was a terrible place, it was a free one, wasn't it?

"Will it risk the others?" Jaska asked.

"Do you want to sit around and wait for them to wake, then take a vote?" Pavel quipped. "I've led people into far more dangerous situations. If left to choose for themselves, they will cow. If they see action, they will follow."

Jaska's hands fisted. "You think them cowards?"

"I think we're wasting time."

"Enough," Matrona said. "Let's take Olia and Roksana back to Pavel's home. Then we'll get the supplies."

"Matrona . . ." Her name was almost a plea on Jaska's lips.

Standing on her toes, Matrona took his chin in her hand and kissed him, paying no attention to Pavel. Peering into Jaska's eyes, she said, "I want to escape. I want to be *free*."

✼

The sledgehammer was too heavy for Matrona to wield, so she fisted a smaller mallet. She felt like a soldier—that was the right word, wasn't it? soldier?—going to war, leaving her loved ones behind. Olia and Roksana had been left in the Zotov *izba* with the dolls. If either of the madwomen wandered, it didn't really matter. Soon, none of it would, if Matrona's theory was correct.

Pavel carried the heavy hammer, and Jaska wielded a sturdy saw. They walked in a line, Matrona in the middle, their paces even. As they approached Slava's house, she saw, again, the illusion of the sleeping dragon—the shingles were its scales, the portico its great head, the hedgerows its tail. She watched it, unblinking, and in her mind saw it shudder with wakefulness, stretch out four massive legs that led to beastly feet with curved claws. Saw its head rise, tilt, and look at them, ready for the challenge.

It's just a house, she reminded herself. An enchanted house. A great doll.

A cage.

"God help us," she whispered, and Jaska nudged her with his elbow.

Pavel must have heard her, too, because he answered, "God isn't in here." They stopped before the house, and Pavel twisted his grip on the hammer. "He's out there."

They stood for a moment. Gray flashed across Matrona's vision. Pavel hefted the sledgehammer with a grunt and slammed its iron head into one of the house's columns.

The ground bucked as the painted wood splintered.

Pavel grinned and swung again. The wood cracked under the blow. The ground trembled; glass rattled in Slava's windows. Matrona heard a very distant shout, though she couldn't pinpoint from which direction it hailed.

The sky darkened.

Pavel swung a third time, breaking through the narrow column. The quaking of the ground didn't cease this time. Thick clouds—were they clouds?—began to bubble in the sky.

Jaska turned around. "This is bad."

"Too late to go back now," Matrona murmured. Gritting her teeth, tensing her shoulders, she walked up to a window and, grabbing the mallet with both hands, shattered it.

She felt power ripple up her arms—not her own strength, but something from *within* the house. Something struggling, or perhaps escaping. Banging and cracking trumpeted Pavel's work, soon followed by the long, rough draws of Jaska's saw. Matrona moved to the next window and shattered it, then grabbed shutters and hung from them until their nails pulled free.

Gray night encompassed them. Blotchy darkness filled the sky, rumbling and flashing with lightning. The ground quaked harder, until Matrona could barely stay afoot. An *izba* down the path began to crumble. A few tiles fell from Slava's roof.

"This is too slow!" Pavel shouted over the rumbling. "There's an easier way to do this!"

He set down the sledgehammer and hurried on shaking legs to the large leather bag he'd brought with him from his house, filled with more tools for dismantling Slava's doll. To Matrona's surprise, he pulled out a flask of kerosene and a box of matches.

She dropped her mallet and ran to him, tripping with every step, until her hands clasped the kerosene.

The quaking had become so terrible, she had to shout to be heard over it, even at such close range. "We don't know how the spells work! You might kill him!"

"Jaska's out of harm's way!"

"Not Jaska!" she bellowed. "Slava!"

Pavel pulled back, hand still on the kerosene. "And?"

Matrona's jaw went slack. "Surely there's a way not to—"

He laughed, the sound of it swallowed by the collapsing walls of buildings in the village behind them. "Do you really think that whoreson would build himself a prison without a way out?"

Matrona's grip on the kerosene loosened.

Pavel leaned closer as one of Slava's walls began to cave in. "Where do you think he does his trades? He goes to *Russia*. There's a *reason* his house has two doors!"

Matrona swallowed and let go. Teetered on the trembling earth.

"We'll chance it." Pavel ran up to the house, near where Jaska struggled to saw through the shuddering portico. He made a few gestures to the potter, who stepped back from the house, leaving the saw embedded in its wood. Jaska walked backward toward Matrona. The ground bucked and knocked him onto his backside.

Matrona hurried to him, falling to her knees beside him. She couldn't see straight from the shaking, couldn't hear over the roar of their breaking world.

The first flames caught her eye, lapping up behind the second window she'd broken. Pavel fell against the house, trying to stay upright. Crawled along its body to his sledgehammer. He unscrewed the head and coaxed flames onto the tip of the handle, trying to spread the fire that was already consuming the dragon from the inside out.

A second burst of brilliance drew Matrona's gaze skyward. Her bones became ash within her.

"Jaska!" she cried, pointing.

The sky was on fire.

Chapter 23

Matrona tried to find her feet, but the earth knocked her down and liquefied her muscles. She clung to Jaska, her eyes watering, her throat itching from the smoke pouring from Slava's house. The orange flames reflected in Jaska's eyes.

A circle of flames whirled above them, eating away at the now-dark sky as if it were parchment, revealing pale gray behind it. Nothing but gray. Though surrounded by heat, Matrona's flesh turned cold. It was as though she stared into the eye of nonexistence, and it stared back at her, laughing in a voice too similar to Slava's.

The flames continued to spread, stretching out like a molten ring, opening the gaping void in the sky. The heat struck Matrona, hitting her in a wave, burning her skin. Jaska turned into her and clutched her shoulders, and she buried her face into his neck.

Was this really the end? Had they trapped themselves inside a kiln? Would their lives truly end in ash?

The blaze brightened white hot. Matrona could see it through her eyelids, through Jaska. She screamed.

The light choked out, and cold settled upon them.

❄

Jaska was warm against her. His breath danced across her ear.

Matrona lifted her head, blinking away spots of color. She exhaled, watching her breath cloud and dissipate. Tall dark trees lingered nearby, their branches bare and crooked like the legs of a dead spider. The sky above them was gray—no, a pale blue. The wakefulness before dawn.

Matrona pulled back from Jaska, shivering in the suddenly frigid air. She turned, her skirted knees scraping on cold, hard ground—a dirt-packed road lined with uneven stones, splattered with shadows, and dusted with . . . ash? A small *izba* barely larger than her bedroom stood lifeless nearby. And another one, farther away.

Jaska shifted, stood. Offered his hands. Matrona took them and let him pull her to her feet. Her muscles still trembled with memory. She turned toward Slava's house, but it wasn't there. In the place where it had stood, there was only a well without a rope or bucket, cold and silent.

Footsteps made her heart jump, and she saw Pavel behind a shed, stumbling as though he had a clubfoot. He blinked rapidly. His right sleeve was singed at the hem and elbow, and ash dusted his shoulders. Matrona thought of the fire that had consumed Slava's house and of the flames whirling in the sky. The ash was all that remained of the world she had known for most of her life.

A moan sounded nearby. Matrona whirled around and saw figures rising from the shadows between structures. Nastasya Kalagin. Georgy Grankin. Whole, restored. The sight of them did nothing to inspire the doll-sight she'd gained after opening her fourth doll. Had awakening to this new world extinguished it?

"They're . . . ," Jaska began, but didn't finish.

"This is it," Pavel whispered, crossing the road to the small *izba*. He pressed his hand to the door. His voice quavered with wonder. "This is it . . . Look at it. Untended, left to rot for what, twenty years? This . . . this was yours, Matrona."

"What?"

Pavel stepped back from the small house. "The Vitsin household." He glanced to Jaska. "If I remember right, your parents lived closer to the wood, that way."

He pointed . . . east. Matrona could see the first pale rays of sunlight licking at the cold sky.

Voices began to murmur in the silence: "Where are we?" "Good Lord, I remember . . ." "How did we come back?" "Where . . . ?"

"Over here," murmured another, a baritone. Matrona gasped and turned to see her father and mother coming down the road from the direction of the trees.

"There!" her mother exclaimed.

"Mama!" Matrona ran up the road, feeling a happiness bloom within her that she hadn't experienced for a long time—a childlike fondness for her parents.

She embraced her mother, pinching away the cold for a brief moment.

"Our home." Her father pressed a palm to his forehead. "I remember . . ."

"This is where we lived," Matrona said, and her mother nodded, her wet eyes darting back and forth as though ghosts surrounded her. Matrona had never seen such an open, emotional expression on her mother's face. It was as if she could see straight through to her mother's soul. In that wordless moment, Matrona understood her mother better than she ever had before, even with the doll-sight.

The other villagers reacted similarly. They were hushed, stiff with cold and memory, walking through a world remembered. The sun crawled up the sky, bringing a touch of life to the dead place that seemed to be on the verge of spring. It wasn't until a plume of wood smoke billowed into the sky that Matrona and the others realized their old village was not completely abandoned.

As Matrona and her parents wound their way toward the smoke, they were joined by several other villagers who had migrated toward the promise of warmth. Jaska had squeezed her hand before leaving to find his own kin, and Pavel had also stayed behind to find his family.

By the time Matrona reached the street before one of the larger *izbas*, a second and third plume of smoke danced into the sky, billowing from large, controlled fires. Her gaze shifted to a handful of unfamiliar people who wore clothes much more ragged and darker in color than any worn by those from the village. There was a thin man with a scraggly graying beard and a thick hat made of fur; he threw some quarter logs onto a haphazard fire pit and waved the villagers forward. Behind him, a woman—perhaps his wife—handed out reedy blankets. She gave a pair of knit gloves to one of the older children.

Matrona began heading toward the couple, questions filling her mouth, but the cry of a babe drew her attention to a dark-haired girl skirting between the collecting villagers, a jug of water and a ladle in her hand. A child was strapped to her chest. There were other strangers, too—an older woman and a man about Feodor's age. Whether they were townsfolk who had been missed by Slava's curse or needy peasants who had moved into the abandoned homes afterward, she didn't know. But there was something about the girl . . . Matrona studied her face as the girl passed by the fire—her black hair, worn in two braids. Strong jaw, thick brows.

Matrona's breath caught in her throat. For a moment, her skin forgot the cold.

Were it not for the shape of the girl's nose, Matrona could have been looking at her own reflection. *It can't be . . .*

She didn't realize she was moving forward until the heat of one of the fires brushed gooseflesh from her skin. But she walked away from it, bearing the cold a little longer. Approached the woman as she offered water to Irena Kalagin. Studied her again—yes. The thick brow, the dark hair. She even had gray eyes. A worn gray *sarafan* hugged her slender body, as though she didn't eat enough, and her hands were even rougher than Matrona's own. But the similarities screamed at her.

Matrona took a few more steps, until only a pace lay between them. "Esfir?"

The name was hoarse on her tongue, and too quiet, but the girl turned her head. She noticed Matrona. A few heartbeats passed before her eyes widened.

"You . . . ," she began, then shook her head. "I . . . No, my name is Sacha. But . . . you—"

"Look like you." Matrona's words were a breath. Her heart beat too quickly in her chest. "I think . . . How old are you?"

"Twenty," Sacha answered, the ladle limp in her hand. "I don't know the exact day. My parents found me when I was just a babe—"

Matrona's hands flew to her mouth, muffling an oath. It was her. Praise the Lord, it was *her*!

Esfir's—Sacha's—eyes watered. "You know me." A smile pulled on her dry lips. "You know me, don't you?"

Matrona swallowed against a sore lump in her throat and nodded. "But you were lost. If you're her—my sister—then . . ." She shook her head. "Slava—"

"Slava?" The name danced on Sacha's tongue, laced with hope.

Matrona shook her head. "Not a relation. I just . . . I thought we'd lost you."

Sacha moved forward—perhaps for privacy, or an embrace—but a wail from the bundle strapped to her chest broke the pull of her body.

Matrona hugged herself. "Y-Your child?"

Sacha shook her head. "No." She placed a hand on the babe's head. "The oddest thing, we found him, just as I was found—"

"A baby boy." Matrona's own eyes watered.

"How did you . . . ?"

"He just appeared?" Matrona pressed.

Sacha nodded.

Her knees felt thin as dried reeds. *Thank the heavens above,* Matrona thought, pulling in a shuddering breath. *Roksana's baby, alive.*

Roksana.

"I'm so sorry"—Sacha looked from Matrona to others trying to build another fire—"but I need to—"

"No, go. See them taken care of. I'll . . . introduce you to our parents, once everyone is settled."

Sacha mouthed the word *parents* and nodded, hesitant to pull away, but duty called, as it always did.

Matrona watched the woman walk away and forced her legs to move. Roksana. Where was Roksana?

"Tumble down into the mud," a familiar ramble sounded from the second fire. Matrona followed the sound and spotted Olia sitting on a fallen log near the flames, Galina and Kostya beside her. Ash speckled her white hair. "Too bright, too hot. Too cold, too dead."

Matrona's heart sank into her stomach, and she hugged herself tighter. The madness was truly permanent, then. If Olia hadn't been cured, Roksana wouldn't be, either. The truth of it panged sharply in her chest, and Matrona closed her eyes for a long moment, pocketing the sorrow for another time. She could not mourn her friend again, not now. Not when there was so much confusion in the village, and so many questions awaiting answers.

She continued her search and found Roksana inside Sacha's home, head resting on her mother's lap. Pavel and Luka had joined a small party scouring the village and examining the houses, most of which remained empty. Apparently the small town of Siniy Kamen was rumored to be haunted, for nearly all its inhabitants had been swallowed up in the night, never to be seen again . . . until now. It was no wonder the homes had stayed vacant, even after twenty years. Few would brave superstition, even if it meant free quarters.

"It's gone," a boy said as Sacha's adoptive mother handed Matrona a shawl—what seemed to be the last of the family's supplies. "The secret house. It's really gone!"

Matrona's gaze bounced between the boy and the woman. "The secret house?"

The woman worried her lip.

"Please," Matrona pressed. "Superstition won't frighten me."

The woman drew in a deep breath through her nose. "It was here when we first arrived. We were not ones to trouble a town of ghosts, but our home had been given to the soldiers, and we were desperate—"

"The yellow house, with the blue tiles," said the boy, hopping from foot to foot either in excitement or to stave off the cold. "It was here, the grandest house in the whole place, but it was locked up."

The woman nodded. "Strangest thing, like a lord's house amid the rabble. But the doors and windows wouldn't budge. The glass panes wouldn't so much as crack under our blows, and the kites . . ."

"Kites?" Matrona glanced back over the village, toward the trees.

"Like sentinels, they were," she continued. "Nasty birds. Sometimes you couldn't see them, but try too hard to get into that house—that empty house—and they'd fly for you with their talons outstretched. So we left the house alone. For twenty years we left it alone. Then it caught fire, and you and yours appeared."

"It's gone," the boy repeated, sticking his fingers in his armpits. "All of it. Just a pile of ash now."

Matrona nodded slowly. "Thank you. For everything." She gestured to the shawl. "We'll repay you in any way we can."

❄

Matrona picked her way through the village lit by morning sun, trying to find something familiar from her dim childhood memories. All of it, however, was strange and surreal. The sky, the cold; even the trees did not grow as they had in the wood around the village, and Matrona could not recall these skeletal monsters from her childhood.

"You did this?"

Matrona looked up to see Feodor walking toward her. His father and mother lingered farther up the road, talking, and gesturing to one of the abandoned *izbas*.

Matrona stared at him until her eyes burned, but no, the doll-sight had truly left her. How pitiful that she could not use the one gift Slava had given her on the man she'd once wished to know the most about. As to his question, she merely nodded. "Me, Jaska, Pavel."

Feodor stopped a pace and a half in front of her, his shirt pulled closely to him. "They say you burned down Slava's house."

She nodded. "Do you remember—"

"A little." He glanced to the side. He would have been ten years old at the time of Slava's spell. "And my father will not be quiet, speaking of Russia and the revolution and everything that might have happened in our absence."

That hadn't yet occurred to Matrona. A lot could happen in twenty years. Was Russia still the way Slava remembered it? The way she didn't? The snows of her memories and the flashing storms were gone, save for traces along the paths. Puddles lay in depressions in the road and in patches where the *izbas*' roofs sank in, their still surfaces dusted with ash. The world was warming. Changing?

"Did you not consider the rest of us?"

The question pulled Matrona from her thoughts.

Feodor frowned. "Look around you, Matrona. How the people shiver. At the hard ground, and these . . . things." He gestured to a squat *izba*, not nearly as fine as the homes Slava had crafted for them. "Why would you do this? Bring us here?"

Matrona licked her lips, but it only made them colder. "It was all or none."

"And you chose for us."

The declaration stabbed knife sharp. Her own words to Slava echoed in her ears: *"Why . . . if this life is so much better . . . did you not give us the choice?"*

But she wasn't like him. She hadn't done wrong, merely undone wrong. This was the real world; the other world, the one he had created, was no more than a mirage.

"You were incapacitated." Hardness leaked into Matrona's voice, and she drew away from him. "Or did you not also hear about the dolls? You were a *doll*, Feodor. Wooden and painted and lifeless."

"We had a pleasant life," he continued, as though her words had dropped before reaching him. "Easy crops, perpetual summer." Looking down into her eyes, he sighed. "I don't know how we're going to mend this."

Matrona shook her head. "There's nothing to mend. Not between us."

Feodor looked at her, expressionless save for the slight downturn of his lips.

"We have a village to assemble," she continued. "Fires to build, homes to repair. Memories to settle. There will be no wedding, Feodor."

He merely nodded. Relief flowed from her core, and yet sorrow tinged it, for Matrona knew Feodor had never truly cared for her, even by the smallest measure. How easily she could have assigned her life to him. The prospect left her colder than the ice lining the road.

Feodor turned up the way, for his family, and she was glad to see the back of him.

Matrona let out a long breath and cut through the yard of another building—house or shop, she couldn't quite tell. A vine of sorts, brown and dead from the winter, climbed up two sides of it. She touched it, and an old, stale leaf crumbled beneath her fingers.

She walked, wondering at Feodor's words. How many more would share his sentiment? Not Pavel, not Oleg. Not Jaska or her parents. Hopefully most of the older men and women would remember their homes and recognize they'd been freed from captivity. There was no returning now.

Slava Barinov's voice chuckled in her imagination. She dug her nails into her palms and hushed it.

Her toe kicked something in the road, and she paused. Its smoothness and colors contrasted against the heap of ash nesting it. Painted eyes looked up at her, squinting and smiling.

Crouching, Matrona picked up the Japanese *Fukuruma* doll and turned it in her hands. Nothing else had survived from the doll world, so why had this?

She ran her hands over the doll, which was a little larger than the ones Slava had crafted. Even if Matrona had not seen his memories of Russia, she would have known this figure had another creator. The hand was not Slava's—it was simple, with fine, black strokes. The large face sat low on the body. It had large eyebrows and a rounded nose.

This was the doll that had started it all, whispering of magic and possibilities to the tsar's mysticist.

Something shifted within its body.

Pressing her thumbs to the seam, Matrona split open the halves. But instead of a smaller version of the *Fukuruma* doll, she found two other dolls. Fourth dolls, judging by the size. One bore the face of a kite; the other of an old man. She recognized the second as Slava, if the years had been harder on him.

Her breath tickled her lips. Cradling the *Fukuruma* doll against her elbow, Matrona took the brown doll and ran her fingers over the detail in its feathers. The wood squeaked when she opened it. Emptiness greeted her.

A cry pierced the air and startled her, nearly causing her to drop the dolls. Looking up, Matrona saw a kite soar above the village. Sun glinted off a copper band around its leg as it flew toward the wood.

"Pamyat?" she whispered, and looked down at the doll in her hands. He had been of this world, and preserved? Then . . .

She placed Pamyat's doll halves back into the *Fukuruma* and pulled out the doll painted to look like Slava. She didn't understand. Slava's doll had been his house. So why did a vessel with his likeness exist here?

The words of Pavel rang ever true in her memory. *"Do you really think that whoreson would build himself a prison without a way out?"*

Her eyes met the blue painted ones of Slava. The irises weren't as neat as the other dolls'. The clothing was oversimple, as though the painting had been done in haste. A new construct? Had Slava created this while Matrona and the others hid in the *Nazad*?

She eyed the seam splitting the stomach of the doll.

"Matrona."

She turned to see Jaska walking toward her, a borrowed hat pressed over his hair. She searched his face for traces of regret, but his eyes were warm, and that singular dimple curved into his cheek ever so slightly.

His gaze fell onto the dolls, and his brow furrowed. "What is that?"

Matrona set the tradesman's doll back into its *Fukuruma* hiding place. She thought of Feodor. "It is a decision that isn't mine to make."

She had already mimicked her mentor and changed the fate of her comrades. The village would choose what to do with Slava's last attempt at immortality. She pressed the *Fukuruma* halves back together.

Jaska's eyes refocused on her, framed with lines of confusion.

"I will explain later," Matrona promised, "but where all can hear."

He nodded slowly. "Now is the time, then. A town meeting." He gestured back toward Sacha's home. "To figure out where to start, I guess. And to learn what we've missed."

He extended his hand toward her.

Matrona tucked the doll beneath her blanket. She reached for Jaska's hand, glancing back to where she had seen the kite.

The *Fukuruma* doll shuddered from within.

ACKNOWLEDGMENTS

Another book done! This one barreled down the pipeline almost out of nowhere, but I'm happy with how it turned out. Many thanks to my husband and kids, who put up with their wife/mother tucking away to punch out words. You all are so supportive (even if the little ones don't realize they're being supportive, yet).

A big thank-you, as always, to Marlene Stringer, Jason Kirk, and Angela Polidoro, who helped make this book what it is, from idea to print. Together we're an unstoppable team.

Thank you to my friends who read this book and helped me get it into shape: L. T. Elliot, Laura Christensen, Caitlyn Hair, Rebecca Blevins, and Kimberly VanderHorst. You guys are dedicated and sharp, and I would flounder without you.

Thank you to Bill Giles, Chris Baxter, and Wendy Nikel, who helped me get religious facts and Russian names correct. Thank you also to Katie Purdie, who shared her research with me.

I'd like to tip my hat to the LDStorymakers conference because I came up with the idea of enchanted *Matryoshka* dolls while putting together a workshop for you. You're the best.

My gratitude to the cover designer, editors, and layout folks who made this book pretty and readable.

And keeping with tradition, thank you so much to my Heavenly Father, who still somehow finds it amusing to let me dabble in my fantasy playground. Cheers.

ABOUT THE AUTHOR

Photo © 2015 Erin Summerhill

Born in Salt Lake City, Charlie N. Holmberg is the author of *Followed by Frost*, *Magic Bitter, Magic Sweet*, and The Paper Magician trilogy, which includes *The Paper Magician*, *The Glass Magician*, and *The Master Magician*. A RITA Award finalist, she majored in English and minored in editing at Brigham Young University. Raised a Trekkie alongside three sisters who also have boy names, Charlie plays the piano and ukulele, owns too many pairs of glasses, and hopes to one day adopt a dog. For more on the author and her work, visit www.charlienholmberg.com.